Black-Irish Setter

ALSO BY BILL STACKHOUSE

(In the Ed McAvoy Mystery Series)
Stream of Death—ISBN: 1-890208-56-6
Hickory, Dickory—ISBN: 0-595-22596-9
Encore to Murder—ISBN: 0-595-25624-4
Wash & Wear—*Forthcoming*
Candle Snuffer—*Forthcoming*
Thin Ice—*Forthcoming*

(In the Caitlin O'Rourke Mystery Series)
Black-Irish Setter—ISBN: 0-595-27063-8

Black-Irish Setter

A Caitlin O'Rourke Mystery

Bill Stackhouse

Bill Stackhouse
2/28/04

Mystery and Suspense Press
New York Lincoln Shanghai

Black-Irish Setter

A Caitlin O'Rourke Mystery

Mystery and Suspense Press
an imprint of iUniverse, Inc.

For information address:
iUniverse, Inc.
2021 Pine Lake Road, Suite 100
Lincoln, NE 68512
www.iuniverse.com

ISBN: 0-595-27063-8

Printed in the United States of America

Chapter I

"Missile ork?!" a voice called out and a pair of large but gentle hands touched me ever so softly. "Missile ork?! Bantu earbee?"

Say what? I thought, but the excruciating pain in my nose prevented me from giving the words my full attention. *Bantu what?*

I had had the dream many times over the years—the nightmare, actually—but rarely had anyone ever spoken to me in it before. The scene usually played itself out in slow motion and in silence—just the visual images and the pain in my nose and head and knee.

And even though I could feel the pain, I had always observed the scene from above, as if I were having an out-of-body experience and looking down from atop the backboard at myself sprawled out on the court below. I had a sort of dual status—the player who felt the pain, and the spectator who watched as it happened—both wrapped into one.

There were other differences as well. *This* time, I seemed to be merely the participant, unable to see anything except blackness. I could hear, but only groggily, just like when it happened for real.

Strangely, though, my knee didn't bother me. Oh, the everyday base discomfort that I'd learned to more-or-less ignore still throbbed dully, but not the wrenching, tearing, piercing agony of the blown-out knee that previous dreams had forced me to relive.

The searing ache in the bridge of my nose was another matter altogether. Magnified tenfold from those other dreams, it made my head feel as if it were about to explode.

Then the voice called out again. "Missile ork?! Missile ork?! Insurgent angbord."

What's going on? Where's Rhonda the trainer? Where's the doctor?

They both were with me in Seoul when it happened, splinting my leg, stopping the blood from gushing out my nose, holding me, and comforting me until the stretcher-crew arrived. And they're always with me in my dreams when the injuries recur. Always.

Where are they now? And what does "missile ork" mean? And who's saying it? It's Russian! It's got to be! That Amazon bitch is standing over me and taunting! "Missile ork" must be Russian for "screw you." Well, missile ork to you, too, bitch! When I get up, I'll...

But I wasn't getting up, that much I knew would be the same as in all the other dreams. I was going to be carried off the court. I had lost the cat fight.

That's how the '88 Olympic semifinals had been billed by the television network in an attempt to garner ratings for women's basketball—*Korean Cat Fight.* For the good guys, Caitlin Kathleen (Katie-Kat) O'Rourke—six-one and a hundred-and-seventy-eight pounds of grade-A prime American beef, averaging twenty-two points and nineteen rebounds per game through four years at Nashville's Regina Caeli College. (To this day I don't know which one of my brothers gave the press my childhood nickname. Oh, I admit to using it when I have conversations with myself, but it was never meant for public consumption.)

In the other corner stood Ecaterina (Big Cat) Kalinovskaya—six-three and weighing in at one-eighty-eight. Big Cat's college had been the Soviet National Team where she had racked up a game average of twenty-eight points and twenty-five rebounds.

The battle had been decisive. Early in the second quarter I, Katie-Kat, lie in a heap after Big Cat missed blocking my jump-shot, then accidentally-on-purpose hammered her fist into the bridge of my nose. Not only had the nose been broken, but I came down twisted on my right leg, tearing up the knee as well.

Again the unseen voice spoke. "Zhecouzin debond. Iride bakinger abiddle."

"Ilbakeober, urgent," a second voice joined in. "Missile ork? Missile ork? Busranginder."

Who's the second guy?

If this is a Russian doctor instead of Doc Berman, this really *is* turning into a nightmare.

Get me Doc Berman, you morons! I don't want some Ruskie quack touching me. And get Rhonda! Jeez, my head is killing me!

Someone peeled back an eyelid and passed a light over my pupil. They might as well have jabbed an ice pick into it. I started to choke, then coughed. Whoever had just arrived propped me up into a half-sitting position. I swallowed. With a metallic taste in my mouth as blood ran down my throat, the vividness of the dream surprised me. I had forgotten that aspect of the injury. It had never occurred before in the dream. Only the pain in my nose and head and knee.

Why isn't the knee hurting?

The fogginess slowly began to lift from my brain.

"Missile ork?...Miss O'Rourke? Can you hear me? Just hang in there."

A blurred image of a man in a blue uniform began to come into focus. He sat on the gray marble floor, holding my head immobile and pinching my nose in an attempt to stop the bleeding. And a woman, also dressed in blue, had a blood-pressure cuff around my left arm.

"Sergeant Langford?" The man in blue turned to address someone else. "She's beginning to respond. I think she's coming around. Broken nose and probably a concussion."

My vision started to clear, but I could see three of everything. The eyes were way ahead of my mind, however. I looked around, unable to figure out where I was. This wasn't a gymnasium and I wasn't wearing my red, white-and-blue basketball uniform. I was dressed in a red-and-white western-cut oxford shirt, jeans, cowboy boots, and a navy-and-red linen blazer. Then I realized that the red color wasn't supposed to be on either my shirt or blazer. It was blood.

The Sergeant Langford, one of two uniformed police officers on the other side of the foyer to whom the paramedic spoke, stepped aside. At his feet lay a white-draped form. One end of the sheet had sopped up something red from underneath it. At the other end, a woman's shapely stockinged leg protruded.

What's going on here? Is this my blood or is it hers? And who is this woman, anyway?

I blinked, trying to focus in on only one of the multiple images.

"She's sure a big one, ain't she?" I heard the second officer murmur to the sergeant, giving a glance and a head-gesture in my direction. "Ever screw anything that big?"

"Watch your mouth, Wittek," Sergeant Langford answered. "That's Pat O'Rourke's little sister you're talking about."

"Little, hell. How'd you like to get those legs wrapped around you?"

The words of the chauvinist were like a Rosetta stone. The veil lifted completely from my mind. I knew where I was and how I came to be there. Glancing again at the leg sticking out from under the sheet, I felt icy tentacles begin to encircle me. I now also remembered who belonged to that leg.

Aw, jeez!

After first clearing blood from my throat, I called over to the piglet cop who had made the crude remark about my legs. "Hey, Wittek, you moron, how'd you like to have a size ten-and-a-half boot that's at the end of one of these long legs kick you right square in that smart mouth of yours?"

Chapter 2

"Man, I'd sure like to get them legs of yours wrapped around me. Hoo, boy!"

I finished the last of my Oysters Kirkpatrick and glanced at the middle-aged man on my right. He, too, had pulled his head out of his plate. We both turned to see which of the three morons who had been loud-mouthing at a table by the door had wandered over.

I had thought as much. The short, thin one. He stood there with an alcohol grin, having just fed a quarter into the juke box. A Hank Williams, Jr. number blared from the speakers. It figured.

"I was talking to the lady, little man," he said, sneering at my companion, who at a mere five-five was even shorter than he. "Why don't you just go back to feeding your fat face?" He sniffed twice and rubbed the sleeve of his faded denim jacket across his dripping nose.

Seeing as how we were in an Irish pub, the sight of a red nose was nothing out of the ordinary. More than a quarter of our regulars suffered from rosacea, the curse of the Irish. But the twerp who faced me now didn't have a skin disease, only a disease of his own making. He clearly enjoyed his nose-candy.

I put a hand on Pat's arm. My brother's neck had already become flushed. He recognized the look in my eye, though. It said, "This one's mine." Pat smiled, turned back to the bar, picked up his spoon and resumed excavating the Irish Stew. In my peripheral vision I could see my other brother Seamus ease over our way a bit as he finished polishing a half-pint mug. It was comforting to have backup, but in this case totally unnecessary.

"Why don't the three of you drink up and hit the road," I said to my new admirer, hoping that he would take the hint, but doubting it. His kind don't take hints more subtle than a ball bat.

"How's about a dance before I go, huh, babe?" His grin got broader and he wet his lips in anticipation as he tipped a once-white but now sweat-stained Stetson back off his forehead.

Well, he wasn't *totally* stupid; I'd give him that. Even though I still sat on my bar stool, he had been able to do the mental arithmetic. At six-one—make that six-three in my Lucchese ostrich-skin boots—his unshaven, pimply face would be oh-so-very-close to my C-cups.

"Dream on, slime ball. And move it out. You and your buddies have had your last drink." I spun around on the stool and once more faced the bar.

Maybe I had given him too much credit for smarts. Although he had done all right on the math section of the test, he failed the logic part miserably.

Here's a tip. (As I periodically give these to you, feel free to write them down—or not; some are more important than others.) Never attempt to sneak up on someone while they're facing a mirror. In the one behind the bar where the bottles were arranged, I could see this moron's every move.

His hand had no sooner touched my shoulder when I grabbed it with my own as I rose and twisted his wrist, turning him around and bending his arm halfway up his back. He was in the middle of taking the Lord's name in vain when his face had a close encounter with the wall, propelled there by one of my size ten-and-a-halfs.

"You, you, and you! Out! *Now*!" I ordered, pointing at each of the three in turn and then at the front door.

From down at the other end of the bar, old Mickey Ryan echoed my command, shaking a palsied finger in their direction. "You here that, lads? Out! Caitlin says for you to leave."

The two at the table took quick looks around, correctly read the faces of Pat, Seamus, and the few other customers in the pub, and headed for the door without challenging me or Mickey. My new friend, however, blood running from a cut on his eyebrow, didn't care about his outer face. His bruised ego demanded retribution. He had been humiliated—and by a *chick*, at that.

"Let it be, cowboy," I said softly. "You had too much to drink; you made a mistake; now walk away." I gave him a no-harm-no-foul smile and nodded, probably a bad move on my part.

The corners of my mouth don't go up by the same amount when I try to smile. One goes up; the other is sort of crooked and turns down on the end. My Aunt Bridget used to call it a *bemused smile*. Sister Perpetua, my eighth-grade teacher who was forever telling me to wipe it off my face, used to call it a *smirk*.

The cowboy must have agreed with the good nun. Instead of walking away, he stuck a hand into the pocket of his jacket and, instinctively, I knew he wasn't reaching for a rosary. Probably because he called me an effing bitch as he did so, spraying spittle halfway across the room.

When you've got legs as long as mine, you can do three things with them. Well, there are more than three, actually, when you consider what the cowboy had in mind, but when it comes to a confrontation, there are three primary things. Number one, of course, is to walk away. Number two is run. I chose the third option.

Reaching behind me, I grabbed the pint mug of Red Mountain Golden Lager that I had been nursing and sloshed the contents into the cowboy's face. A split-second later I let him have the right Lucchese where he'd be sure to remember it the next time he sang the descant to *O Holy Night* with the boys' choir. As he doubled over, dropping a pearl-handled stiletto to the floor, I cracked him upside the head with the empty mug. End of confrontation in about five seconds.

Mickey Ryan led the applause and the cheers of, "Way to go, Caitlin!"

A distinguished looking, middle-aged man, dressed expensively in tan slacks and a brown glen plaid linen sportcoat, had just come from the hallway that led to the rest rooms, pay phone, and the back door. Seamus had directed him there about five minutes earlier when he had entered the pub wanting to call road service. As my would-be admirer spun around on his way to the floor, he had hooked a flailing arm around the gentleman. A red streak now spiraled down the side of the man's sportcoat where the cowboy's bloody head had rubbed against it.

The gentleman went two shades paler than Casper and looked furtively around the pub. He had probably debated with himself about coming in here in the first place and did so only out of necessity. Being ten-thirty in the p.m., the other businesses on the block had long ago locked their doors. Now, his worst fear was becoming a reality—getting mugged in a redneck bar.

As I approached him to apologize, he backed up a step or two and a look of stark terror flooded his face. Following his gaze, I realized I still held the beer mug with which I had dispatched the cowboy. Obviously, he thought he was next on my hit list. I tossed the mug to Seamus behind the bar and raised a calming hand.

"It's okay, it's okay," I told him. Then, nodding toward the man on the floor, I said, "He won't be causing anymore trouble tonight. Here, let's get that jacket off of you."

Before he could protest, Mary Grace, Seamus' wife, rushed from the kitchen with a dish towel and a pitcher of water. "A little ice water'll get it out," she cooed. "Here, give it to me. Quickly, now, or the blood'll set. In three minutes time, you'll never know you've had any dealings with the likes of...that." She gave a disparaging glance at the cowboy as my brothers half-dragged him toward the front door.

The appearance of short, plump, middle-aged, motherly Mary Grace must have counteracted the image of the big banshee with the beer mug. The gentleman calmed immediately and allowed her to help him off with the sportcoat. As it came off, I could see the Brooks Brothers label and, underneath, a custom-made shirt and accessories that didn't come from the Lands' End catalogue. I had to smile at the tie, though. It showed a largemouth bass jumping from a pond with a hook in its mouth.

"Come on over here," I said, crossing to an empty table in the far corner. "Mary Grace will have your jacket looking like new in no time. And, if not, we'll take care of the cleaning bill."

Dutifully, he followed me to the table. I stuck out a paw as I pulled out a chair for him. "Caitlin O'Rourke. Kate, for short. What can I get you to drink?"

He shook the hand with a firm grasp. And made eye contact, too, without first looking at my boobs. I like that and chalked up a few points in his favor.

"Matt Denning," he said. "You had me worried there for a second."

I doled out a few more points. He was secure enough in his manhood to acknowledge that he had been scared. I didn't hold it against him that he had been worried for much longer than one measly second, though. A man, even the best of them, can only admit to so much.

"What do you have?" he asked in answer to my question about the drink.

"Red Mountain on tap. Golden Lager, Red, and Wheat. Also Harp in a bottle, if that suits your taste." I had become so used to our regular clientele, it never crossed my mind that he might want a mixed drink or an aperitif.

As Matt Denning took the proffered chair, Pat called out from the doorway. "Katie, do you want to press charges against one Junior Lee Thigpen?"

My brother stood there holding the door open, half in and half out. Seeing the badge and ID case in his hand, I assumed he had dispensed some official advice to the cowboy.

"Junior?" I asked, letting the amusement clearly show in my voice.

"Honest to God. That's his given name."

"As long as *Junior* and his friends agree not to show their ugly faces around here again, let him go."

Pat winked, nodded, and went back outside.

"A glass of the Wheat, I think," Matt Denning said, once I had turned my attention back to him.

I signaled Jimmy Tuohey, who had quickly stepped behind the bar in Seamus' absence. "A pint each of Wheat and Lager, please, Jimmy."

He acknowledged me with a grin and a wave.

I sat opposite Matt with my back to the wall, hoping that Seamus would get back inside soon. Jimmy was an extremely nice, but not too bright, little leprechaun of a guy in his late twenties, and helped out around the neighborhood doing whatever odd jobs came his way. He was also a regular customer—actually a *very* regular customer—and that's why I wished for Seamus' prompt return. Jimmy would be his own *best* customer if left alone behind the bar for very long.

"That's you," Matt remarked, pointing to the walls behind and to the side of me. The tone of voice and the expression on his face showed that he was impressed.

I gave an abbreviated snort-laugh and corrected him with, "It *was* me. In another life."

Pat, Seamus, and Mary Grace and, I guess, just about all the regulars referred to the area where we sat as *Caitlin's Corner*. My brothers and sister-in-law had framed just about every picture of me they had gotten their hands on, with the exception of the very first one, showing me in a pastel-pink receiving blanket.

Thank God, they hadn't used *that* photo. You've heard people talk about puppies, I'm sure. They all look at an animal's big paws and say,

"Jeez, check out the size of those, will you. He's going to grow into them."

With me it wasn't my hands or feet, but my nose. When I was born, I was practically *all* nose. Of course, no one ever said it to Ma and Da, but I'm sure they must have thought, "Jeez, check out the size of that honker. I sure hope her face gets big enough to balance it out."

Well, it did, almost. My schnozz is still good-sized and a bit bent, but my face *did* grow into it and, with the right hairdo, no one actually stares at it much anymore.

As to the pictures of me that my relatives *had* used: Around the outside of the display were magazine ads with me hawking sportswear, volleyballs, footwear, athletic equipment, lip balm, an energy drink, spring water, and a few other more-embarrassing items of a female nature.

Then came the group photos—the '88 U.S. Olympic Gold Medal Basketball Team (me on crutches and with raccoon eyes), the '92 U.S. Olympic Bronze-Medal Volleyball team, and various pages from Italian magazines (I don't know how they got those), showing me either with my Italian Pro Volleyball League teammates or singly in profile pieces and when I was voted League MVP.

Still further toward the center of the exhibit were basketball and volleyball pictures taken during my four years at Regina Caeli and, earlier still, at Nashville's Immaculata High School.

The picture at the very center, though, and the largest one at 11 x 14, was a photo of me at age twelve, the day I placed third in the 12 to 13 year old *cailini* category of the Eastern Region *Oireachtas*. The camera caught me in mid high-step—chin out, confident smile, jet black Shirley Temple curls cascading down over my shoulders and blending in with my black velvet dress. Having naturally dark skin, the only items of color were the green, blue, and white Celtic symbols embroidered on my dress.

I had to smile whenever I looked at the display. The position and size of that one picture spoke volumes. My family took pride in all my accomplishments but the most important, in their eyes, was my third-place trophy in Irish step dancing.

That had been my last year to compete. A full one-foot growth spurt during the next year had pushed me to five-foot-eight at age thirteen and sent my coordination into a tail spin. By the time I had recovered it, I had discovered basketball and volleyball.

"Looks like you were good," Matt remarked as Jimmy set our mugs of beer down and scurried off back to the bar. "Why'd you give it up? You certainly don't look that old."

Assuming he referenced the sports photos and not the Irish step dancing picture, I stuck out my right leg. "The eventual scourge of all athletes. Blew out a knee…twice."

He nodded to where I had finished off the cowboy. "Didn't seem to bother you much over there."

"Oh, I can do that with no trouble at all and, with a brace, I can still kick the guys' butts in pickup games of B-ball and V-ball over at the Y. It's just not a world-class knee anymore."

"You seem to be adjusting well."

I gave a noncommittal shrug of my shoulders. That way I neither had to vent my frustrations nor fib about how well I was adjusting to forced retirement from that which I loved doing more than anything else in the entire world. Bitter? Who, me?

Instead, I deflected his question with one of my own. "What brings you here at this time of night with a broken car?"

As it turned out, Matt, an investment counselor at Reis-Wiedenkeller, had been meeting with a client in one of the high-rise condos down the street. With the appointment over, he had come out to a dead Mercedes. Rather than bother the client, he had seen the lights of the pub and hoofed the half block over here.

I made the usual observations and asked the requisite questions.

He wore a wedding ring. "Are you married, Matt?"

"Twenty years."

Too bad, I thought. "Any kids?"

"No, it just never happened." There seemed to be a trace of regret in his voice.

I wondered if his wife felt the same way. Why did I care, you ask? I'll admit, I was attracted to him. Hey, he was a good-looking man. All right, a little old for me, perhaps. Well, okay, old enough to be my father, but he had the kind of looks that every girl hopes her husband will have at his age. Of course most men don't, but then you hope you'll love him so much it won't matter.

In an attempt to shift the conversation to items of a less personal nature, I pointed to his tie and asked the obvious, "You a fisherman?"

He was kind, though. He didn't say, "Duh, no, I'm a bowler." Instead, he smiled broadly and nodded. "With a passion. Got a small place down on Nickajack Lake."

The almost simultaneous appearance of Mary Grace and the guy from Capshaw's Euro-Care prevented me from asking any more stupid questions.

"Hey! Somebody in here send for a wrecker?" the Capshaw's guy shouted out from the doorway.

Although Euro-Care advertised twenty-four hour service, it was obvious that the driver had been hauled out of his home to make the run and was none too happy about it. When Matt waved, the man's surly demeanor softened considerably.

"Oh, Mr. Denning. They didn't tell me it was you. I…I'll be out in the truck whenever you're ready, sir." He backed out the door with a subservient half-salute.

"I got the stain out," Mary Grace told Matt, holding up his sport-coat. "But I want you to get it dry-cleaned tomorrow, anyway. And then bring the bill here. Do you understand me?"

Having raised four sons, Mary Grace had become accustomed to tagging most of her directives with the do-you-understand-me phrase. It carried over into her dealings with everyone else.

Before Matt could protest, she continued. "And when you bring it, you come for dinner. It's on the house. And you bring your wife, too, you hear?"

"Yes, ma'am," Matt answered with a laugh, recognizing an order when he heard one. "And it was nice meeting both of you."

He allowed Mary Grace to help him on with his jacket, then crossed toward the door. "What time do you get here after those pickup games of yours, Kate?" he asked over his shoulder.

"About nine-thirty, give or take."

"We'll come then," he said. "Oh, and thanks for the beer." With that, he waved and headed out into the night.

"Now, that's a real gentleman, if ever I laid eyes on one," Mary Grace said, gathering up the used mugs from the table. "We could do with more of his kind around here."

I looked around the nearly empty pub. "We could do with more of *any* kind, Mary Grace."

"And don't I know it," she replied with a cluck of her tongue.

The Friday and Saturday-night crowds here at Kehough's were substantial. Those two nights were *ceili* nights with an Irish band and dancers and poems and stories—the whole works. Irish and would-be Irish from all over the Greater Nashville area would flock to the pub to receive an infusion of their heritage. Because our clientele was made up mainly of working people who had to rise early during the week, Monday-through-Thursday attendance was limited. On those four nights we were simply another neighborhood bar, catering to a more-or-less local patronage. With no band or dancers (we couldn't afford them), the music on the Wurlitzer reflected the varying tastes of the weeknighters—a fifty-fifty mix of Country-Western and Irish.

This being a Thursday, we could, indeed, as Mary Grace had pointed out, use more Matt Denning-type customers. Even carrying beer on tap from a local microbrewery here in Nashville had failed to have any influence on the clientele. Figuring that the serious beer drinkers would rather get their suds directly from the brew-pub itself, we switched to Red Mountain, from a microbrewery down in Birmingham, to give them a little variety. That hadn't worked either.

If you're even vaguely familiar with Nashville then you know about the two main areas of the city for nightlife. The District is located downtown, with such establishments as the Wildhorse Saloon, Bourbon Street Blues and Boogie Bar, Club Mère Bulles and the "other place" (at Kehough's we never mention Mulligan's Irish Pub by name). The second area is over by the Opryland Hotel on Music Valley Drive. That's where the big showplace theatres like the Stardust and Nashville Nightlife are located.

Don't look for Kehough's in either of these areas. We're over on Wooten Pike, which runs at a Northeast to Southwest angle between Nolensville Pike and Old Hickory Boulevard. It's an area blessed with none of the top three items for which realtors are so very fond of reciting. It's strictly a working-class/small-business neighborhood. Even the new high-rise condos down the street, where Matt Denning had met his client, were populated by only the fairly well-off.

As I walked toward the door at the rear of the pub, I said my goodnights and gave Pat a small hand-gesture in the direction of where Mickey Ryan sat nodding off.

Pat took the hint and called out, "Are you ready to go, Mr. Ryan?"

Michael Aloysius Ryan had been one of our father's closest friends. Although we referred to him as Mickey among ourselves, we always respectfully addressed him directly as *Mr. Ryan*. Retired and not at all financially well off, Seamus let him run a tab at the pub. In Da's memory, though, he only billed Mickey for about a quarter of what the old man actually ate and drank.

"And where is it we'd be going, Patty?" Mickey asked, slurring his words slightly after snorting himself awake. The question had become a ritual between them whenever Pat offered him a ride home.

"To Innisfree, Mr. Ryan," Pat said, providing the correct response as he got up from his stool. "To Innisfree."

"'Ahh, I will arise and go now,'" Mickey quoted Yeats, putting on his Donegal tweed tradesman's cap. "'And go to Innisfree,

And a small cabin build there, of clay and wattles made:

Nine bean rows will I...'"

The door closed behind me and I mounted the steps to my living quarters. Thinking back to Mary Grace's comment, I made a mental note to have some fliers designed and stuffed under doors at the high-rise. Even fairly well-off customers would be an improvement to what we had.

* * * *

I can't remember Kehough's Irish Pub as having actually been owned by a Kehough. When I was a little girl and Ma used to send me down here to drag Da home, it had been run by a Billy Wiggins.

In my early teens, when Ma used to send me down to drag Da and Pat home, a Stan Skulski owned the place. By then, Pat was back taking his supper with us. As a uniformed officer in the Patrol Division of the Metro Police, he had been wounded in the line of duty. His wife Eileen, after seeing him through to his recovery, had packed up their two kids and left, having had, as she put it, "a belly-full of sitting up and waiting for someone to come and tell me that you've gone and gotten yourself killed."

In high school, it was Seamus' wife Mary Grace who sent me down to drag Seamus and Pat home, and a Tony Rogers was in charge. My parents had passed away within six months of each other when I was a freshman, and Seamus and Mary Grace had not only inherited the old homestead but me with it.

When I started college, I turned over the fetching duties to Sean, Seamus and Mary Grace's firstborn. He had just turned fourteen during my first year at Regina Caeli and after the third time he had *accidentally* walked in on me while I was in the shower, I had opted for a dorm room.

I lost track of who owned the pub after that. The year I graduated and went to the Olympics as part of the Women's Basketball team (and recovered successfully from my first knee surgery), a representative from Metodo Minetti, a volleyball team in the Italian Professional League, had approached me. He had scouted me in college after I had been named to the All-South Region First Team in Volleyball for the third time. Badly in need of a setter (I was outstanding in that position and could double as middle blocker), the rep had made me an offer I couldn't refuse. (Women's sports are much more highly regarded across the pond.)

Armed with a *Langenscheidt Italian Phrasebook* and not much else, I set out for Vicenza, not having given Pat, Seamus, and Mary Grace what they considered to be a satisfactory explanation for going overseas. Why, they had wondered, if I wasn't going to play for America, didn't I at least sign on with Ireland. None of my many thousands of dollars worth of reasons seemed good enough. I did, though, take a brief leave of absence to play setter/middle-blocker on the U.S. National Team in the Barcelona Olympics.

I had also planned on coming home for the Atlanta games. However, this second, and what turned out to be my final, return home had been an order of magnitude less glamorous—surgery at the Vanderbilt Medical Center after a second blowout of the knee I had injured in the '88 Olympics. This injury, though, had been caused by a double-block collision with one of my own teammates rather than an opponent. The prognosis from the orthopedic surgeon had been that which every athlete dreads.

"I'm sorry, Miss O'Rourke, but I'm afraid your playing days are over."

"But what will I do? I'm only twenty-eight years old."

"Have you considered coaching girls basketball or volleyball? As long as you wear a knee brace, you can still demonstrate all the moves and keep up with the best of them."

"The best of whom?"

"The girls you're coaching."

"You don't understand, Doc. I've got at least five good playing years left in me."

"*You* don't understand, Caitlin. You've got *no* playing years left…no playing months, no playing weeks, no playing days. At least not on the same level. Your knee won't take it anymore. And any playing of *any* sport from here on out will have to be done with a knee brace."

It wasn't the money I'd miss. Six years of playing in Italy plus product endorsements, combined with some sound financial management, had left me quite well off indeed. I'd miss the competition, the challenge, and the winning. For half my life I had been competing against the best—middle school through the pros—and had always been a winner. All right, except maybe once.

But even then, in the '88 Olympics when Ecaterina Kalinovskaya had kicked my butt in the semis, my team had won 102 to 88 and had gone on to beat Yugoslavia 77 to 70 in the finals. And after all, I had helped get them there and had a gold medal that testified to my prowess.

The urge for competition, the challenge, the winning were all in my blood. And since my forced retirement, not one waking moment went by that I didn't miss them terribly, especially during the Atlanta Olympics.

I couldn't bring myself to go to there, even though it was only a six-hour drive from Nashville. Instead, I watched the games on TV, beating up the arms on my La-Z-Boy while cheering for the women's B-ball team as they captured the gold medal. The chair took a further pounding during the volleyball matches as I punched it in anger and frustration, tears rolling down my cheeks.

Never would I trash one of my teammates—make that, former teammates; they all played their hearts out. But had I been there with a good knee, in my setter/middle-blocker position, there's no way we would have finished an ignominious seventh. No way!

The pickup games at the Y did precious little to fill the void in my life. Even though I was competing against guys and winning, these guys (and I'd never say this to their faces) were not in the same league as the girls I played with in college or on the pro circuit.

* * * *

A meow from W.B. and a blinking red light on the answering machine greeted me as I entered my living room. I picked up the little black-and-white Manx and scratched her ears, walking toward the kitchen with her and pushing the PLAY button on the machine as I passed it.

"How you doing, Dub? Did you keep the place mouse-free while Mom was gone? Huh?"

W.B. purred in the affirmative.

Oh, come on, now. Don't tell me you don't carry on conversations with your pets. And those of you who don't, should. Animals can be very wise about some things. W.B. gives me a good read on first dates. Any who toss her off their laps when she affectionately hops up to greet them never get to be second dates.

The tape had rewound itself while I was getting the Fancy Feast out of the pantry, and W.B. and I listened to the recording as I spooned Ocean Whitefish & Tuna into her bowl.

"Hey, girl!" The caller didn't identify herself. She didn't need to. There was no mistaking Laurissa Green's earsplitting shriek. "I assume you're still thinking it over. You damn well better be. I'm leaving on a two-week vacation. When I get back I'm gonna need an answer one way or the other, so you think real hard about this. I definitely want you, girl, but I can't hold the damn job open forever. Take care now."

Laurissa, a former college basketball teammate and roommate of mine, had been an all-state guard during her last two years of high school in Hattiesburg, Mississippi, as had I at center for Immaculata. However, where I had passed up offers to go elsewhere, choosing, instead (with Mary Grace's arm-twisting), to go to Regina Caeli, Laurissa had come by default. Due to her lack of height (5′-4″), she hadn't been recruited by any of the Division I or II schools and had ended up as a Regina Caeli Bobcat in Division III. What she lacked in size, though, she more than made up for with her knowledge of the game. Laurissa had a fantastic sports mind. She knew the exact moment to pass the ball and when to shoot it, and had an uncanny ability for being at the right place on the floor at the right time. Upon graduating, and to no one's surprise, she had landed an assistant coaching position at Notre Dame College for Women in Fond du Lac, Wisconsin. In two years time she had been named basketball head coach and, three years later, Athletic Director.

The woman who had replaced Laurissa as basketball coach had opted for the mommy-track. The present volleyball coach would be moving into that slot in the fall and Laurissa wanted me for the V-ball position. I wasn't so sure.

On the one hand, I *knew* I could coach. But, on the other, I didn't know if I *wanted* to. On the third hand, even though I didn't like it, I had finally come to accept that my playing days were over and that I needed to do something with the rest of my life. But, on the fourth hand, did a nice Southern girl really want to freeze her nicely-shaped derriere off in Wisconsin? I'd watched Packers games on TV, and Fond du Lac is only sixty-some miles south of Green Bay.

Maybe, on the fifth hand, coaching would give me back some of the sense of competition and challenge I craved. But, on the sixth hand, maybe I didn't really know as much about coaching as I thought I did. Always having a goal to play professional V-ball, I'd gotten a Bachelor's of Philosophy degree while most of my teammates, Laurissa included, had majored in Phys. Ed. On the other hand…

I needed an octopus to consider all the various pros and cons of the decision. Not having one, I resolved to postpone making it. What the heck. Laurissa wouldn't be calling back for another two weeks, anyway.

With W.B. fed and watered, and the litter-box scooped, I got ready for bed. My nighttime ritual culminated with me undoing the French braid and running a brush through my mane a hundred strokes. Although I wasn't actually counting, I thought I detected a few more strands of silver among the black.

When you conjure up an image of a typical Irish lass, or lad for that matter, what do you see? Someone with red or reddish-brown hair, blue or green eyes, ultra-fair skin, freckles, full of face, not too tall, and pleasantly plump, right? Then you've got a pretty accurate picture of my brothers Seamus and Pat—and Mary Grace and my late parents as well. I, on the other hand, am what my countrymen and women refer to as *Black Irish.*

With olive skin, violet-blue eyes, jet-black curly hair, I have nary a freckle (at least none that show in V-ball gear). I'm also exceptionally tall and have high cheekbones and an aquiline nose (which, after the third time it was broken, now takes a pronounced turn to the right because some moron in Italy reset it crooked).

The neighborhood washerwomen used to whisper about changelings and substitutions by the *Sidhe*. Even Da and my brothers would sometimes get into the act, particularly when, as a little girl, I became a pest while they were together doing guy-things. One of them would call me *nig*, knowing that it would drive me wailing away in search of my mother.

Ma, though, would dry my tears and reassure me that not only hadn't the fairy-folk switched me for her own daughter, but that I wasn't a Negro, either. (Back then, the term African-American was only just beginning to be used—at least in our Middle-Tennessee household.) She would always serve up a quite logical explanation for my looks. Something about survivors of the Spanish Armada being washed up on the Hibernian shore and being assimilated into the culture and recessive genes and the like.

I never knew if the story were true, but, somehow, it always comforted me—that and Ma's homemade oatmeal-raisin cookies. There's nothing like milk and cookies to take your mind off your troubles.

Having finished the hair ritual, I climbed into bed, with W.B. curled up at my feet, and said my nightly prayers, sarcastically thanking the Lord, His Holy Mother, and all the Saints for giving me the talent to become a world-class athlete, then pulling the rug out from under me at my prime.

Turlough McInerney, Mary Grace's brother, was the pastor of Our Lady, Queen of the Universe, the parish where we all had been baptized, gotten our religious education, and still worshiped (some of us not as regularly as others). Soon after I had returned home from the hospital, Mary Grace went to him, concerned because she had heard me yelling at God about my situation. As reported to me by Seamus, Turlough chuckled and told her not to worry and that it was a good sign. It showed that I was still on speaking terms with the Almighty.

That night, like so many others, God punished my sarcasm in His usual way. He saw to it that I dreamt about tearing up my knee and getting my nose broken at the '88 Olympics. However, with His infinite sense of humor He had added a new twist. A gang of pimply-faced, drippy-nosed cowboys wrenched my leg back and forth while wee-folk repeatedly punched me in the schnozz.

And through it all, Laurissa Green stood on the sidelines shouting, "You wouldn't have to worry about no rednecks and fairies up here in Fond du Lac, girl!"

No, Rissa, just snow clear up to my butt for half the year, that's all.

CHAPTER 3

The weekend had gone the same as most others before it. Although I did make time for a game of V-ball at the Y on Saturday afternoon (my team won three out of five), Friday and Saturday nights were spent at home, dateless as usual. I'm not sure why that is, but when I ask friends who have fixed me up, the word *intimidating* seems to come up quite often.

After being pressured by my adoring fans (Mickey Ryan yelling, "Hey, now, Caitlin, how about giving us a dance?"), I changed out of my boots into hard-shoes, donned the knee brace, and impressed the crowd with a Hornpipe on both Friday and Saturday. Pat, Seamus, and Mary Grace beamed with pride.

Thought briefly about the Fond du Lac deal, then promptly put it out of my mind.

* * * *

Sunday morning I met Seamus, Mary Grace, and Tim (their number-four son, who still lived at home) at Our Lady, Queen of the Universe, for 9:30 Mass and managed to garner more black marks in God's book by calling his holy priest a wise-ass. Turlough had it coming, though. His remark about putting my picture on the side of a milk carton was totally uncalled-for. I had been there just two…no, three…well, maybe four weeks ago, tops.

At the afternoon B-ball game, my team won by eight points. This particular win was exceptionally gratifying. A new kid had showed up to play, Reginald Baker, a six-four basketball player extraordinaire (self-proclaimed) from Middle Tennessee State. Reggie, a cousin to one of the regulars, was going to show this Y crowd a thing or two, or so he thought.

The designated captains rock-paper-scissored for first pick; Bobby Curtis won and picked me. Reggie did his Kermit the Frog impression, eyes bulging out of his skull. Talk about a blow to the ego. Not only didn't he get selected first, but an old *chick* wearing a knee brace did.

It wasn't too long into the game, however, before he found out why. I surely hope this kid liked the taste of rubber because I stuffed a good fifty percent of his shots down his throat and outscored him thirty-three to eighteen.

On Sunday evening, I couldn't help but think of Laurissa's offer. Just me and W.B. doing our laundry. Actually, if the truth be told, W.B. hates doing laundry. She usually has me wash up her blanket for her.

Still no closer to making a decision, I opted to postpone it yet again, choosing, instead, to look over Kehough's second-quarter earnings statement. Nadine Weisbaum, the middle third of Shamansky, Weisbaum, and Polhemus, CPA's (also my personal financial manager) had finally gotten it prepared and had dropped off the paperwork the evening before.

I had bought Kehough's for two reasons. Primarily I wanted to give something back to Pat, Seamus, and Mary Grace for looking out for me after Ma and Da passed away. They wouldn't take money; I knew that all too well. Many times over the years I had tried slipping them some.

Even when the apparel manufacturing plant where Seamus had worked for twenty-six years (the last twelve as a foreman) had closed and moved to Mexico, he had put on a brave face and claimed it to be only a temporary setback. But after almost a year of him finding only part-time jobs and having to rely almost totally on Mary Grace's income as a cook at Cracker Barrel, I knew something drastic had to be done.

The first six weeks or so after getting out of the hospital, I had lived in brother Pat's spare bedroom. We didn't cramp each other's style. With the hours he worked as a Detective Sergeant in the Robbery Division and my luck with men, neither of us had much of a love-life.

There's a three-bedroom flat over Kehough's. Using the reason of needing a place of my own to live, I made a very nice offer to Jerry Steggman, the then-owner, and stood back so that he and his wife wouldn't trample me to death. I could swear I heard the wife shouting, "Cash the check quick, before she changes her mind," all the way out to their pickup truck.

While none of my family would take cash from me, no one had a problem accepting a piece of Kehough's, their home away from home anyway—twenty-five percent each to Pat, Seamus, and Mary Grace. And, of course, I made sure to let Seamus and Mary Grace know just how big a favor they'd be doing me by running the place. Everyone agreed. In addition to Seamus and Mary Grace's fifty percent, they would also draw salaries, the same as what their former jobs paid. Pat and I would be content with our respective quarter shares of the profits, plus free food and drinks, and lodging for me.

In looking over the accounting figures, those profits were negligible. We were just barely covering Seamus' and Mary Grace's salaries and benefits. But that was okay by me. After all, that was the primary purpose of the investment. Besides, I hadn't spent a dime on food or drink in the seven months since we opened.

Nadine had also dropped off my personal financial statement. A note paperclipped to the report cover read, "I never thought I'd say this to a client, but you're allowed to spend some of it, Caitlin. It's yours. You've earned it."

After performing my hair ritual, I went to bed thinking that if I took the job in Wisconsin, I'd be spending plenty of money on warmer clothing.

* * * *

Monday, also, started the same as all the Mondays before it. I slept in late, did my six miles around the neighborhood, and tormented Duke, the Larsen's Dalmatian, by banging my hand along his chain-link fence as I ran by. It does a cat-person's heart good to watch that fool-beast growl and snarl and snap until he runs headfirst into the garage. Besides, it was my way of getting even with him.

Every once in a while, usually late at night, the Larsens let Dukie out to get a little exercise prowling the neighborhood. His exercise consists of making a beeline for Kehough's and strewing our trash all over the alleyway. God help him if I ever catch his spotted butt out there some night. God help *me* if the Larsens ever leave their gate open during the day as I'm running by and banging on the fence.

After an hour on the Nautilus, I showered, dressed, and went downstairs for lunch, wondering what I'd do to kill the six hours before V-ball at the Y. The aroma of Salmon Chowder greeted me as I opened the downstairs door to the pub. Opting for that and a Grilled Cheese Sandwich, I reviewed the high points of the quarterly statement with Mary Grace. (Seamus figured that if we had cash in the till, we must be doing fine.)

With lunch over, I now only had five more hours to kill. I've got to get a life. Maybe Fond du Lac really *is* the answer. Deciding that perhaps Nadine Weisbaum had been right about me spending some money, I got Liddy out of the garage and tooled down I-65 to the Cool Springs Galleria.

Liddy, you ask? In the garage? Of course. Where else would you expect to find a car. And don't tell me you never named any of your cars or boats.

My very first was Eldred, a white Ford Escort that brother Pat had given me as a high-school graduation present, bought at a police auction. It had been used by some very bad people to do some very bad things, but I could tell that El really hadn't been a willing participant. He had served me faithfully, all through college.

In Italy, with my new-found V-ball wealth, I had a succession of flashy sports cars that I could barely fit into, among them Franco the Ferrari. My last vehicle, before being forced to come home, had been Rollo the Range Rover, built for comfort and durability, not for speed. Rollo, as it turned out, was far more durable than yours truly.

Back home and once again able to drive, I was drawn to a mocha-colored Toyota Land Cruiser. Liddy, my first car with a girl's name, and I have gotten on well together.

I wonder what a shrink would make of that? While a hotshot jockette, I had cars with male names. Now, as a has-been, I have a female car. Hmm.

Shopping turned out to be a chore. First of all, I don't *need* anything. From my endorsement contracts, I have one closet chock-full of athletic wear—enough now to last another ten years. Boots, jeans, and western shirts from Sheplers are my standard everyday garb. For semi-dress-up occasions I add one of a dozen or so blazers. A step up on the dressy-meter are prairie skirts and western blouses (again from Sheplers), usually for church. Mary Grace would die of embarrassment if I ever showed up for Mass in slacks.

I really don't have an occasion to get more dressed up than that and if I did (like, maybe, get a date who would take me somewhere really special) I have a second closet full of Italian designer originals, mostly unworn.

While totally unproductive, the trip did, however, kill the required time and I showed up at the Y ready for action. Unfortunately, the pickings were pitiful that night—some high-school kids and guys a few years older who all wanted to be spikers.

Why is it so hard for kids to understand that you can't make a really good kill unless someone sets up the ball properly? And if no one blocks, you never get a chance to score. With some rudimentary coaching tips from me on how to set, block, dig, and not poach in each other's territory, my team won four straight—one by a shutout. Maybe I *would* do all right as a full-time coach.

* * * *

Kehough's is the middle establishment in a five-building strip that takes up the entire block on Wooten Pike between Plainview and Deford. All the parking places are in front, except for a few proprietors' spots in the rear. An alley separates the businesses from their respective garages-slash-storage buildings.

I had tucked Liddy into her stall, locked the garage door, and, with Mary Grace's Dingle Pies on my mind, walked across the darkened alleyway toward the pub. It had rained earlier that evening and was still overcast. With the August heat, the dampness in the air magnified the slightest sound.

"Let go of me!" a woman's voice cut through the silence of the night.

I turned toward the voice, at the Deford Street entrance to the alley. In the dim light, I could see a man in a cowboy hat struggling with a blond woman. Holding her from behind he appeared to be trying to yank her purse away from her. Defiantly, the woman hung on securely to the strap end.

"Hey!" I shouted, dropping my gym bag and starting out at a jog in their direction.

I must have startled them, unfortunately the woman more than the man. She let go of the purse strap and the man threw her up against the Claridge Cleaners garage. As she sank into a heap in the bushes, he took off like a rabbit, down Deford in the opposite direction from Wooten.

Two reasons kept me from giving chase. First, I had taken off my knee brace after the V-ball game and my leg wouldn't have held up under a strenuous run. Secondly, the woman now sprawled out in the wet alley was crying, and I didn't know how badly she had been hurt.

"Please, someone?" she whimpered. "Please, help me?"

I knelt down beside her. Although probably in her early forties, she kept herself in excellent shape. The now-tousled-once-perfectly-coifed blond hair framed a very pretty oval face (aside from the mud caked on the left cheek). And, with her skirt hiked up past mid-thigh, I could see that those legs would certainly turn more than their share of male heads. The other thing I noticed was the dress itself (an expensive mock two-piece in taupe linen), not the type we normally see in this neighborhood.

The woman didn't appear to be all that badly hurt but, then, I shouldn't judge everyone by my personal standards for pain absorption. Resisting the urge to rehearse for the Fond du Lac job and say, "Get up and walk it off!" (a coach's standard response to almost any injury), I tried to be comforting instead.

"Don't worry," I told her, trying to affect the Mary Grace motherly coo but coming up way short. "He's gone. Nobody's going to hurt you. Are you able to move everything?"

After trying each limb individually, the woman nodded and squeaked out an, "I think so," between sobs.

"Come on," I said softly, moving behind her and taking her by the armpits. "Let's get you up and inside."

With my help, she struggled to a standing position.

"I'm Kate," I said, attempting to brush some of the mud off her shoulder. "What are you doing out here at this time of night?"

"I'm supposed to meet my husband. In that bar," she said, still sniffling while pointing toward the small neon sign over the back door of Kehough's. "My name's Delane....Delane Denning. I can't thank you enough for rescuing me. I don't know what would have happened if you hadn't come along."

With that, Mrs. Denning stood on the toes of her muddy, bone-colored Ferragamo pumps and kissed me on the cheek.

I was touched. Really. Now I knew how guys felt when they rescued damsels in distress.

No, don't go reading anything between those lines. Just because I intimidate men doesn't mean that I go the other way. I like men. Really. I just can't seem to keep one for very long.

"Well, he's gone now," I said to Mrs. Denning. "Come on with me."

As I shepherded her to Kehough's door, I hoped brother Pat occupied his usual stool, second from the left end of the bar. There had been a third reason why I hadn't given chase to the purse-snatcher. I really didn't need to catch the thief. He had turned toward me when I yelled.

In that brief moment, the light from the solitary bulb above the back door of the dry cleaners had clearly illuminated the pimply face of Junior Lee Thigpen.

CHAPTER 4

Now that the shock had worn off, a semi-hysterical Delane Denning sat curled up at one end of my sofa. Mud from the alley, mixed with streaks of mascara, still encased half of her pretty face. A blue ice bag partially obscured the other half. With her free hand, she held a tumbler of B & B, from which she freely and frequently gulped.

W.B. had snuggled in on the woman's lap, attempting to let her know that everything would be all right. Although not buying any of it, Delane did reward W.B. for her efforts by periodically setting the glass down on the end table, then using that hand to scratch the kitty's ears. You could hear the purring from halfway across the room.

The accent tables in my apartment are all made of English Oak. (I tell Seamus and Mary Grace that they're Irish Oak, just to keep peace in the family.) Delane put my paranoia to rest right off. Although visibly shaken, she still had the presence of mind to take a coaster from the stack and use it for her drink.

Matt Denning, intent on wearing a path in my needlepoint rug, circled the sofa like a caged animal. He apologized profusely over and over again, trying his best to assume all the responsibility for what had happened because he had let his wife drive by herself "in this neighborhood."

I let the slur pass. He was, after all, understandably upset.

Having driven Matt over to Capshaw's Euro-Care in her BMW to retrieve his Mercedes (with its brand new starter motor), Delane was supposed to follow her husband over here. In compliance with Mary Grace's orders of Thursday last, Matt had gotten his sportcoat cleaned and was bringing the bill to us and his wife to dinner. Delane had lost him two traffic lights back on Wooten Pike, then, when she got here, had driven past both parking lot entrances before seeing the Kehough's sign. Rather than turn around, she had parked on Deford just beyond the alleyway and had barely begun to walk the thirty-or-so yards to the back door when Junior had accosted her.

Pat had taken down all the particulars—my eyewitness account and precious little from Delane, since she had been attacked from behind and hadn't seen much of anything. He had just finished phoning in the report and had requested limousine service for our friend Junior.

"Just in case it takes a day or so for us to find him," Pat told the Dennings, "better get those credit cards canceled and the locks changed on your doors."

"The locks?!" Delane wailed.

"Your house keys were in the purse, ma'am. And your ID. He knows where you live."

I made a mental note to smack Pat on the back of his rapidly balding head. Like he couldn't have told that to Matt in private?

"I'll have it attended to first thing in the morning," Matt promised.

That was not the answer Delane wanted to hear. "Tomorrow? What about tonight? My God, Matthew, he might think that I can identify him. He'll come and murder us in our beds."

W.B. beat a hasty retreat for her wicker basket in the kitchen while Matt tried to calm his wife.

"Lanie, honey, I can't do anything about it tonight. If it really bothers you, I'll give the Maxwell House a call. You can spend the night there."

"Me? What about you?"

"Well, under the circumstances, I don't think I should leave the house empty overnight. We'll go home so you can get cleaned up and change, then you can pack a few things and I'll drive you over to the hotel."

Delane had made up her mind on the subject. "I am not setting one foot in that house until those locks have been changed. And I certainly am not checking into a hotel looking like *this*."

Pat had ducked out while Delane had been talking, pantomiming that he had to give a piano recital—either that or type up the robbery report, I'm not sure which.

Clearly frustrated that his wife would neither go home nor to a hotel, Matt tried another suggestion. "What about Cove Creek?" He gestured toward the clock on my mantle. "It's only ten. If we leave now, we'll be there by eleven-thirty. You've got plenty of clothes there. I'll drive back, spend the night in the house and get everything arranged with the locksmith tomorrow."

She thought about it for a second or two, then acquiesced but with a caveat. "You know I won't get a wink of sleep but, I guess, if it's only for one night."

"Actually, Lanie, unless you want to drive yourself, it will have to be for three nights. I'll be in Memphis on business for the next few days, remember?"

"Then you'll just have to cancel. I'm *not* spending three nights by myself in the middle of nowhere while there's a maniac on the loose."

Matt's patience was growing thin. "He couldn't possibly know you'd be there. And, I would hardly call a gated resort community with twenty-four-hour security patrols, a golf course, tennis courts, private beach, not to mention our own pool, hot tub, and sauna, *the middle of nowhere*." With hands thrown up, he turned to me for support. "Does that sound like the middle of nowhere to you, Kate?"

"Hey, beach, pool, sauna, golf course. It sounds like fun," I answered cheerfully, trying my best to be helpful.

"Then would you come with me, Katie?" Delane pleaded, dropping the ice pack and grasping my hand in both of hers. "I'd feel so much safer if you were there with me and it wouldn't cost you a cent. Matthew would pay for everything, wouldn't you, dear?"

I made a mental note to smack myself on the back of the head. Wouldn't a noncommittal shrug have been in order instead of such unbridled enthusiasm on my part?

Matt did a deer-caught-in-the-headlights impression. "Lanie, you can't expect Kate to just pick up and leave on the spur of the moment." Then, as he thought about it, he seemed to change his mind in mid-sentence. "Although, Kate, since you did say you were sort of retired…could I impose…I mean, I'd be happy to pay you for your time. In fact, I'd insist on it."

Delane bobbed her head up and down like one of those rear-car-window dogs. "An all-expenses-paid three-day vacation, Katie. Oh, please, say you'll come with me? It'll be so much fun. And Matthew will be very generous with his wallet. After all, you *did* save my life in that alley."

I was watching the Dennings the entire time and since neither one moved their lips, it had to have been me that I heard say, "Well, okay, what the heck."

On the way downstairs to let Seamus know where I'd be for the next three days and to ask Mary Grace to feed and water W.B., I gave myself a smack, though not on the back of the head. This open-handed smack I directed solidly to my forehead. One down, one to go. I'd get Pat when I returned from *vacation*.

* * * *

The eight-hundred-acre resort community of Cove Creek is located on Center Hill Lake, just west of Silver Point, Tennessee. Delane had talked almost nonstop all the way up, alternating between two topics, the wonderfulness of her husband and whether Junior Lee Thigpen would be caught by the time we returned to Nashville.

I had volunteered to drive; Delane was in no shape to attempt it. Matt promised his wife that he'd have someone from Capshaw's pick up her BMW and keep it until he got back from Memphis and we returned from Cove Creek.

It was around twelve when I started to brake Liddy to a stop at the main gate but the old geezer on guard-duty raised the pike, smiled, and thumbed us on through. Either he had recognized Delane (she had washed her face and redone her hair at my place before we left) or he figured two white women belonged there. Although I had Matt's gate pass in my shirt pocket, I never got the opportunity to show it. Instead, we both waved and kept right on going. I wondered if two black men arriving at midnight would have gotten the same warm reception.

Home sites in Cove Creek were in three, five, or eight acre parcels that started around eighty-five grand (that's just for the land) depending on their proximity to the lake. The Denning manse was, as were all the other shoreline homes, built on three acres, complete with private beach and boathouse. I'm just guessing but figure two-hundred grand for the lot and another seven-hundred for the house (2,500 square feet).

During the twenty-five-cent tour, I dutifully checked the locks on all the windows and doors, then I again had to rescue my damsel in distress by helping her undo the clasp on a garnet-and-pearl lavaliere.

I don't know why they make those little springy-things so small. I have a gold pendant like that, myself. When fastened, the chain is too small to fit over my head. And to get it fastened or unfastened, you need both another pair of hands and a second set of eyes.

While Delane showered and got ready for bed, I put away the few provisions we had bought from the Zippy Stop bandit at the Interstate exit, then brushed my hair. After assuring my house-mate that I had double-locked the front door and set the chain, we both turned in.

Here's a tip if you ever consider going on vacation with someone you don't know very well. Make a list of your likes and dislikes beforehand. If there aren't at least two likes that match up, stay home. Either that or plan on spending quite a bit of time apart. Delane and I, as it turned out, had just the bare minimum.

On Tuesday morning I did my six miles on the jogging trail through the forest. Delane slept in.

We breakfasted together, then I hit the links. Delane laid out by the pool in a low-cut top and high-cut bottom one-piece gold mesh bathing suit that seemed more suited for table-dancing then for swimming.

After golf (the two old sandbaggers the golf pro set me up to play with took me for twenty bucks apiece), Delane and I drove down to Smithville for the remainder of our provisions.

Why? Beats me. There was a market within the confines of Cove Creek but Delane claimed that the prices were too high.

Now, as I've told you before (and I'm not bringing it up again merely to brag), I'm financially well off; however, not nearly in Delane Denning's league, judging from the house on the lake. But, had it been *my* money and not part of the five-large that Matt had peeled off and given to me for expenses, I certainly would not have driven fifteen miles to save a dime on Post Toasties.

That afternoon, while Delane laid out by the pool, I played tennis. The tennis pro apologized afterward for pairing me with Ashley Leighton-Murdock. Thirty-something, blond, pretty face, and a gorgeous figure, Ashley looked great, sitting around the court in her designer duds holding her three-hundred-dollar racquet. I kicked her firm little butt six-zero in the first set, then played pitty-pat with her for another hour or so before taking the second set seven-five. Jerry (the pro) promised that if I came back mid-morning of the next day, he'd give me a real game himself.

After tennis I hit the sauna, then took a swim in the lake, both while Delane laid out by the pool. She didn't want to muss her hair.

As I came up from the small beach, tying the wrap skirt that matched my brown-and-metallic gold snakeskin-print swimsuit, I caught up with her on her way to the house. She stepped gingerly in her bare feet, picking her way along the pebbled walkway, trying to avoid stepping on the sharp pieces of stone.

"You ought to get yourself a pair of sandals," I said, pointing to my own Birkenstocks.

"Oh, I have some," she replied in a tone laced with disgust. "But the strap rubs my little toe raw."

I offered my arm and helped her the rest of the way.

We *did* go to dinner together that night. Although the country club had what looked to be a fairly upscale restaurant, Delane insisted on taking me to Frank's Harbor, a "cute little place just up river."

Now, being born and bred in Tennessee, I know this may seem like heresy to some of my fellow Southerners, but while I *do* like properly-prepared catfish, I can't, for the life of me, understand the purpose of hushpuppies. *They have no taste*! There, I've said it. So sue me.

Back at the manse, I took a nighttime swim in the lake while Delane watched TV (CMT, of course).

Since we both had big days (apparently laying out by the pool can take a lot out of someone), we called it a night just after the ten-o'clock news.

* * * *

Wednesday turned out to be an almost Xerox copy of Tuesday, except my golf and tennis times were swapped around and we went to a different dive for dinner—The Golden Ginzu.

Here's a tip for selecting a Japanese steakhouse. If there are no Asians of any persuasion involved with the operation, take a pass. The chef at this one was a dead ringer for Gaylord on the old *Hee-Haw* TV show.

"And what will you purty little gals have tonight?" Bubbamoto (my name for him, not his own) asked with a moronic grin.

We both ordered filet and got round steak, either that or the sole of someone's boot. And I'll be darned if they didn't serve hushpuppies, Japanese-style with ginger sauce. I won't bore you with the details on the remainder of the meal. Suffice it to say, you'll find nary a star next to The Golden Ginzu's listing in the Triple-A book.

That morning during my tennis match (although Jerry beat me three sets to one, they were all close) the FedEx guy had shown up. The envelope he brought contained keys to the new main and garage door locks on Matt and Delane's Forest Hills home.

Since Matt would be arriving from Memphis about mid-afternoon of the next day (Thursday), Delane decided that we'd spend another night and morning at Cove Creek and get back to Nashville just in time to meet her husband. It was okay by me. That afternoon the two sandbaggers had each taken another twenty bucks from me at golf and I hoped to get some of it back before we left.

I conducted my nightly ritual (checking the doors and windows, helping Delane out of her lavaliere, and brushing my hair), then went to bed. For the third night in a row I slept soundly, without dreaming of tearing up my knee and breaking my nose. Maybe all I needed to exorcise my demons was to get some semblance of a life. And, just maybe, taking the Fond du Lac job would do the trick permanently.

* * * *

On Thursday I lost another forty bucks, thanked the old geezers for the pleasure, took a swim in the lake, and got ready for the trip home.

Delane came into my room, lavaliere in hand. She had opted for a low-cut, black-and-white linen coatdress, hemmed about four inches above the knee, and white pumps with a black patent leather cap-toe and heel.

"Where's the garden party?" I asked as I fastened the pendant around her neck.

"I haven't seen my man in three whole days. I want him to realize what he's missed." She gave a throaty laugh as she walked away and then struck a sultry pose in the doorway. "So, what do you think?"

"That'll do it all right," I agreed. "Give me a couple minutes to make the bed and I'll be right with you."

"Don't bother with that," she said, gesturing toward the rat's nest I had made out of the room. "I'll phone the maid service from home. They'll change the towels and bedding when they clean the rest of the place."

After she had gone, I glanced over at the mirror on the dresser. In my standard boots and jeans and, today, wearing a white oxford western-style shirt with turquoise beads and silver conchas, I looked a bit underdressed compared to Delane. I unzipped my suitcase, retrieved a navy linen blazer and checked the mirror again. Still nowhere near Delane but, now, at least, I'd be passable in polite society.

After a final inspection inside (windows, doors, stove, burners, and thermostat), Delane double-locked the front door and rehid the key in the porch light while I checked out back to make sure she had shut off the pump for the pool. She had, although it escapes me why she had bothered turning it on in the first place. Not so much as a pinkie toe had ever gotten wet in that pool.

The trip didn't turn out to be a total waste, however. I did find Delane's sport sandals by the chaise, along with an old towel. She hadn't brought a suitcase with her and wasn't taking anything back except the outfit she wore. Rather than open up the house again, I rinsed the sandals off in the pool, wiped them down thoroughly with the towel, and tucked them away in my own bag. The towel I left on the chaise.

With that last little task taken care of, I came back around to the front of the garage, tossed the bag into Liddy's second seat and we set out for home.

The drive back to Nashville turned out to be very similar to the trip up to Cove Creek. Delane chattered on and on, upbeat one moment and talking about how wonderful a man Matt was; the next, worried about whether Junior Lee Thigpen would find her before the police found him.

Although I had enjoyed my mini-vacation, I was glad to be getting back. Nudging the cruise-control up a notch, I decided to risk a ticket. Delane's blathering was beginning to get on my nerves ever so slightly. Besides, while it's true that I thought Matt Denning to be charming, handsome, and debonair, I've found that women who constantly brag on what great husbands they have are usually trying to convince themselves.

After a short pit-stop at the I-40 and Briley Parkway Marriott (Delane's bladder couldn't hold out for another fifteen minutes), we took the Hillsboro Pike exit off of I-440 and drove south to the Denning home. The 4,000-square-foot Georgian estate, located in the center of an acre-and-a-half parcel on Marylebone Drive, backed up onto Forest Creek Park in the city of Forest Hills. A twelve-foot high black wrought-iron fence ringed the entire complex. I steered Liddy into the drive and up the fifty yards or so to the circle in front of the house, the only area outside the fencing.

"Did you have fun?" Delane asked as I braked the car to a stop.

"I sure did. It was just what the doctor ordered."

As I set the shift selector in PARK, Delane put her arm around my neck and gave me a quick but warm kiss on the cheek. "I'm so glad," she said. "You're a very special person, Katie." Her deep brown eyes were moist.

Thankfully she didn't wait around for a response. There would have been one heck of an awkward silence while I attempted to think of one. Instead, she smiled, opened the door, hopped out of the car, and ran up the steps to the portico. I slowly got out on my side, still a little taken aback by the kiss.

Delane, having used her new key to open the front door, had no sooner entered the house when a car horn honked behind me. A Mercedes had just turned into the drive and, through the windshield, I saw Matt Denning raise his arm and wave. I started to wave back at him, but a sound from inside the house caused me to stop abruptly.

The hair on my neck and arms stood straight out. I took in a short gasp of breath and my heart missed a beat. Although not a hunter, I have shot skeet numerous times. The sound that I had heard was unmistakably that of two shotgun blasts, fired in rapid succession. Not waiting for Matt, I bolted toward the portico, taking all three steps in one bound, screaming, "*Delane!*"

I reached the open front door and pulled up short, gulping down air in an attempt to keep my lunch from making an encore appearance. At the far side of the foyer, my damsel in distress lie on her back, limbs at odd angles with one shoe off and the other on. The garnet-and-pearl lavaliere hung down the side of her neck. What had been Delane Denning's pretty, oval face, though, now resembled raw hamburger, with the blood already starting to pool about her head.

No sooner did I step though the doorway toward her when my own head exploded in a kaleidoscope of colors, the crushing pain slamming me up against the door jamb. Then, as if in slow motion, I felt myself falling.

* * * *

"Missile ork?!" a voice called out and a pair of large but gentle hands touched me ever so softly. "Missile ork?! Bantu earbee?"

Chapter 5

The paramedics had just given me something for the pain (after determining that I had no allergies to any medications) when a pair of detectives arrived, a white male and a black female. The detectives conferred quietly with the uniforms for a half minute, then the female lifted a corner of the sheet and they took a brief glance at the remains of Delane Denning. Both winced, looked at each other and shook their heads.

The female member of the team came over, hitched up the slacks of her light sage pantsuit and squatted down next to me. "I'm Detective Osborn, Miss O'Rourke. Metro Police Homicide. I worked with your brother some years back when I was in Robbery. How's the Sarge doing these days?"

She looked to be about my age, but small and wiry. Although reasonably attractive, she used no makeup and had her hair shorn to about a quarter-inch in length. Underneath her professional politeness there was a hard edge that had to have come from many years of proving herself to white, male peers. I'd have bet money that she drank her beer straight from the bottle.

I managed an "okay," in response to her question about Pat and she continued. "I won't keep you long, but I do need to ask a few questions."

After a minuscule nod from me, she went down her mental list. "Did you see who shot Mrs. Denning?"

I replied with a small shake of my head.

"Did you see who hit you?"

The same.

"Did you see anyone else around the house when you arrived?"

Ditto.

"Do you happen to know where Mr. Denning was when Mrs. Denning was shot?"

"Matt?" I asked, letting her feel the full force of my incredulity at her question.

"The husband's always a possibility, Miss O'Rourke. Do you?"

"Do I what?"

"Do you have any idea where he might have been?"

"I know *exactly* where he was. The driveway."

"This driveway?"

"He was just pulling in."

"Are you sure?"

"He honked and waved to me. I saw him clearly."

One of the paramedics touched Detective Osborn on the shoulder. "Officer?"

"Detective," she quickly corrected him and her coal-black eyes flashed for just an instant.

"I'm sorry, Detective. But we really need to be going."

She gave me a pat on the shoulder. "Hang in there; you'll be all right. I'm sure you've experienced much worse pain on the court."

At first I thought she might tell me to get up and walk it off. Instead, she said, "The rest can wait. I'll talk to you later." Then turning toward the one uniformed cop (Wittek, the chauvinist piglet) who still stood by the sheet, she said, "Where's the husband?"

Wittek pointed through the foyer toward one wing of the house. "Sergeant Langford put him in the den, ma'am. He and Detective Sykes are in there with him."

"Detective?" I called out, choking again on some blood as the paramedics raised the stretcher. She looked back and cocked an eyebrow. "You forgot to ask me who did it," I said.

Detective Osborn walked back toward me. "You said you didn't see anyone."

"Not seeing and not knowing are two different things. Talk to Pat. He's got an APB out on a Junior Lee Thigpen. Junior stole Del…Mrs. Denning's purse last Monday."

"I'll check it out. Thanks." She gave me a wink, then motioned to the paramedics.

* * * *

"Ahh, but you are a big one, are you not, Miss Caitlin O'Rourke?" Dr. Bhitiyakul chirped, noticing my feet and lower legs hanging over the edge of the gurney. In his accented singsong delivery, the word *big* came out *beeg*. "You must be an amazing woman, hey?" When he grinned, his teeth looked extra-white against his nut-brown skin.

"Amazing?" I asked. "In what way?" *Is this little camel jockey trying to make a pass at me while my proboscis swells up like a banana?* I wondered.

"The amazing women. You know? The warriors? With the bow and the arrow? They are reputed to be big, like you. Yes?"

"You mean, Amazons."

"Quite so. Amazingons. Yes, indeedie."

I had been at the hospital for just under three hours. One of the paramedics had gotten my purse from Liddy before we left Forest Hills so I had been able to prove to the white dragon at the triage desk that I did, in fact, have health insurance. Armed with the knowledge that everyone would be well paid for their services, she had started me on my snail's pace through the maze. At last, I had reached the inner sanctum and was now graced with the presence of a real, honest-to-goodness doctor, well, Kamul Bhitiyakul, the resident on duty, anyway.

"You do not seem to have a broken head," Dr. Bhitiyakul said, examining the x-rays against a light-board. "But your nose, that is another matter altogether. Also, I see this is not the first time you have broken it, Caitlin O'Rourke. You must learn to watch where you are going, yes?" Again the grin.

"Yeah," I answered. "I guess I should."

"Yes, indeedie, you should. But you are most fortunate that you have broken this nose many times before."

"Yeah. That's me, Doc. The luck of the Irish."

"No, no. I do not make joke, Caitlin O'Rourke. I am quite serious. Yes, indeedie." He crossed back over to me. "Here, I show you. Are you able to stand?"

I swung my legs over the edge of the gurney and either I or the room started to sway, maybe both. As soon as my feet touched the floor, Dr. Bhitiyakul stopped me.

"That will do just fine and dandy. You do not have to stand all the way. Stay sitting there and I will show you."

Balancing my tush on the edge of the gurney, I tried to affect a skeptical expression. That's plenty hard to do with a cucumber growing out of your face.

"Do you know with what you were hit?" he asked.

"No. It felt like it could have been a baseball bat."

"It was a shotgun, Boo," a familiar voice spoke up from behind me. Brother Pat stood there, badge in hand, flushed and puffing from having run down the corridor.

I wondered about the badge until I remembered the triage white dragon. Apparently the phrase "the girl is my sister" hadn't impressed her. The badge, on the other hand, had. Although he tried acting nonchalant, now that he could see I'd be all right, I knew he had rushed down here with his siren blaring. The use of my childhood nickname was a dead giveaway.

* * * *

As I've told you, both my brothers are considerably older than me. When Pat, the younger of the two, entered junior high, Ma convinced Da to let her take a job outside the home. I understand it had been a tough sell. Anyway, Da reluctantly agreed and she went to work as a part-time bookkeeper at a restaurant. Owned then as it is today by Nikolaos Panacopoulos and named after the Ionian island of his birthplace, Zakinthos is one of the few four-star establishments in Nashville.

Ma had been on the job for only six months or so when she became pregnant with yours truly and had to quit (at Da's insistence) three months later. Because the pregnancy had been unplanned and, therefore, quite unexpected, I had been affectionately tagged early on with the nickname, as in, when you jump out from behind a door and yell, "Surprise!" or…"Boo!"

* * * *

"A shotgun?" I asked.

"Twelve gauge. Over and under," Pat said. "According to Ozzie Osborn, the same one used on Mrs. Denning. Lucky for you, the perp didn't have time to reload. Instead of blowing your head off, too, he just tried to knock it off."

"See?" Dr. Bhitiyakul said. "Did I not just say that you were lucky, Caitlin O'Rourke? This policeman, he agrees with me."

"This policeman is my bother, Patrick, Dr. Bhitiyakul. Pat, Dr. Bhitiyakul." Before they could exchange pleasantries, I quickly followed up with, "But why does having a thrice-broken nose make me lucky this time?"

The good doctor grinned again. "We will use your brother Patterick in our little demonstration. Patterick, you will come and stand over here by me, please, okay? Yes."

Pat stuffed his badge case into the pocket of his hunter-green sport-coat, flashed me a "What the hell is this all about?" look and crossed over to the doctor.

Dr. Bhitiyakul handed him a tongue depressor. "Here, you will pretend that this is shotgun. Yes? Now, pretend to strike me on nose with it."

Pat stood there, looking back and forth from the doctor to the tongue depressor to me.

"Come, come. Quickly," Dr. Bhitiyakul said, clapping his tiny palms together. "You are criminal and I am coming into house to catch you. Yes? Now swing at nose."

Pat dutifully swung his tongue depressor in slow motion. Just before making contact with the bridge of the doctor's nose, Dr. Bhitiyakul caught Pat's wrist.

"You see, Caitlin O'Rourke. Patterick, he is taller than me, and shotgun, it hits me in downward motion. Yes?"

Even though my brother is on the short side, he still had Dr. Bhitiyakul by quite a few inches.

"But you," the doctor continued, "are much taller than he. Go, Patterick. See what happens when you hit your big sister with baseball bat."

Pat, being a quick study, didn't need to play out the charade. "It's going to hit her on the upswing," he said.

"Ahh, quite so. Yes, indeedie, it is. And there is high probability that this upward blow will drive one of the nasal bones into her brain.... Except..." He looked over at me and grinned.

I finished his train of thought. "My nose turned to mush with little broken pieces."

"You can tell the angle of the blow?" Pat asked.

"From position of broken pieces, yes, indeedie," Dr. Bhitiyakul answered, pointing toward the x-rays on the light board. "Quite clearly."

"Then the person who hit Caitlin is shorter than her."

"Oh, yes, indeedie. But is not almost everyone?"

"Junior Lee Thigpen certainly is," I said.

"Junior Lee pig what?"

"Never mind, Doc. How long are you going to keep me here?"

"Your CT scan looked to be okay. You just have minor concussion. We will not be doing surgery on nose now. We will just pack it and give you something for pain."

You're damn right you won't be doing the surgery, I thought. *I want someone with a degree from a med school whose name I can pronounce.*

"On your questionnaire, you listed Dr. Reorden as your orthopedic surgeon. A good man. An excellent physician. We have called him and told him of your misfortune. You are to be back here at nine o'clock in the a.m. on Monday morning. He has arranged for Dr. Neely, a plastic surgeon, to fix nose then. Okay, Caitlin O'Rourke?"

"Okay, Doc." I bit my tongue to keep myself from saying, "Yes, indeedie."

A nurse came in and helped him pack my nose with what looked to be miniature tampons and, with precious little regard for fashion, she taped a plastic nose guard to my face.

* * * *

Pat pulled his car in next to Seamus' Windstar, parked at the back door of Kehough's, so that I could quietly sneak upstairs to my quarters without walking through the pub. I wanted to shower and change clothes before having to do the replay commentary for Seamus, Mary Grace, and the regulars. To that end, Pat agreed to wait at the foot of the stairs until I got into my apartment before going into the bar. I had only gotten midway up when Mary Grace came bursting through the downstairs door, bawling her eyes out. That woman must have the ears of a bat.

"Oh, Katie, we were so worried about you!"

She came scampering up the steps, threw her arms around me and hugged me tightly. Adding the seven-inch stair tread to the difference in our heights, her head came to about my bellybutton.

"You poor thing," she went on, reaching up and touching the dried blood stains on my blazer and shirt. "Just look at what they've done to you. I've got some Beef Broth with Barley on the stove. It'll be just what the doctor ordered."

There is absolutely no wrong in God's wide world that Mary Grace doesn't think can be set right again with a little food.

"Let me get cleaned up first," I said, "then, I promise, I'll come right down."

"Is she going to be all right?" my brother Seamus asked Pat, as he, too, came through the downstairs door.

"Another busted nose, black eyes, a slight concussion but, otherwise, none the worse for wear," Pat answered.

Seamus peered up the dimly-lighted staircase. "God, I hope you don't feel as bad as you look, lass. 'Cause you look like bloody hell."

"And isn't that just what she needs to make her feel better," Mary Grace answered. "Get yourself back in there and see to the customers. I'll handle things up here."

"Is that Katie?" Jimmy Tuohey asked, wedging himself into the small anteroom. "How you doing, Katie?" He grimaced at the sight of me, but didn't give voice to his thoughts.

Mickey Ryan, though, shuffling in right behind him, never had a problem finding words for any occasion. One look at me and he chose a passage from Mangan's *Dark Rosaleen.*

"'Woe and pain, pain and woe,
Are my lot night and noon,
To see your bright face clouded so,
Like to the mournful moon.
But yet…'"

"Kate?" Matt Denning's voice called out from just inside the bar. "Kate, is that you?"

Seamus, Pat, Jimmy, and Mickey all squished together so that Matt could enter.

"Kate, I am *so* sorry," he said, looking up the stairway once he had joined the six of us. "The police wouldn't let me talk to you at the house. Then I just missed you at the hospital. Please believe me when I say that I never thought you'd be in any…"

"I'm okay," I told him. "And it's me who's sorry. I shouldn't have let Delane go in first. I should have…"

"Nonsense, Katie," Mary Grace protested. "It's not your fault that…"

The final interruption came from brother Pat in the form of a shrill whistle, both pinkie fingers in his mouth. Once everyone had quieted down and turned to give him their attention, he continued, firmly in charge of the situation. "We all know who's really at fault, here. And there's an APB out on him. No one else is to blame…for anything. Not you, Katie. And not you, either, Mr. Denning. My condolences, by the way. Now, Jimmy and Mr. Ryan, why don't you both go back out there and have one on the house, huh?"

As both men scurried back through the doorway, Pat turned to Seamus. "Let's you and I get Mr. Denning a drink and leave Mary Grace to help Katie clean herself up a bit." He held open the door to the pub for the other two men and, after they had passed, he looked up the stairway at me. "Don't sit up there and brood. Do the bare minimum you need to make yourself presentable, then get your butt back down here. Believe me, it's the best thing for you." He waited until I nodded, then he followed Matt and Seamus into the pub.

* * * *

Despite what Pat had told us, I did harbor feelings of guilt over Delane's death. I could see that Matt did, also. We had difficulty making eye contact, even though we sat directly across the table from each other in Caitlin's Corner.

I still thought (just possibly exaggerating my own skills a bit) that had I entered the house first, my superior reflexes might have allowed me to dodge the first blast. Then I might have been able to take Junior Lee Thigpen down before he could aim and fire again. A couple of very iffy mights, there.

Matt, I imagined, felt guilty about leaving on that Memphis business trip over Delane's objections.

"To top it all off," Matt said, after a long discourse on the sheer emptiness he felt now that Delane's death was beginning to sink in, "Detective Sykes and that...that other one questioned me for hours. Oh, I'm sure a lot of it was routine, but I got the distinct impression that they actually thought *I* did it. Especially the black girl."

"Detective Osborn?" I asked, thinking it interesting that he had remembered the name of the white male detective but not that of the black female.

"Yeah, I guess that was her name. Oh, she was polite enough...a little *too* polite, actually, but I could see it in her eyes. I'll tell you, Kate, as a well-off, Southern white male, I'm getting pretty damn sick and tired of apologizing for what my great-great-granddaddy did to them. Enough, already!"

"Don't worry about it," I said, reaching across the table and giving his hand a friendly squeeze. "I told her you were just pulling into the driveway when it happened. I also told her about Junior. She's going by the book. Covering all the bases. That's all it is."

I couldn't think of any other clichés to use in my attempt to put Matt at ease so I concentrated on the beef broth instead. As I slurped, though, another thought struck me.

"If the locks to the house had been changed," I asked, looking up from my bowl. "How could Junior have gotten in?"

"The French doors from the patio out back had been jimmied. I guess when he discovered that Lanie's old key didn't work, he decided not to waste the trip. Because of the brick wall around the patio, the neighbors wouldn't have noticed him."

"But how did he get there, Matt? I don't remember seeing any other cars around."

"The black detective conceded that *if* it was someone other than me, and she was damn reluctant to make that concession, he must have left his car in Forest Creek Park. Probably on Tottenham Court Road. Although there's a back entrance from my place to a service drive, the gate's always locked. He must have climbed the fence and planned to leave the same way. My rifles and shotguns were sitting by the French doors wrapped in a throw rug...except for the one that..."

Matt had to pause a moment to collect himself. "After he hit you, he must have seen me coming up the drive and just took off without them. All he had time to get was Lanie's jewelry box."

"That fence is a good ten feet high," I said. "A heck of a climb with a jewelry box. Can the back gate be opened from the inside?"

"No, it takes a key both ways and there are only two. I have one and Lanie..." He let the sentence tail off, then grimaced and shook his head as tears once more filled his eyes. "Lanie's key was in her purse. Oh, God, it never dawned on me to have *that* lock changed! We use the back gate so seldom. If only I had..."

I squeezed his hand again. "You couldn't have known, Matt."

"I *should* have known. But my mind was preoccupied with Memphis. And because of it, Lanie's..."

"Hey, it's not your fault....It's *not.* The only difference the gate made was that Junior was able to take the jewelry box with him. Otherwise, he still would have climbed the fence, but with the jewelry stuffed in his pockets."

I hesitated a moment, wanting to ask, then not wanting to, and finally just doing it. "When will the funeral be? I'd like to come, if...if that's okay."

Matt rotated his hand palm up and returned my friendly hand-squeeze. He forced a smile but his gray eyes were still moist. "Lanie would want you there, Kate. She usually didn't warm up to people very quickly, but with you it was different. I could tell Monday night. I'll call tomorrow after I've made the…the arrangements."

We both stood, gave each other a brief hug and I watched him leave by the front door, shoulders drooped.

Pat sat there on his stool, just finishing up a telephone conversation. He hung up, shoved the phone across the bar, and Seamus returned it to its customary place under the counter.

"Anything?" I asked, assuming what the call had been about.

"Junior's car has been parked out front of the dive where he lives since Monday, but the scumbag's disappeared down a rabbit hole. Don't worry, Katie, we'll find him. He'll surface in a day or so. He's not bright enough to stay hidden for very long. Just in case, though, we've got the airport and bus terminal covered."

"What can *I* do?"

Pat gave me a perplexed look. "About what?"

"About helping. What can I do?"

Mary Grace passed by our end of the bar after having collected my soup bowl and Matt's empty beer mug from the table. She-with-ears-like-a-bat had overheard the last exchange between Pat and me.

"You can get yourself upstairs, young lady," she said. "That's what you can do. A good night's rest is what you need. And before you climb into that bed of yours, you can get down on your knees and thank the good Lord and His Holy Mother for watching out for you this afternoon."

"Luck of the Irish," I quipped.

"It's not the *luck* of the Irish that kept you from being murdered," she replied heatedly. "It's the *faith* of the Irish."

I started to snicker. Bad move. Mary Grace had been serious.

"Now, go!" she ordered, pointing toward the hallway that led to the back stairs. "You heard me. Off with you, now!"

Giving her a little half salute, I said, “Yes, ma’am,” then headed in the direction she pointed. As I rounded the corner, I could hear her tear into Pat.

“And don’t you be encouraging her, either, Patrick. It’s bad enough we have to worry about *you* being out there every day with that element of our society. I absolutely forbid you to drag Katie into it, too.”

“But, Mary Grace,” Pat started to protest the wrongful accusation, “I didn’t…”

“But, nothing! I forbid it!”

* * * *

There were three messages on my answering machine. Mary Grace had not let me check them when we had been up in my quarters earlier so I punched the button as I walked by the phone. All were from Bobby Curtis.

“Hey, it’s Bobby. It be Tuesday night about ten in the pee emm. We done got our asses kicked up here tonight in round ball, girl. And do you knows why that might be? You don’t get no vacation, y’hear? You got what they call commitments. Yeah, commitments. See you *mañana*, babe.”

Bobby was one of the few persons I let get away with calling me *babe.* The way he used the word, it had no sexual connotation. To Bobby, everyone—male, female, young or old—was *babe.*

BEEP.

“Hey, babe! It now be Wednesday night and we ain’t seen or heard from y’all. What gives?! You out loafin’ or you out gettin’ laid? It don’t make no never-mind which. You do it some other night than Monday through Thursday. On them nights, your fine ass belongs to us. Sheeeet, girl, we embarrassed ourselves out there tonight. Lost five straight. One by shutout. Sheeeet, I ain’t never been shut out before and I don’t plan on it happening again. You best be here tomorrow, you dig?”

BEEP.

"It's Thursday night and you damn well *know* who this is, babe. And what's more, you damn well *know* why I's callin', don't you? This shit's gotta stop, Katie. That son-of-a-bitch Reggie done scored forty points tonight. People's laughin' at us, Katie. They's laughin'. *Please* be here on Saturday afternoon? Reggie done goes back to school on Tuesday for registration. Please come Saturday and kick his ass good before he goes. I's beggin' you."

I made a mental note to call Bobby the next day. With the upcoming operation, he and the guys were on their own for the next few weeks. And if I decided on the Fond du Lac job, maybe forever.

Having been by herself for a few days, W.B. needed lots of attention. She didn't seem to care that my eyes were blackened and that I had a gourd growing out of the center of my face. I was the one holding the catnip mouse and scratching her ears. That's all that mattered to her.

Later that evening, as I gazed into the mirror at my atrocious-looking honker while conducting the before-bed hair ritual, my mind struck on the solitary positive aspect of the entire situation. This time, having the plastic surgeon reset the bones, at least my nose would be straight once again and I wouldn't have to go through life looking as if I were sniffing around corners.

Mary Grace would be happy to know that I did, in fact, say a prayer of thanks that night, without complaining about my busted-up knee. (Come to think of it, the knee hadn't crossed my mind once in the past four days, except while I lay in the Denning foyer half unconscious.) I also said a prayer for my damsel. Although she was no longer in distress, I vowed to see her killer brought to justice. Somehow.

My dreams that night were filled with surreal images of a row of pimply-faced cowboys shooting skeet. In place of the target disc, each time one of them yelled "Pull!" I would reach behind me and toss a flailing Delane Denning into their line of fire.

CHAPTER 6

On Friday morning I skipped both my six-mile run and the Nautilus. I would just as soon have skipped Friday altogether. My head throbbed like an engine misfiring on two of its cylinders. How do I know what that's like? Eldred the Escort used to do it quite regularly.

After making my way zombie-like into the bathroom, arms extended and hands touching the walls like feelers, I downed a couple of Orudis from the paper envelope that Dr. Bhitiyakul had given me the evening before. Nothing would have felt better than standing under a hot shower for a half-hour or so and letting the water run on top of my head. I couldn't figure out how to do that, though, without getting my nose wet. There seemed to be quite a lot I couldn't do without my nose interfering. I had hit it with the edge of the drinking glass when I took my pills. And I found it impossible to brush my front teeth without jamming my upper lip into it.

In the end, I settled for a neck-down shower and a wipe around the edges of my face with a washcloth, then pony tailed the hair, dressed, and staggered downstairs to the pub at about ten o'clock. Evidently Batwoman had heard the shower running. A large mug of steaming Jamaican Blue Mountain sat in front of my end-stool at the bar.

Bless you, Mary Grace.

"Well, let's have a look," she said, coming from the kitchen with a full stack of buckwheat pancakes and a stoneware pitcher of hot maple syrup. She set the plate and pitcher down, took my chin in her hand, and rotated my face, inspecting every square inch of it.

"Has Pat called?" I asked, once she had given me back the use of my mouth.

"No. And why should he, now? He knows I'll be looking after you."

"That's not what I meant, Mary Grace, and you know it. Would you hand me the phone, please?"

"Eat your breakfast, young lady, and let the police do their jobs. After all, that's what we're paying them for, isn't it?"

Twice in less than twelve hours she had called me *young lady*. She hadn't done that since I was in high school. Even though many years intervened, I still remembered the not-so-veiled meaning of the phrase: "I'm on the verge of losing my temper, so do as you're told and don't answer back, if you know what's good for you."

Believe me, I knew. As a five-eleven, one-hundred-and-fifty pound tenth-grader, I had figured I was too big to spank and ignored a school-night curfew that Mary Grace had set. I had figured wrong. Maybe I was too big to spank now but, then again, maybe not. Rather than press the phone issue I dug into the hotcakes instead. I'd call Pat from upstairs after breakfast.

Mary Grace must have read my thoughts. No sooner had I finished eating when Seamus stuck his head out of the kitchen. "Come on, Katie," he said, jingling the keys to his Windstar. "Let's run over and get your car before we open up."

"Give me about ten minutes, will you?" I answered. "I need to run upstairs and get my purse."

From the other side of the kitchen door I heard, "Ten minutes seems like a lot of time to be fetching a purse, dear."

My getting whacked in the nose must have shaken them up more than I had imagined. Although I had been injured before in a variety of sports-related accidents during high school and college, my brother and sister-in-law had never before gone into an overprotective-parent mode. I guessed this was the first time they had seen me injured deliberately (except for the Big Cat incident but, then, they hadn't *seen* that, just *heard* about it).

"Start the car, bro," I told Seamus. "I'll be with you in thirty seconds."

* * * *

We drove most of the trip in silence. Finally, I said, "Mary Grace seems a bit overprotective, don't you think?" I tried my level best to make the question sound conversational rather than accusatorial.

After reminding some moron who had cut us off of his (the moron's) canine ancestry, Seamus made a right turn off of Hillsboro Pike onto Otter Creek Road. "Yep," he said, answering my question but without any elaboration.

"Well?" I prodded.

"Well, what?"

"Will you speak to her about it?"

"Nope."

"Why not?"

"Same reason as you."

Sometimes talking to my brother could be maddening. "And that would be what?" I asked.

"I'm scared of her."

We both laughed and as I reached over to smack him on the back of his head, I remembered that I still owed brother Pat one from Monday night.

Liddy the Land Cruiser was not the only car in the Dennings' driveway. Parked over by the side of the three-car garage was a white Dodge Colt. I guessed that it belonged to friends, there to offer Matt their sympathies, and, although I hated to intrude on his grief, I didn't think it would be polite to just get in my car and drive off.

Goose bumps broke out over my arms and neck as I climbed the three steps to the portico and approached the front door, remembering the only other time I had done so. In answer to the Miniature Ben chimes, a rather short and thin Hispanic woman of indeterminate age (somewhere between thirty and fifty) came to the door. She opened it about three inches and peered out with reddened and still-teary eyes. I assumed she had been crying about Delane.

"Yes? May I help you?" she asked suspiciously, looking at my nose guard. That's the translation of what she meant, anyway. What she actually said was "Dyes? May I hep dyou?"

"I'm Caitlin O'Rourke," I told her. "May I speak to Mr. Denning, please?"

"I sorry. He no home right now."

"Oh. Well, would you tell him I stopped by to pick up my car?" I spoke slowly and loudly as I pointed at my chest, then cocked a thumb toward Liddy out in the drive.

Her eyes grew large as she made the connection, then she opened the door wider. "You were the one with poor Missy Denning." She crossed herself, sighed, and shook her head as the tears began to flow again. "Mr. Denning, he tell me you probably come today. You take car. It okay. I tell him." She dabbed at her eyes with a well-used tissue.

After thanking her, I descended the steps and waved to Seamus. He eased his Windstar around the circle, down the drive, and turned right on Marylebone. I started up Liddy, fully intending to follow him back to the pub. At the end of the drive, though, I had just begun my own turn when, in the rearview mirror, I caught a glimpse of my suitcase in the second seat. Swinging the wheel to the left, I reentered the circular driveway through the other entrance.

I don't know why I felt compelled to return Delane's sandals that I had hurriedly stuffed into my bag the day before. It wasn't as if she'd need them, unless the afterlife featured a heavenly swimming pool for her to lay by throughout all eternity. But I knew I'd feel guilty about just tossing them out. It wouldn't be right. With Matt away, the timing couldn't have been better. I'd leave them with the housekeeper and avoid any awkwardness.

This time the door opened a full two feet. Apparently I was now an old friend.

"*Si?*" the housekeeper said, trying for a smile, but missing it big-time.

"Hi, it's me again. I...uh...what is your name?"

"Anita Mendoza," she answered. "And you are Caitlin O'Rourke. I no forget. I no speak the good English but I no *estúpido*."

"No, no, Anita," I said, trying to erase any ugly-American impression I might have given her. "That's not why I came back. It's that I had these in my suitcase." I held up the sandals. "They were Mrs. Denning's. I just thought that...well, that you'd know what to do with them."

"Ahh, *si*, I put them with others."

She opened the door wider and took the sandals from me. There were about a dozen black Hefty bags lined up in the foyer. Anita stuffed her tissue in an apron pocket and stooped to open one of the bags, then straightened up again and turned to me.

"These no belong Missy Denning."

"But she had them with her up in Cove Creek," I said.

"They no hers," Anita insisted. "They...oh, how you say...*demasiado pequeño*?"

Giving up trying to figure the translation, she motioned me over to the trash bag. "Here. You see."

Anita shoved the sandals into my hand and opened up the yellow ties on the bag, then reached in and grabbed a handful of different-style women's shoes. Taking them one at a time, she pointed to the size imprinted inside the heels.

"*Siete y medio! Siete y medio! Siete y medio! Siete y medio!* You see?"

I nodded. "Seven-and-a-half." Each one bore that number.

"*Si*," she said. "Seven-half." Then she tossed them back into the bag and took one of the sandals from me. "*Seis!*" she said, pointing to the number six embossed into the bottom of the polyurethane sole. "Missy Denning, she take seven-half. These *seis*. Six. They no fit Missy Denning."

I must have sounded like a half-wit. "All those shoes in that bag are size seven-and-a-half?" The bag was three-quarters full. Imelda Marcos had nothing on Delane Denning.

"*Si, sigñorita*. All seven-half. Mr. Denning, he no can look at Missy Denning's things without big sadness. He have me pack them to give away."

She bit her lip to control her own obvious big sadness, reaching into the apron for the tissue, then pointed to the sandals in my hand. "Those no belong Missy Denning, but I put with others if you no want."

Deciding not to argue with the grieving housekeeper, I said, "Thank you, Anita, but I'll hang onto them and try and find their owner."

As I turned to leave, two competing theories crossed my mind in rapid succession. The first was, *No wonder these sandals rubbed her pinkie toe raw if they're a size-and-a-half too small.* And the second, *But, what if Anita's right and these aren't Delane's? Then some neighbor lady is gonna be mighty ticked off that I stole her shoes.*

My train of thought was broken by the arrival of a royal blue Toyota Tacoma pickup truck. It pulled up into the circle as I reached the bottom step of the portico and a pair of full-size Ken and Barbie dolls hopped out. They were both dressed in expensive tennis togs and carrying on a string of exaggerated banter, using the phoniest British accents I'd ever heard. It was like watching a very bad *Saturday Night Live* sketch. (Is that a redundancy?)

"Hello, love," Ken said when they reached me, looking me up and down in a manner that might have cost him his teeth in different surroundings. "I most certainly hope the other bloke looks worse than you, say what?"

"Jason!" Barbie scolded, swatting him on the arm. Then she shot me an apologetic look and dropped the Royal Duchess act. "Sorry. He gets a bit carried away sometimes. I hope he didn't offend you."

Jason stayed in character. "No, no offense meant, love. Furthest thing from my mind, really. Furthest thing, love."

Had there not been an audience (in addition to Barbie, Anita Mendoza still stood in the open doorway), I would have made certain that ever again calling me *love* would be the furthest thing from Jason's mind. Instead, I shot him one of my bemused smiles, not much caring if it, indeed, came across as a smirk.

Barbie tried her best to ignore her partner-in-stupidity and offered me a limp hand. "I'm Taylor Hollingshead," she said, "and that's Jason Scarborough. We're from The Foresters."

She made that last pronouncement as if it should explain everything, including Jason's asinine behavior. In answer to my blank stare, she elaborated.

"The local community theatre group here in Forest Hills? Over on Otter Creek Road just before you get to Granny White Pike?"

"Oh," I replied, giving her delicate little paw a very gentle pump, fearing that I might break it with a genuine handshake.

"Really, off, off, way off Broadway, don't you know?" Jason piped in.

Again Taylor ignored him. "A real tragedy about Mrs. Denning," she said. "We didn't know them personally, but the Dennings were big supporters of The Foresters. They were Game Wardens."

That also failed to register on me so she went on to explain the half-dozen or so levels of contributors to the theatre group. On the lowest rung at a twenty-five-dollar donation were the Rangers. The highest honor, that of Game Warden, was bestowed upon those who forked out over one-thousand dollars annually.

"If you're here to pay your respects," I told them, "Mr. Denning isn't at home."

"We know," Taylor said. "When he called Bobbie, the managing director, earlier, he said he wouldn't be."

"Said the clothing would be ready for us to pick up late this morning," Jason added. "Awfully decent of the old chap, considering, say what?"

"Clothing?" I asked.

"Ahh," Anita, spoke up. "You from theatre? I have Missy Denning's things all ready like Mr. Denning say. They here." She opened the door to its full extent and gestured to the trash bags. "You take now?"

While Jason answered Anita's question and helped himself to the first two bags, Taylor nodded to me. "A donation to our costume department. It's done all the time. Rather than give a loved one's things to the Goodwill or Salvation Army, they'll donate them to the theatre."

I didn't much care for her tonal inflection on *Goodwill* or *Salvation Army*. The implication was that at least the clothing would be put to good use at the theatre, entertaining rich people, instead of going to waste keeping bums warm.

I didn't much care for either Ken *or* Barbie.

* * * *

Fortunately by the time I got back to Kehough's, the pub was open and the lunch trade had arrived in full force. I say *fortunately* because Mary Grace was too busy to scold me for not having tailgated Seamus all the way home.

After making a stop upstairs to dump my purse and take care of a few items of a personal nature, I entered the pub and discovered that, apparently, my brother had not been so lucky. He whispered a "Stay the hell out of her way!" to me as he delivered a pitcher of Red Mountain Red Ale to one of the tables.

Old Mickey Ryan called out a greeting from his end of the bar. "You made the papers, Caitlin." He sat there next to Jimmy Tuohey, waving a copy of the *Tennessean* at me.

"No picture of you, though, Katie," Jimmy chimed in. "Just one of that poor lady that went and got herself killed yesterday." He made it sound like it was Delane's fault.

Shame on you, Delane, I thought. *Purposely going and getting yourself killed like that.*

Out of curiosity, though, I crossed down to where the two of them sat so I could take a look. I knew that the only reason Mickey would ever get off his stool was for his hourly trip to the men's room or to shuffle off home at closing time.

The photograph that the newspaper had used was an old one, ten years at least, judging by the clothing style. In it, Delane wore her hair in a poodle shag that covered most of her face. Had Mickey not pointed it out to me, I wouldn't have recognized her, except for the ever-present garnet-and-pearl lavaliere. Something about that picture, though, bothered me.

The Delane Denning I had spent the last three days with had been warm, friendly, and almost childlike at times. She had smiled continually. The Delane Denning in the photograph had a severe look to her and a face that seemed incapable of smiling—ever. Maybe this had been a difficult time in her life, but I preferred to remember the Delane I had gotten to know in Cove Creek.

I thanked Mickey and was returning to my end of the bar when all conversation in the pub came to an abrupt halt. Turning toward the front door, I spotted the reason straight away—Detective Osborn, sans partner, had entered.

A Country-Western bar/Irish pub is not the watering hole of choice for those of the African-American persuasion. But I don't believe there was any animosity in the silence, just surprise.

The detective's light sage pantsuit of the day before had been replaced by its navy sister, the ecru shirt by a white one with blue stripes. Seeing her with a clearer head did nothing to change my opinion of her. She still looked like a tough broad, even though she tried dressing softly.

"More questions, Detective?" I asked, sitting on my end-stool and gesturing her into Pat's customary spot next to me.

"Hoped maybe you might have remembered something useful," she answered, not bothering to hide the doubt that she felt. Then she looked up at Seamus, who had come over to us, and said, "A bottle of Harp, please, and whatever's good for lunch. Surprise me."

"I've thought about it all morning," I said, as my brother first got the requested beer, then passed the lunch order in to Mary Grace, "but nothing other than what I told you yesterday comes to mind. I heard the shots, ran to the door, saw Delane lying there, and, as I started toward her, bammo...lights out."

The detective reached into her large brown shoulder-strap purse, removed a brass business card holder and slid one of the cards along the bar toward me, then dropped the holder back into her bag.

"You'll call if you do think of something?" Although she phrased it as a question, having been partially raised by Mary Grace O'Rourke, I knew an order when I heard one.

I nodded, wondering what the E in E. Osborn stood for, then asked a question of my own. "Find Junior, yet?"

Seamus had delivered a wedge of Chicken and Ham Pie to each of us and a cup of coffee to me. With a mouthful of lunch, she shook her head, then swallowed and qualified the answer. "Not yet."

"Anything at the Denning house that ties him in?" I asked.

"Nada. I was hoping it would be your eyewitness testimony. Otherwise, until we find him and break him, we've got nothing. The crime scene was clean. There were no scratchings of skin under Mrs. Denning's nails. In fact, aside from the obvious, the Assistant Medical Examiner reports that there wasn't a mark on the body."

"Except for her toe," I said, then shoveled a forkful of pie into my mouth.

In answer to Detective Osborn's arched eyebrow, I explained about Delane's penchant for lying by the pool during the past three days and how she had complained that her sandals had rubbed her little toe raw.

"The AME said, not a mark," the detective repeated, getting up from her stool. "Where's the phone?"

Rather than point her toward the one by the rest rooms, I got up, went around to the back of the bar, and pulled the house phone up from under the counter. That way I could satisfy my curiosity without having to look like a moron by following her to the pay phone. She nodded a thanks, then dialed a number from memory.

"This is Detective Osborn," she identified herself, once the connection had been made. "Let me talk to Dr. Zelasko."

In the twenty seconds she waited, she managed two more mouthfuls of pie and a swig of beer, ignoring the glass that Seamus had brought and drinking it straight from the bottle. How's that for my intuition, huh?

Eventually she said, "Trish, Ozzie."

So much for finding out what the E stood for. She didn't even call herself by her first name.

"When you said not a mark on the Denning woman's body," the detective continued, "did you mean not a mark that could have contributed to her death or not a mark period?"

Her frown deepened as she listened to the reply. "What about her toes?" she asked, then looked over at me and repeated the question she had obviously been asked by the AME. "Which toe?"

"Don't know," I answered. "One of the little ones."

She relayed the answer, then elaborated with my story about the sandal strap.

During the next five minutes we sat there in silence while the detective finished her pie and beer, and I almost wet myself, so anxious was I to say, "Well, what the heck's going on?"

Finally she said, "You're sure?" and immediately pulled the receiver away from her ear as the Assistant Medical Examiner for Davidson

County came partially unglued. All I was able to make out clearly was the phrase *arrogant bitch*.

"Trish, calm down," Detective Osborn said, and I could tell she was using every ounce of restraint to keep the conversation from degenerating. "I'm not questioning your thoroughness. It's just that I'm here with the girl who spent the last three days with the victim."

The girl? I thought. *We're the same age. In fact, I'm probably a year or two older.*

"She says that Mrs. Denning's sandals had rubbed one of her toes raw."

The detective looked over at me and said, again repeating what I'm sure Dr. Zelasko had asked, "Then why don't you know which toe?"

"I didn't actually *say* that the toe had been rubbed raw, I said that *Delane* said that it had been rubbed raw. I never saw it for myself."

Detective Osborn had held the phone out during my answer so that she wouldn't have to repeat what I said. Again putting the receiver to the side of her head, she asked, "Did you get that?…No, it's me who's sorry, Trish. I should have clarified that first.…I agree. It bothers me, too, but if the girl didn't actually see it, the Denning woman could have been exaggerating. Maybe the sandals were just tight."

While the doctor continued the conversation, Detective Osborn held the receiver between shoulder and cheek and pawed through her purse for a small spiral pad and pen. "Give me the address," she told the doctor. "I'll check it out." When she had finished scribbling in her pad, I waved a finger in front of her face. She said, "Just a minute, Trish," and covered the mouthpiece with her hand.

"Would you ask her what size shoes Delane was wearing?" I asked.

"Not until you tell me why."

I explained about the size-six sandals. Apparently she considered it a fair question and repeated it to the doctor.

"That explains it, then, Trish," she said, once the reply had been given. "The girl, here, says the sandals were a size six. No wonder they pinched her toes."

Again, I was *the girl.* But now I had figured out that it had nothing to do with chronological age. It was a euphemism for *the civilian.*

After a few more pleasantries, the detective broke the connection. "Can I get another beer?" she asked, shaking her empty bottle.

Rather than bother Seamus, I got it myself, plus more coffee for me.

"The doctor seemed pretty upset," I remarked, hoping to loosen Detective Osborn's tongue.

"She always gets touchy when there's no direct means of identification. It's rare, but there *have* been cases where a body has been misidentified. Never by Trish, and she intends to keep it that way."

"There certainly isn't any question about it being Delane Denning, is there?"

"Maybe not to you or her family and friends. She's gone, that's all you know. But the law isn't as sentimental. It needs proof. With her face blown away, we can't have anybody ID her by sight. She never applied for a gun permit or anything else that would require fingerprints, so hers aren't on file. Aside from an appendix scar, which nearly everyone has, she never had any major operations or broke any bones, so medical records are next to useless. The blood type checks out. So all we have are dental records. Now, let's say that you *had* personally seen an injury to one of her toes. Then we'd be on our way to the morgue right now for you to do a foot-check because, according to the doctor, there isn't a mark of *any* kind, *anywhere* on that body."

We were interrupted by the arrival of brother Pat. Had I just woken from a coma and didn't know what day it was, I'd be able to tell it was a Friday by Pat's clothing. After living with him while I recuperated from my knee operation, I had gotten to know his routine.

Friday was gray slacks, burgundy sportcoat, and white shirt day. The only thing that changed, with no pattern that I could discern, was his choice of tie. He had three that went with that outfit and, on this particular Friday, he had opted for the burgundy-and-gray paisley.

Midway through Detective Osborn's briefing of Pat, Seamus had brought her check. I picked up a pen from the bar to sign it, but she plucked it from my hand and shook her head, all the while never missing a beat in her conversation with my brother.

With the shoptalk finished, she said to him, "You own a piece of this place, don't you, Sarge?"

"Yeah," he answered proudly. "You like it?"

She nodded and said, "Nice place. But I can't let your sister sign my tab. That wouldn't be right. She's a material witness in a case I'm working. You, on the other hand, aren't." She tucked the bill into Pat's breast pocket, patted him on the cheek, and walked toward the front door.

"Sorry about the sandal thing," I said.

The detective stopped and turned. "Don't be. Whatever you remember, no matter how insignificant or irrelevant you might think it is, you tell me. I'll decide what's important, okay?"

"Okay," I agreed. "But I *am* sorry if I caused any problem between you and the doctor."

"Trish?" She snorted a laugh through her nose. "Don't worry about it. We argue over every case. The only thing this'll cost me is the half hour it'll take to verify the authenticity of the dental records."

"You think they might have been switched?" I asked.

"Nope. But you raised a question in Dr. Zelasko's paranoid mind so now I've got to check it out."

I started to apologize again, but she waved it away and said, "It's probably something I should have done anyway."

It was at that instant that I understood what had compelled me to try and be helpful by providing Detective Osborn with the sandal information in the first place. My sports-oriented brain had transformed Delane Denning's death into an athletic metaphor—a loss. Not a loss, as in the loss of a friend or loved one (although, in our short time together, I had come to think of Delane as a friend), but a loss in the competitive sense.

In my mind, Junior Lee Thigpen and I were engaged in a competition. I had beaten him in the bar; he had busted my nose at Delane's home. Our record stood at one apiece.

Now in most athletic competitions when you lose, there's always an opportunity for a rematch that tides you over—the we'll-get-'em-next-time philosophy. In the Olympics, the next time isn't for four more years, but, still, there *is* a next time. Even when Big Cat bested me personally, I had had the satisfaction of seeing my team kick her team's collective butt.

In the Katie-Kat vs. Junior Lee Thigpen contest, though, there would be no rematch—no best two out of three. I was now a spectator and not part of the team that would eventually bring him down.

As Detective Osborn opened the front door, I called out, "Detective? Can I...uh...can I tag along with you?"

My plea to her might have been the pathetic appeal of every athlete or would-be athlete who ever rode the bench during the big game. "Put me in, Coach? Please, let me play?"

She stopped and turned and a quizzical expression came over her face. "To Delane Denning's dentist?"

"Yeah. If it's not too much trouble."

Her gaze shifted briefly from mine as she glanced to my left and, out of the corner of my eye, I saw Pat give a minuscule nod of his head.

"Sure," she said, again looking at me. "My partner and I are working solo today. I could use the company."

Someone else had seen Pat's nod as well. Over all the noise in the pub, a voice from the kitchen doorway cut through loudly and shrilly. "By God, Patrick, if you let her get involved in this, you'll answer to me!"

She-with-radar-like-a-bat had spoken and brother Pat, sitting on his bar stool, turned into a statue on a pedestal.

I held up a finger to the detective as I rose from my own stool and said, "I'll just be a minute."

We met in the doorway. Gently but firmly, I spun Mary Grace around by the shoulders and hustled her back into the kitchen. She howled in protest and, in the middle of her third young-lady speech in two days, I interrupted.

"Mary Grace, I love you." Her mouth remained open but the words had stopped. So far so good. I continued. "I love you like a sister; I love you like a mother. You've been both to me. But this is something I *have* to do."

The words started up and I placed the first two fingers of my right hand to her lips. Again the words stopped.

"No matter what you or Seamus or Pat say, I feel partially responsible for what happened yesterday. A woman who looked up to me as her rescuer got killed and I want...no, I *need* to do something. I don't know *what,* but something...anything. And, while I appreciate your concern, really I do, I'm a big girl now. Look at me, Mary Grace, I'm a...an Amazon, for God's sake."

Thank you, Dr. Bhitiyakul.

"And, yesterday, I went up against a guy with a shotgun and all I got was a busted nose. I can take care of myself."

Okay, so I failed to mention that the gun had been empty at the time and I also neglected to tell Mary Grace that were it not for a thrice-broken nose, I'd be a dead Amazon. But my point in confronting my sister-in-law was to get her off my back. It wasn't as if I had lied to her; I just didn't tell her the whole truth. Even Turlough would buy into that, wouldn't he? Well, wouldn't he?

Okay, so I'll ask him next time I go to confession. Satisfied?

Chapter 7

Here's a tip for you. If you're tall and going somewhere with someone who's much shorter than you, offer to drive. Better yet, insist on it. I'm sure a Pontiac Sunfire is a very good car, but I'd hate to take an extended trip with my chin resting on my knees. The fifteen minutes or so to Delane Denning's dentist's office was plenty long enough.

It was also long enough to find out everything Detective Osborn knew about the case. In fact, thirty seconds would have sufficed. Aside from hunting for their number one—scratch that—their *only* suspect, Junior Lee Thigpen, the police were more or less spinning their wheels.

Although she didn't come right out and admit it, Ozzie (she said I could call her that when I asked about her first name) gave me the distinct impression that she wished I hadn't seen Matt Denning in the driveway just moments before the shooting. Before agreeing with Matt and chalking up her attitude to an inward hatred of rich, middle-aged, white guys, I felt compelled to ask her why.

"Since Pat will probably keep you updated anyway," she said with a purposely-exaggerated sigh, "I might as well give it to you firsthand. The husband not only played around but, despite appearances to the contrary, he has money problems as well."

"How do you *know* that?" I asked and, as I did so, the defensiveness in my tone of voice surprised me.

"I'm a detective. That's what I do, detect things. You think I've been sitting on my backside since last night, doing my nails and waiting for someone to locate Junior for me?"

After pausing a few seconds for a response and not getting one, she calmed herself and continued. "Denning's been losing accounts at the investment firm where he works and they've put him on notice. He's got just one of the six months left to bring his totals up or he's out. It doesn't look like he's going to make it. Senior VP or not, apparently in that business, past performance counts for squat. It's, 'What have you done for me this week?'"

Ozzie glanced at her notebook, where she had written the dentist's address, then at the building numbers on Hillsboro Pike. Once she had gotten her bearings, she started up again.

"According to info we got from his co-workers, his friends, and his wife's friends, the wife came from money and spent it as if she had a goose that laid a daily golden egg. Also, some of her friends say that she knew about her husband's indiscretions and had talked to a lawyer. To limit his liability, in case he was ever sued for giving people bum financial advice, the houses, the cars…all paid for, I might add…and the bank accounts are…were…in the wife's name. If she had divorced him, he'd have nothing. No house, no car, no money. And now, in one month, he'll have no job. However, my partner Sykes has turned up an insurance policy on Mrs. Denning for one mil. Double indemnity for accidental death and payable to Matthew Denning. How's that for motive?"

"You're wrong, Ozzie. Flat out. On the drive up and back from Cove Creek, all Delane Denning talked about was what a wonderful man Matt was. She loved him."

Again I caught myself defending Matt Denning, a man whom I barely knew. Would I have been that quick to speak out for a short, fat, bald guy as I was for someone tall, handsome, and distinguished? I hoped so, but I wouldn't want to swear to it under oath. And, during the trip back from Cove Creek, hadn't I mentally questioned Delane's reasons for constantly bragging on her husband? Hmm. Methinks I've been too long without a date.

"Rich people are strange," Ozzie replied, then quickly followed up with, "No offense, Kate."

"None taken," I said, flashing my smirk.

"I meant rich, social butterflies like the Dennings," she qualified herself. "They live in a fantasy world where money can buy virtually everything, including happiness. Image is important to them. Their whole lives are facades. They don't hang their laundry out on the line for fear everyone will see them for the phonies they really are. Delane Denning was probably just going through her standard we-live-a-perfect-life act for your benefit."

"So you think what? That Matt put out a contract on his wife for the money?"

"It's a possibility, Kate. When we eventually find Junior Lee Thigpen, you can bet I'll ask him."

We had arrived at our destination so I didn't press the issue any further. From the parking lot, I could tell that the Delane who had just been described to me must have felt very comfortable with this particular dentist. A Lexus, a BMW, and a Mercedes sat parked out front.

Dr. H. Bennett Frost, DMD, ran a five-man operation out of a quaint old building on the historic register that had once been a small six-room schoolhouse. Actually Beth Ann Downey, the receptionist/office manager, ran it and *it* turned out to be a one-man, four-woman operation. Besides Beth Ann, there were two hygienists and a dental assistant. H. Bennett himself was the only man, and a very lucky one at that. All four of these women with whom he had surrounded himself could have come from Petticoat Junction.

Detective Osborn got only the words, "Good afternoon, I'm…" out of her mouth when Beth Ann looked up at me and made the connection, despite my bandaged nose and black eyes.

"I know you!" she shouted in a little-girl-like, breathy voice, getting up from her chair and extending her hand across the counter. "You're Caitlin O'Rourke, the volleyball player. This is *such* a treat."

"Thank you very much," I answered, wracking my brain to figure out where I might have met this woman, "but I'm not sure…"

"Oh, you don't know *me*," Beth Ann said. "My daughter has posters of you all over her bedroom walls. She'll be a sophomore over at McGavock High this coming year. Plays both basketball and volleyball, just like you did. Oh, how she cried when you got hurt over in Italy. She felt so terrible about it. And last night, when we heard the news about you and poor Mrs. Denning? Why, I can't tell you how upset that made her."

Beth Ann stopped gushing just long enough to release my hand, reach down, and pick up a pen and a prescription pad. "Would you please give me your autograph?" she said, forcing them into my still outstretched hand. "Make it out to Heather Ann. Heather Ann Downey. Oh, she'll be so thrilled. I'm Beth Ann, by the way. Beth Ann Downey. I wish I had one of those posters here with me now for you to sign."

"I hang out at Kehough's Irish Pub over on Wooten," I told her as I scribbled on the slip of paper, *The prescription for success: Practice, practice, practice!* and signed it. "Bring one by anytime and I'll be happy to autograph it for you."

"Oh, thank you. That would be so wonderful," Beth Ann said, tucking the prescription into a pocket at the end of one of her double-D's. "But I didn't notice your name in Dr. Ben's appointment book for this afternoon. I would have remembered if it had been. There's no problem, though. I'm sure I can get him to squeeze you in if it's an emergency. Did a tooth get broken when you were hit yesterday? Is that it?"

Throughout this whole rather embarrassing incident, Detective Osborn had stood to one side, silent and unnoticed by Beth Ann. Outwardly she appeared calm but I could tell that she seethed on the inside. Not knowing when the next pause in the receptionist's string of prattle would likely occur, I used the opportunity to bring the focus back to our original mission.

"No, no, Beth Ann. My teeth are fine. I only got a broken nose out of it. Besides, I'm just along for the ride on this trip. Detective Osborn, here, has some questions she needs to ask."

Beth Ann's big baby-blue eyes grew wide in amazement as she realized that the black woman with me was not my cleaning lady. "Detective?" she asked (and I fully expected an "I *do* declare" but didn't get one).

"Osborn," Ozzie told her, flashing a badge and ID. "I'm working the Denning case."

"A man from the Medical Examiner's Office was here first thing this morning," Beth Ann said. "Before we even opened up. He was standing on the front steps when Betty Jo and I arrived. She's one of the hygienists and she helped me pull Mrs. Denning's records for him. Was that all right? Or should we have waited for you?"

As Beth Ann blathered on, I had to admire Ozzie. She had summoned every ounce of self-restraint to keep from shouting, "Will you please just shut the hell up and let me ask my questions?!"

Instead, she smiled (I could tell that it was a grimace, but it appeared to Beth Ann like a smile) and said, "No, Ms. Downey, that won't be necessary. The ME appreciates your cooperation. I just need to verify the authenticity of those records."

"In other words, you want to know if they really *were* Mrs. Denning's?" Beth Ann's baby-blues opened even wider.

"Not in *other* words, Ms. Downey. Those are the *exact* words. Is there any possibility that Mrs. Denning's records could have been...tampered with?"

Although a gusher who came across as somewhat of an air-head, Beth Ann Downey really did *manage* the office. It wasn't just a title given to her because of her considerable physical assets. She opened a file drawer and produced the employee folders for herself, the dental assistant, and the two hygienists.

"If the records were tampered with," she said, "it could only have been done by one of us." In answer to a skeptical expression on Ozzie's face, Beth Ann walked us through the procedure.

All patient records, even x-rays, were keyed to a patient ID number and filed by that number, not the patient's name. To find the records for a specific patient, someone other than the staff would have had to break in, disabling the alarm system; know which file cabinet contained the key to the computer system, and, because it was locked, pick the lock to get it; know the computer password (changed on a quarterly basis) to access the patient files; find the patient ID Number; pick the lock on the file cabinets containing the patient records; and substitute new records and x-rays, having the same patient ID Number on them; then relock everything and reset the alarm on the way out.

At the end of the show-and-tell, Ozzie held up her hands in mock surrender. "You've convinced me," she said. "And it would have been difficult even for one of you because of the patient number imprinted on the x-rays. Thanks for your time, Ms. Downey."

I gave a smile and a wave. As we turned to leave, Ozzie's beeper went off.

"May I?" she asked, looking at the number on the beeper and pointing toward the phone.

Beth Ann punched a button for an outside line, handed the receiver to Ozzie and stepped aside. While we waited for the detective to complete her call, I gave Beth Ann directions to Kehough's and reminded her to bring a poster by for me to sign. When Ozzie had finished, we again said our good-byes, then headed out to the Sunfire.

"That was Sykes," Ozzie said, as she drove out of the parking lot. "Matt Denning just went down a few notches on our list of suspects."

"Why so?" I asked, curious, yet relieved.

"He doesn't inherit. Sykes just got a look at the will. It had been changed less than two weeks ago. Everything used to go to the husband. It now goes to Mrs. Denning's sister in Chattanooga, a Melinda Huntington. And that includes the insurance money."

* * * *

There were three new messages on my machine when I got home. The first one was from Nikolaos Panacopoulos. He had just seen a copy of Friday's *Tennessean.*

"Katie, this is your Uncle Nico. Are you all right? Why you no call me? Shame on you. Why for you let me read about you getting your head busted in newspaper. You call. Delia and me, we worry about you. Okay? Okay."

Yeah, Uncle Nico, I thought. *I'm sure Delia is just worried sick about me.*

* * * *

Although Ma had only worked briefly at Zakinthos, her bookkeeping skills must have made one heck of an impression on Nikolaos Panacopoulos. Uncle Nico (that's what I had always called him) had kept in touch through the years, Christmas cards to the family and birthday cards and small gifts for me.

At Immaculata I had gotten to know his daughter Artemis fairly well. Although the Panacopoulosses were Greek Orthodox, they felt that Arti could greatly benefit from the disciplined regimen of the Catholic School system (we had IHM nuns—enough said?). Despite the fact that I was three-years Arti's junior, we both played B-ball and V-ball together and had become friends, as much as any freshman and senior could be.

As I was dateless for the Spring Spectacular (Immaculata's big dance of the year), Arti had fixed me up with her brother Khristophoros who was my age. Chris (very tall, very dark, and very handsome) and I had hit it off so well, we had made a follow-up date for the next Saturday night—a date which never took place.

Da had gone through the roof when he found out about it. "There are no kids named O'Brien, Kennedy, McDougal, or Flynn in all of Nashville for you to date?" he had bellowed. "You have to go out with a foreigner? Can you imagine what your kids would look like if you were to get serious with him? My God, lass, with you being Black Irish and him as dark as a dago, they'd have to ride in the back of the effing buss, for Christ's sake!"

Ma, usually a calming influence, had sided with Da. No amount of tears nor number of tantrums could change their resolve. I was to call Chris and cancel. No discussion; no appeal.

All week long I struggled with what I would say, developing an extensive list of ailments so that I wouldn't have to tell him the truth. By Friday night, I couldn't put it off any longer. As I sat there in my room staring at the phone, it rang.

I picked up the receiver. "Hello?"

"Caitlin? It's…it's Chris Panacopoulos."

"H…hi, Chris."

"I'm afraid I'm going to have to…uh…cancel our date for tomorrow night, Caitlin."

"You are?"

"Yeah, I…uh…something's come up. It's a…a family thing. I…I hope you aren't too mad at me."

"No, Chris. That's okay. Believe me, I understand about…about family things."

"So, I guess I'll see you around, huh?"

"Yeah, I guess so."

I had been dumped. And I was angry. *I* was supposed to do the dumping, not him.

On Monday at school I had found out why from Arti. Their mother Delia had gone as ballistic as Da when she found out about the date.

Apparently she thought there were plenty of Greek girls in Nashville and that Chris didn't have to settle for "shanty Irish."

That remark had ticked me off even more than being dumped, and although I had maintained contact with Uncle Nico after Da and Ma died later that same year, I never did warm up to Delia.

* * * *

The second call on the machine was from Bobby Curtis. He, too, had apparently just seen the *Tennessean*, although I was surprised to learn that he read anything other than the sports page or the comics.

"Hey, babe, it's Bobby. I just read about what happened yesterday. Forget about them other three messages, okay? I was acting like a jerk. Take care of yourself. Give me a call when you get a chance."

I started to laugh. Bobby was really a sweet guy underneath his line of BS. Only half a laugh managed to escape, though, when the third message kicked in and stifled it.

Matt Denning had called to tell me that Delane's memorial service would be held at two o'clock the next day at the Chandler Mortuary in Brentwood.

I hit the rewind button and felt sorry for both the Dennings—Delane, because her life had been snuffed out; Matt, because, in addition to no longer having a wife, would now have no house, no car, no job, and no insurance money. I really didn't know which would be more upsetting to him, but tried to take a pragmatic attitude about his situation. You play, you pay.

But that hadn't been the side of him that I had seen. On Monday night when Delane had been attacked in the alley, I had observed what I thought to be a loving couple. I wondered how many other people, having problems with their relationships, put on happy faces for company. Probably lots of them.

Due to the pain in my nose and head, I didn't dance at the *ceili* that night. I did, however, sit in for a few sets with Brian Mulcahy and the Tara-Diddles and played the bodhran respectably.

The noise and laughter of the pub had temporarily cheered me up. In my quarters after closing time was another matter altogether. W.B. tried her best to help, but there are times when you need more than a cat to curl up with. I wondered what Chris Panacopoulos was doing. The last I had heard (a letter from Uncle Nico when I was in Italy), he had shortened his last name to Poulos (much to his parents' dismay), had begun calling himself Kit, and had opened up his own restaurant in the Greek Town section of Detroit. Delia had probably forgiven him, though, since he had married a nice Greek girl by the name of Daphne.

Daphne. What a stupid name. Sounds like Daffy. Jealous? Me? You bet.

My dreams that night were again of Delane Denning, but pleasant dreams this time, unlike those of the night before. Delane, modeling the various expensive outfits that she had worn on our vacation, would strike a series of seductive poses as she walked down a fog-covered runway. At the end of the dream, dressed in the ensemble that she had worn home and died in, she did a pirouette, then turned toward me, smiled, and blew me a kiss.

I awoke, briefly, at three-thirty in the morning with tears running down my cheeks.

God damn you, Junior Lee Thigpen!

Chapter 8

A steady rain had begun to fall during the night and had continued on through Saturday morning. By the time I left for the memorial service, it had slowed to an intermittent drizzle. I had hoped for a sunny day—one to match the personality of the Delane Denning I had gotten to know. Instead, it more-closely resembled the Delane in the newspaper photograph—gray and somewhat gloomy.

I reached the Chandler Mortuary down on Old Hickory Boulevard at about one-forty-five, thinking that would be plenty early enough. Instead, I found the huge parking lot already full and had to leave Liddy halfway up Timber Hollow Lane. The rain had let up for the moment and, after debating as to whether or not to take an umbrella, I hopped out of the car without it and quickly walked the half block to the funeral home.

As I entered, I said a silent prayer of thanks that I had dressed up more than normal for the occasion, having selected light-taupe silk crepe-de-chine slacks and a matching top, and a jacket-overshirt of the same material in dark taupe. With my jet-black hair in a French braid, the only items of jewelry I wore were diamond stud earrings. All in all, I blended in very nicely with the posh crowd who had come to pay their last respects.

One thing I would have done differently would have been to wear a different pair of shoes. The bone CK sandals with two-inch heels gave me two more inches of height that I really didn't need. Of course, had I not been under doctor's orders I would have left the nose guard behind, also.

In an alcove on the other side of the large foyer, a somber, but just as distinguished-looking, Matt Denning stood next to a Queen Anne wing chair in the small sitting area. With the number of people around him, I'd have bet he hadn't had time to make very much use of the chair.

An officious, middle-aged woman hovered close by, prompting Matt with names and keeping the traffic flowing smoothly by. Short (at about five-four or so) and a bit on the plump side, she, nevertheless, had a pleasant face and a very nice figure. Had she taken her chestnut hair out of the granny bun, used some makeup, and swapped the black-rimmed specs for contacts, she would have improved her appearance dramatically. As it was, she more or less faded into the background.

Although I saw no resemblance whatsoever, I wondered, because of the tears that she constantly blotted with a handkerchief, if she were Melinda Huntington, Delane Denning's sister that Ozzie had told me about the day before.

While I moved through the throng toward Matt and Miss Mousy, I was aware of the looks my own presence generated, and not just due to the nose guard and raccoon eyes. Dr. Bhitiyakul had been right on the money when he called me an Amazon. I *am*, with my one-hundred-and-seventy-eight pounds proportioned very nicely, if I do say so myself.

I was used to those looks from males and females alike—jealousy from the women as they instinctively drew their mates closer to them; admiration (with a trace of lust) from the men whose gaze followed me. One rather portly elderly man even let a whispered "Wow!" escape his lips, unaware that he had done so. An elbow from his wife let him know in no uncertain terms that he had best take more care with his thoughts in the future.

A kiss on the cheek, a squeeze of the hand, whispered regrets, and a brief introduction to a very bloodshot-eyed Miss Mousy—a Sharon Ross, not the sister-in-law that I had wondered about—were all I had time for with Matt. The minister (I'm not sure which denomination) asked everyone to enter the chapel and observe a few moments of silence.

While Sharon Ross guided Matt down to the front row, then took a place for herself in the second, I opted for a spot near the rear where I could watch without my height blocking anyone else's view.

There were quite a few faces I recognized, not from a personal relationship of any kind but from having seen their photos. Aides to both the Mayor of Nashville and the Governor of Tennessee were present as were minor politicos, movers and shakers of the Greater Nashville Metropolitan Area, and a dozen or so medium to well-known recording stars. The Dennings may have been on the road to bankruptcy but they traveled that road in the best of company.

Another familiar face I spotted (and the only black one in the place) I *did* know personally—Detective E. Osborn, dressed in another one of her pantsuits (russet with a white blouse). Ozzie must have turned to a single page in the Lands' End catalogue and told the operator, "Give me the suit and the blouse on page seventy-two in a size eight-petite in every color you've got."

Don't get me wrong. She looked good in the suits, but a little variety wouldn't have hurt. She had put on just a trace of makeup for the occasion. It worked. I'd never tell her that, though. She'd probably run straight for the ladies' room to wash her face. Being one of the boys seemed to be really important to her.

Delane's remains had been cremated earlier in the day. A pewter urn with her ashes sat on a white-cloth-covered pedestal in front of the altar next to a blowup of the photo used in the obituary column. One by one, friends and dignitaries got up and spoke eloquently of her devotion to husband and a multitude of charities throughout the area.

Had it been me, I would have tread lightly on the wonderful wife bit, considering the shaky circumstances of the marriage. *Don't they know the Dennings were having problems?* I wondered as the fourth or fifth speaker started in. *Or are they all actors in the same play?*

By the end of the eulogy, I had heard Delane described as devoted, upright, principled, benevolent, considerate, and a whole bunch of other adjectives. With the addition of brave, clean, and reverent, they could have been describing a Girl Scout. But not once did anyone say that she was loving…or fun-loving, for that matter.

Maybe they all had known the grim-faced Delane Denning in the photograph and not the woman I had spent three days with in Cove Creek. Why didn't anyone say that she liked to lay out by the pool, or shop for clothes, or eat in tacky restaurants, or anything that would have given her a human touch?

Matt finished up his remarks, fighting back the tears, with, "And now, the person who knew Delane for most of her life would like to close this service with a few words…Delane's sister Melinda."

A woman dressed in a black sheath with a black mantilla covering her blond hair rose from the first row of chairs and crossed to the lectern. She and Matt exchanged air-kisses and, as Matt retook his place in the front row, she turned to face the assemblage.

"My sister cared deeply about people and their pain," she started out and went on to describe how even the young Delane had volunteered as a candy-striper at the Red Bank Memorial Hospital in their childhood hometown, Chattanooga.

The resemblance between Melinda Huntington and the photograph of Delane Denning was striking. Anyone could tell they were sisters. They both had the same eyes and nose and Melinda wore her hair in a style similar to the Delane in the picture. I wouldn't have been as certain had I seen them together a week ago. Delane's newer hairstyle definitely flattered her face more than the old one.

What Melinda Huntington said after the candy-striper story was completely lost on me. I didn't hear another word. All my concentration had zeroed in on the necklace she wore—a garnet-and-pearl lavaliere. It was the same garnet-and-pearl lavaliere that I had fastened around Delane Denning's throat at Cove Creek before we had set out for home—the same garnet-and-pearl lavaliere that I had seen hanging down from her neck as she lay in a pool of her own blood.

One of the better known Country-Western personalities brought tears to most everyone's eyes (mine included) with a soulful rendition of *Amazing Grace*. After another few moments of silence, the minister announced that a private ceremony would be held to scatter Delane's ashes somewhere. I'm not altogether sure of the exact location, either the Botanical Gardens at Cheekwood or the Grassmere Wildlife Park or some such place where she had served on some committee. I wasn't paying attention at that point.

With the service over, Matt, Melinda, and the minister formed a short reception line (with Sharon Ross once again performing sentry duty, slightly behind and to Matt's right). The other guests queued up to again express their sympathies while I elbowed my way over to the far corner of the chapel.

"Turn quite a few heads when you enter a place, don't you?" Detective Osborn asked with a wry smile when I reached her.

"So do midgets," I answered, trying to appear humble.

During her snicker I plowed right ahead. "Have you released Delane's personal effects yet?"

"Late yesterday evening. With the body. Why?" The smile disappeared. She suspected I had asked the question for a reason.

"Do you remember what was on the list?"

"I have a copy in my purse. Why do you want to know?"

"Ozzie, humor me. Show me the list."

She dug a thrice-folded sheet of paper from her shoulder-strap bag and handed it to me. It detailed each article of clothing that Delane had been wearing along with a size and a description. No items of jewelry appeared on the list.

"What about her jewelry?" I asked.

"She wasn't wearing any. Mr. Denning has given us a copy of the insurance rider describing her wedding and engagement rings. We assume your friend Junior took them off the body before he left."

I refolded the paper and passed it back to her. "There's no mention of a necklace."

"Necklace?" Ozzie replied, unfolding the paper again and scanning it.

"I fastened the clasp for Delane before we left Cove Creek, Ozzie, and I distinctly remember seeing it around her neck just before I was hit."

A slight shake of her head, accompanied by an audible expulsion of breath through her nose, was the detective's first reply. Then, after a pause, a reluctant, "Come with me."

I dutifully followed her outside to the beige Pontiac Sunfire sitting in the NO PARKING zone. She unlocked the door, took a black leather briefcase from the back seat, set it on the hood, snapped the locks, and opened it halfway.

"These are photos of the crime scene," Ozzie said, turning to me. "They're not pretty."

I swallowed hard—as hard as is possible with a mouth that felt like the Sahara. "Go ahead," I told her.

"They're not pretty" could be classified as the understatement of the century. I had only glimpsed Delane's body for a moment before I was hit. Here, looking at the photographs, was a couple orders of magnitude worse, especially the close-ups of what had been her face. None of the pictures, however, showed a necklace.

"It was there, Ozzie. I swear. It was there."

She closed the folder with the photos and opened another containing a single sheet of paper. "Junior probably took it along with the rings. See if it's on this list of missing jewelry that Mr. Denning gave us."

I read through the inventory of items that were reportedly contained in the jewelry box stolen from Delane's bedroom. The lavaliere was number seven of the twenty-some pieces that had been itemized.

"This one," I said, stabbing the paper with my finger. "Garnet-and-pearl lavaliere."

"That explains it, then. The husband probably didn't know she was wearing it and assumed it was in the jewelry box."

"Maybe so, Ozzie, but can you explain why it's now hanging around Delane's sister's neck? A sister who you said inherits everything."

From the arch of her eyebrow, I could tell that Ozzie was remembering the big deal I had made out of the sandals the day before.

"Are you sure?" she asked, not bothering to disguise the skepticism she felt.

"Positive."

After returning the briefcase to the car, sans jewelry list, we reentered the mortuary. Ozzie stood on her tiptoes to look above the crowd, then reread the description of the missing necklace from the list.

The reception line had just ended and the funeral director was in the process of announcing that tea would be served in the Sycamore room, one of the eight parlors that surrounded the centrally located chapel. Rather than being designated by numbers or letters, all were named after trees.

As the crowd gravitated toward where the director had pointed, I hoped there wasn't an Ash room. That would have been a bit tacky.

"Stay close, but don't say anything unless I ask you a specific question," Ozzie directed, then moved out toward Matt Denning, Melinda Huntington, and Sharon Ross.

I had fully intended to follow Ozzie's orders, but Matt saw me approach and touched his sister-in-law on the shoulder. "Kate, there you are. I had hoped you were still here. Please come and meet

Delane's sister. Melinda, this is Caitlin O'Rourke. Kate, Melinda Huntington."

Ozzie, about to get sandwiched, simply stepped aside and, as she had done at the dentist's office the day before, became the invisible observer.

Melinda extended a hand to me and said, "Matthew has told me so much about you, Caitlin. I'm so sorry that you were injured."

The coolness of her handshake and her expression belied the warmth of her words. She wasn't the least bit sorry that I had been injured. And what *had* Matt told her? That I had gotten to the door too late to help her sister? Maybe she thought I should have gotten there first and that it should be *me* in that urn. Who could blame her. It wasn't as if the thought hadn't crossed *my* mind. A simple "How do you do?" would have been preferable.

Being raised a proper Southern girl, however, I didn't voice any of my thoughts but simply said, "Thank you, Ms. Huntington. And I'm terribly sorry for your loss. I didn't know your sister well, but I'll miss her." At least the last part was true.

"Come and join us for tea," Matt said, putting a hand on Melinda's and my shoulders and ushering us toward the Sycamore room.

"Uh…Matt," I started, attempting to return the focus to the investigation. "You remember Detective Osborn, don't you?" I stepped aside so as not to block his view.

"Oh…yes, of course," he said. "Thank you for coming. Would you care to join us as well?"

I had thought Melinda Huntington's remarks to me were somewhat on the cool side. Matt's to Ozzie were downright frosty. Have you ever watched one of those B movies from Japan with the English dubbed? Where the facial expressions and body language don't seem to agree with the words? Seeing Matt invite Ozzie to tea was reminiscent of that.

"Thank you, Mr. Denning, but I have just a couple of questions," Ozzie answered politely. "They won't take too long. Perhaps if we could step into one of the vacant parlors for just a few minutes?"

"By all means. Melinda, why don't you and Kate go on ahead. I'll be with you shortly."

I stayed put, serving as an anchor for Melinda so that she couldn't walk away. That gave Ozzie the two seconds she needed to clarify her request.

"Actually, I need to speak to Ms. Huntington as well. Why don't the four of us step into the Beech room." She gestured toward the closest parlor.

A little bantam rooster of a man from the governor's office had been hovering as close as Sharon Ross permitted anyone to get. As I opened the door to the Beech room, he swooped in.

"Is everything all right, Mr. Denning? Can I be of assistance?"

Matt smiled. "It's okay, Carlton. This policewoman just has a few questions about Delane. Why don't you go with Miss Ross and she'll get you a cup of tea."

We turned to enter the parlor and Sharon Ross started to herd Carlton in the direction of the Sycamore room. "Well, you just let me know if there's anything I can do," he called out over his shoulder after us.

Ozzie had stood to one side, tactfully letting pass the use of the term *policewoman*, and allowed the three of us enter first. She closed the door and took the list of missing jewelry from her shoulder bag.

"Mr. Denning, this is the list of your wife's jewelry that you reported stolen, would you look it over for me, please?"

Matt took the sheet of paper and gave an audible huff, then said, "And this is what was so important that it couldn't wait? I thought you had a break in the case or something. We have guests out there. Some of them extremely important people."

Ozzie ignored the protest. "Take a look at item number seven, if you would, Mr. Denning. Ms. O'Rourke is sure that your wife was wearing that particular piece on the day she was killed."

His voice softened as he addressed me. "Well, if you say so, Kate, okay. The police just asked me to list everything I could think of that was missing. This was one of the items I couldn't find at home. Does it matter, Officer, if the killer took it from the bedroom or from…from Delane?"

Ozzie choked down another objection to being called *Officer* and, in her best police-speak, answered with a question of her own. "Could you please describe the item in more detail for me, sir?"

"Well, let's see. It had…oh, I don't know, maybe about…"

"Matthew, which piece is it?" Melinda asked, speaking up for the first time and turning his hand so that she could read the list.

"The lavaliere. Number seven."

"It looks just like this." She held up the pendant hanging around her own neck, showing it first to Matt, then to Ozzie and me.

"There, Officer, are you satisfied?" Matt asked, a bit testily. "Now, get out there and catch the person who killed my wife and leave us alone with our grief." He took Melinda Huntington by the hand and brushed past Ozzie and myself, yanking open the parlor door.

"Are you saying that the necklace you're wearing *is* your sister's, Ms. Huntington?" Ozzie asked, bringing them up short.

"No, not this exact one," Melinda replied, turning around. "One just like it. They were our paternal grandmother's favorite earrings. When she passed away, our mother had them made into lavalieres for Delane and me."

"Is there a problem, Mr. Denning?" It was Carlton, the governor's toady. He and the mayor's aide had been waiting just outside the Beech room like two loyal guard dogs. Sharon Ross, still with tears in her eyes, raised her hands in resignation and shook her head apologetically at Matt.

Melinda tried to diffuse what was slowly becoming a tense situation. "Not a problem per se. Just a point of confusion, I'm afraid." She looked at Sharon Ross. "Would you be a dear and fetch my purse from the cloakroom? It's a black-beaded bag. The girl there will know which one it is."

As Miss Mousy, the ever-obedient servant, rushed off, Carlton's companion moved in. "I'm Ray Bob Gardner," he said to Ozzie, with an air of self-importance. "And I'm representing the mayor here today. What's this all about?"

Ozzie took in a deep breath and showed him her credentials. "I have a witness who claims that Delane Denning was wearing a necklace similar to that one when she was killed. I just needed to ask Ms. Huntington about it."

"And you had to do it *now*?" Ray Bob answered, his voice dripping with a mixture of sarcasm and incredulity. "You found it necessary to embarrass these people at the funeral of their loved one? It couldn't have waited until a more...appropriate place and time?"

"I'm investigating a murder, Mr. Gardner. The sooner I get my questions answered, the better my chances are of finding the killer."

Sharon Ross had returned with the purse. Carlton grabbed it from her and pushed his way to Melinda's side as if he had fetched it himself. Then he waited for a pat on the head and to be told what a good lap dog he was. Melinda rewarded him with a smile, then delved into the bag for her wallet.

"Here," she said, opening the wallet to the glassine picture holders. "This was taken many years ago but it clearly shows both lavalieres."

The picture she presented to Ozzie was a head-and-shoulders shot of two girls, both blond and attractive, one in her early teens, the other a few years younger. They both carried fishing poles and both wore identical garnet-and-pearl lavalieres.

Had we been in a cartoon, smoke would have spiraled out of Ozzie's ears. She gave me one quick, icy glare, then returned her attention to Melinda.

"Thank you for your time, Ms. Huntington; I'm sorry for your loss." That said, she turned, ignoring my presence completely, and walked out of the room toward the front door of the mortuary.

Ray Bob called out after her. "The mayor will hear of your conduct, Officer. And, believe me, he *won't* be pleased."

Ozzie didn't even break stride and remind him, either, that she was a detective. She just pushed through the front doors and headed out to the driveway.

Matt put a hand on my shoulder. "Kate, how could you?" The hurt in his voice and in his eyes made me want to cry.

"I'm sorry, Matt. I thought it might be important to the case." Looking at Delane's sister, I gave a schoolgirl shrug. "Sorry, Ms. Huntington."

"It's all right," she replied, giving me just the glimmer of a smile. "I know you were just trying to be helpful. Now, we really mustn't keep our guests waiting any longer. Will you join us, Caitlin?"

Even though her voice sounded sincere, I couldn't face Matt any longer. He felt that I had betrayed him and, in reality, I guess I had.

"No," I told her. "I really have to get going."

She smiled at me again, then nodded knowingly.

As I left, the foursome (led by the faithful Sharon Ross, who hurried ahead to hold the door for them) made its way toward the Sycamore room and the waiting guests.

Outside, an early winter had come to Nashville. Detective E. Osborn stood leaning up against her car, arms folded across her chest, ankles crossed, and a deep scowl on her face.

"Sorry," I said softly, walking up to her, unable to look anywhere higher than her mock-croc loafers.

"Sorry?" The volume of her voice matched my own.

I made no reply.

"You're sorry?" she repeated a bit louder.

I looked up and made eye contact. "What else can I say, Ozzie. You told me to tell you everything, no matter how small and that you'd be the judge of whether it was important."

"Oh?" This time her volume rose quite a few decibels. "You mean this is *my* screw up, not *yours*?"

"Both, I guess. I was just trying to help."

"You're going to help me right into a job as a school-crossing guard, Kate." She walked around me and opened the door to her car. "Forget about what I said. From now on, don't tell me anything unless you can remember who hit you or who shot Delane Denning."

"Okay," I answered. "But where do we go next?"

"*Next? We? We* don't go anywhere! There is no *we* anymore! And as far as *next* goes, *you* go home and *I* go about the business of finding Delane Denning's killer. I tried to accommodate your brother by letting you tag along with me, Kate. But now you've become a liability that I flat out can't afford. I've worked too long and too hard to get where I am. I'm sorry. It's nothing personal, but go home and stay out of it."

She didn't wait for me to respond. She just climbed into the Sunfire, started the engine, and pulled away from the curb without ever looking at me again.

Ozzie was steamed and I guess I couldn't really blame her. Twice, now, I had given her information that I thought was important and both times she had gotten into trouble acting on it—once with the Assistant Medical Examiner, now, most probably, with the Mayor's office. But, although I couldn't blame her, I couldn't just give up trying to help, either. Delane Denning was murdered on my watch.

During the homeward drive, something kept nagging at me—those damn sandals.

The traffic light at Old Hickory Boulevard and Franklin Pike changed. As it did so, I switched my gaze from the signal to the road ahead and caught a glimpse of the Cove Creek gate pass, still sitting on Liddy's dash where I had left it. The digital clock read three-oh-five. I verified it with the Omega Speedmaster on my wrist and, instead of continuing on to Wooten, I took the turnoff to northbound I-65.

While we had been inside the mortuary, the sun had finally burned its way through the cloudbank. It promised to be a nice afternoon—in fact, a perfect afternoon for a drive.

Chapter 9

A different gate-geezer from any I'd seen during my three-day stay guarded the entrance to Cove Creek; however, his reception turned out to be the same as that of his colleagues. At my approach, he raised the pike, smiled warmly, and waved me on through, not seeming to care that I hadn't flashed the gate pass.

Maybe I should reconsider going to Fond du Lac. I could stay here where the winters are mild and have a fairly decent career as a burglar just by driving in and out of Cove Creek every day, robbing the residents blind.

I always figured Mrs. Nash, the woman who comes in on Wednesdays to clean my place, to be the absolute tops. The people providing maid service at the resort community, though, sure come in a close second.

After retrieving the key from the porch light, I opened the door to a completely spotless home. Not one spec of dust, dirt, or clutter could I find anywhere. The floors had been washed and waxed, carpets vacuumed, bedding changed, and beds remade, and the kitchen appliances and bathroom fixtures sparkled. Had I not known better, I would have sworn this was a builder's showcase home—unoccupied.

You're probably wondering what I was doing, prowling around the Dennings' Cove Creek home and, I have to admit, I'm a bit embarrassed to tell you. I know, there are some perfectly logical explanations for a woman with size seven-and-a-half feet to have a pair of size six sandals. One, she liked them and the store was out of her size; two, she had gotten them as a gift and couldn't return them; or three, they weren't hers and actually belonged to a friend who had left them by the pool. But, the discrepancy still bugged my compulsively-tidy mind to no end.

One of the things Matt had said to Delane that Monday night at my place when he first suggested she go to Cove Creek was, *You've got plenty of clothes there.* Truer words were never spoken. While I had merely changed shirts with the same jeans and blazer ensemble during our stay, Delane had been able to wear a different outfit each day. Including clothing changes for going out to dinner, by my rough count I had seen her in five different pairs of shoes, shoes that I intended to check for size.

Unfortunately, the twin walk-in closets in the master suite were as bare as Protestant crosses. Maybe Ken and Barbie had driven up here before or after their trip out to the Dennings' Forest Hills home.

I started with one of the few people I knew at Cove Creek—Jerry, the tennis pro. Delane's murder had made the ten o'clock news Thursday night, with regular updates the past two days on the lack of police progress in finding the killer. Consequently, the Cove Creekers were aware of the general circumstances surrounding the case. I filled in some specifics for Jerry, which would allow him to play BMOC with inside information. In return, he got me an intro with the cleaning service supervisor.

No, I was told, there had been no clothing at the Denning home when his crew arrived at nine that morning. Someone had phoned in the cleaning order the night before. He didn't know who, but he promised to ask the night person and have the information for me on Monday. I thanked him and decided to check with a few of the neighbors.

No one answered the Avon-calling chimes at the house to the right of the Dennings. Hearing laughter coming from the rear, I traipsed around back to find three middle-aged women in swimsuits lounging around a pool and slurping margaritas. It was a little past five-thirty and, from the sound of their voices, I guessed they had been at it awhile.

"Well, ding-dong, the witch is dead," a big-bosomed redhead toasted, holding up her glass when I explained who I was and asked if I could bother them with a few questions.

"Now don't speak ill of the dead, Rusty," the blond member of the trio cautioned, pulling up the straps to her halter as she rolled over and raised herself to a sitting position.

"Oh, Tess," the one called Rusty shot back. "We've been doing it since we heard the news Thursday night. And, unless someone drove a stake through her heart, I wouldn't wanna bet that the dearly departed Delane will stay dead for very long."

They all giggled like school girls.

A tiny woman with a cute face but mousy-brown hair and the figure of a twelve-year-old patted an empty chaise next to her. "I'm Cece Prendergast," she said, still giggling. "And as you can tell, we were *not* members of the late Delane Denning's fan club."

"We hated the bitch," Tess confided over the back of her hand.

"But, girls," busty Rusty (I'll bet she had heard that once or twice before) pointed out. "That means Matt is now available." She sung out the word *available*.

They all laughed and made animal-snorting noises.

After attempting to shush the other two women and get serious herself, Cece said, "Now that you know how broken up we are, Caitlin, what did you want to ask us?"

I waved away a margarita, unsure of how it would mix with the Orudis I was still taking for my sore nose, and started with the easy question. "Did you happen to see anyone around the Denning place yesterday or early this morning?"

"No one after you and Delane left on Thursday afternoon," Tess answered.

The other two nodded in agreement.

I couldn't hide my surprise. "You knew I was here?"

"Our husbands were real quick to point you out to us, honey," Rusty said, with a shake of her head. "When you rose out of that lake in your snakeskin suit and walked back up to the house, there wasn't a man within a mile who didn't strain his eyeballs following your every step and shimmer."

"They usually watch for Delane," Cece added. "I'm surprised she didn't swim with you, she's such a water rat. And she rarely misses an opportunity to bounce those boobs of hers up and down the beach."

"But no one saw anything after we left?" I asked again.

"When Matt's not there for us to ogle and without Delane for the menfolk, no one has much of a reason to look," Tess replied pragmatically. "I live on the other side of the Dennings and we didn't notice anything. Of course, if it had been after dark, there's not much you *can* see with the houses spaced this far apart and all the shrubbery. And, believe me, my husband has tried."

Again a joint snicker.

I asked my second question, holding up the pair of sandals that I had brought with me. "I found these over by the Dennings' pool. They're not Delane's but I was wondering if you or any of her friends might have left them there."

"Friends?!" Rusty shouted with a horse-snort. "Now that's a good one."

Cece explained. "We admit it, Caitlin. We're spoiled little rich girls who have too much time on our hands. We're catty and bitchy, but we are nowhere, and I mean *nowhere*, in Delane Denning's league. Oh, we associated with her, of course, if you can call trading snarls at social gatherings *associating*, but we weren't friends by *any* stretch of the imagination."

Both Tess and Rusty nodded their heads in agreement and raised their glasses.

"Delane had no friends," Tess added. "Just jealous wives."

I had to agree with one thing Cece had said. These women certainly *were* catty and bitchy. From the three days I had spent at Cove Creek, I had found Delane Denning to be *very* likable. I could see why they'd be jealous, though. Delane had a figure that put all three of theirs to shame. But something in Tess' tone of voice told me there was more to their animosity than mere boob-envy.

Just to make sure that I had picked up the correct signals, I asked, "She hit on your husbands?"

"Not ours," Rusty corrected, waggling a cautionary finger at me. "Others who don't keep as close an eye on their men as we do."

This time only Tess joined in with Rusty's laughter. Cece, with the prepubescent figure, tried forcing one, but it came up way short. I could see the hurt in her eyes but her companions were too preoccupied with their own amusement to notice.

"Then these sandals wouldn't belong to any of you?" I asked.

They all looked, but shook their heads in the negative.

"The Dennings had a pool party two, maybe three weeks ago," Cece said. "There had to have been three dozen of us there." Then her expression changed to one of concern and I could see her trying to figure out why someone would be asking about a dead woman's sandals. "Is this important, Caitlin? Does it have something to do with Delane's death?"

"I really don't know," I confessed. "Maybe. Maybe not."

"I've got a digital camera. If you'd like, I could make a picture of them and stick a note up on the lost-and-found board at the club. Other than that, I'm not sure what to tell you."

Since I didn't know what else to do either, I agreed. Cece got her camera and took four shots, one of the sandals and the other three of me with each of the women individually.

After another fifteen minutes of listening to gossip about Delane (all of it unflattering), I thanked them for their time. Cece had printed out the photos and I autographed the prints of me with each of them. Then, climbing into Liddy, I headed for Nashville.

* * * *

During the drive back, alone with my thoughts, depression began to set in big-time. In trying to understand why, I remembered a scene from an old movie. A little kid had just found out that his idol was not the person the kid had thought him to be, but, in reality, a bum.

"Tell, me it ain't so!" the kid had pleaded with his former hero, tears streaming down the little tyke's cheeks.

Tell me it ain't so!—the universal cry when our sports, movie, or political celebrities get busted for drugs, illicit sex, illegal gambling, or anything else that tarnishes our images of them. *Tell me it ain't so!*

I had thought Delane and Matt to be happily married; the police had uncovered evidence to the contrary. The Delane I had known, if only briefly, had been warm and friendly; yet, at her memorial service, her family and friends had merely given her a businesslike eulogy. Now her neighbors had engaged in a little postmortem back-stabbing, accusing her of being a bitch and an adulteress, as well. I was beginning to think that for three days in Cove Creek I had seen only a facade, not the real Delane Denning.

Tell me it ain't so!

But Delane had seemed so genuine when we talked and laughed and watched CMT and, yes, even when she had kissed me before running up the front steps to her death.

Perhaps, though, it was *I* who had seen the real Delane Denning and everyone else had known only the facade. Maybe the fear brought on by being mugged outside the pub or extreme gratitude because I had rescued her had cracked her shell. If so, it buoyed my spirits to know that she had opened up to me. At the same time, it saddened me to think of all those people, including her own sister, who would forever think of her as cold, calculating, manipulative, and, according to the neighbor-shrews, involved in charity work only to enhance her own social standing.

Maybe the people the police had interviewed or the ones I had talked to were not the most impartial of sources. There was one person I knew who rubbed elbows with the same people as the Dennings and, although, he could probably buy and sell them twice over, didn't have a mendacious or deceitful bone in his substantial body. And, since I hadn't yet returned his phone call, I decided to drop in for a quick visit.

Chapter 10

"Hey, Katie," the valet parking attendant said, opening the car door for me. "They did some job on you, huh? Get in a few good licks of your own, did you?" He feinted the old one-two punch.

"Never laid a glove on him, Carlos."

"Too bad. They find this slime-ball yet?"

"Not yet."

"Well, when they do, maybe your cop-brother can arrange for you to spend a little quality time alone with him, if you get my drift."

"That would be nice," I told him with a smile. "That would be *real* nice. And Carlos, don't take it too far. I won't be long."

"You got it, Katie," he said, sliding behind the wheel and moving the seat up so that his feet touched the pedals.

Zakinthos, located on Broadway near the West End split, had been designed to look like a Greek temple on the exterior. Subdued strains of bouzouki music filtered through the din of the crowd as I entered and nodded a thanks to Georgios, the doorman who greeted me warmly.

A second greeting came from Nikolaos Panacopoulos himself. "My darling Katie," he boomed out in his deep bass, catching sight of me above the crowd of people waiting for their reservations to be called. Abandoning the couple with whom he had been schmoozing, he politely elbowed his way over. "Why you no call your poor Uncle Nico, heh?"

At six-one and two-hundred-eighty pounds with a full mane of white hair to complement his large mustache, Nico looked like a walrus in a tuxedo.

"I decided to come in person, instead," I told him in between double cheek-kisses while making sure that my poor sore nose didn't get hit by his hawk's beak. "It's been awhile. Isn't this better than a phone call?"

"Much better. Very much better." He took my face in his hands as Mary Grace had done the day before and gave me the once over. Satisfied that I would be all right, he nodded and said, "You come; I fix you something to eat and then we talk."

Nico snapped his fingers at a fustanella-clad waiter and rattled off a few sentences in Greek as he pushed me gently in the waiter's direction. "You go with Andreas. He's the best. I go to kitchen, then I bring you big surprise. Okay?"

"Okay, Uncle Nico. But not too much food," I cautioned, shaking a finger at him. "Some of us have a figure to watch."

"You eat; everyone else watch," he answered with a laugh, then lumbered down toward the kitchen.

I followed Andreas and the eyes of the crowd followed me. These were not the usual looks that I had grown accustomed to, like the ones I had received at Delane Denning's memorial service earlier in the day. These were daggers. They said, "Who the hell is she that she gets to waltz right in and sit down. We've been waiting for over half an hour."

I'm the boss' niece. I'm the boss' niece…sort of. I mentally sang out to them as I sashayed over to a table for four that Nico always kept open for dignitaries.

Most restaurants hide the kitchens from their patrons. Just try asking to see one sometime and you'll know what I mean. Health regulations forbid it; insurance won't allow it; or a half-dozen other lame excuses. We always honor such requests at Kehough's, although, I'll have to admit, they are very rare. But, then again, we have nothing to hide.

Nikolaos Panacopoulos had nothing to hide, either, and didn't even try. Quite the contrary. He was so proud of his kitchen, he made it the centerpiece of the restaurant.

The interior of Zakinthos resembled an ancient Greek theater, having tables set in three horseshoe tiers so that the patrons could look down onto a thrust stage. The ovens were set along the back wall of the stage, with the ranges down center. Although enormous exhaust hoods had been placed above each cooking surface to draw off the smoke and smells, enough of the aromas wafted up to the tables to keep the patrons in a perpetual state of mouth-watering anticipation.

Center stage contained the preparation area for the main courses. Appetizers and salads were readied stage left, leaving desserts to occupy the stage right position so that they could be viewed from the lobby. Coolers and food storage rooms were backstage, accessed through two sets of double doors up left and up right.

Because of the Orudis, I declined Andreas' offer of wine and asked for an iced tea (unsweetened), instead. I'd add a few packets of the blue stuff when the drink got there.

From my vantage point in the center of the second tier, I had a clear view of everything that went on in the kitchen. I settled back and watched as Nico made his rounds, inspecting what his chefs were preparing and offering little gems of fatherly wisdom at each stop. One of the chefs sautéed veal sweetbreads. When he squeezed a lemon into the pan, my mouth went sour.

Ooo, I hope the sweetbreads are for me, I thought, completely forgetting my earlier admonition of "not too much food." Of course, I thought the same thing about the shrimp in tomato, wine, and feta cheese sauce as well as the moussaka.

A tuxedoed arm slid a plate in front of me. On the plate sat a large, frosted glass of iced tea.

"Would the big Amazon lady with the broken nose care for anything else?" a voice asked with just the trace of a snicker.

I knew that voice, a mellow and seductive baritone. It had been many years since I had heard it, long before I had left for Italy, but, nevertheless, I *knew* that voice.

"This big Amazon lady, broken nose or not, can certainly kick the ass of anybody with a wimpy name like Kit Poulos," I fired back without turning around.

"Please don't start on that," the voice pleaded and its owner kissed the top of my head. "It's back to Chris again, along with the full impossible-to-spell last name."

Chris Panacopoulos sat in the chair at my right, and my heart went into fibrillation. *God,* I thought, *he's still as handsome as ever. Maybe even more so. Lucky Daphne.* What I said was, "So much for being your own man, huh? Long time no see. Home for a visit?"

"The restaurant in Detroit went bust. Not bust, really, but just never became what I had hoped it would."

"Yeah, sometimes that happens. So you and...uh...Daffy?" I asked, raising a hand to my forehead, feigning forgetfulness.

"Daphne," he corrected.

"Daphne, right. You guys going to be living here in town?"

"There is no *us* anymore, Kate. Another something that didn't work out. I've moved back in with the folks. Temporarily, until I can find a place of my own."

"Sorry," I said, trying my best to sound it. "I mean about Daphne, not about you moving back."

He shrugged. Before we could get any further, though, Nico arrived, followed by Andreas and a busboy, each bearing trays.

"Hey, waddayu on vacation or what?" Nico bellowed at Chris. "You just supposed to stop and say hello. I take care of Katie. Get back out there and make nice with the people." He thumbed at the crowd in the lobby.

Chris squeezed my hand and winked as he rose. "Can I call you?" he asked.

"If your mom will let you," I answered, returning the wink.

As he walked away, I could see him wince, knowing that I hadn't forgotten being stood up in the ninth grade all those many years ago. That was good. Now he'd feel that he had to make it up to me, unaware of how badly I really wanted him to call.

During the Dolmades appetizers (steamed grape leaves with rice, pine nut, and currant stuffing, topped with a yogurt-mint sauce), Nico and I talked about family. I got the scoop on what had happened between Chris and Daffy (he hadn't realized he'd have to marry the mother, too).

I explained about the Delane Denning murder (and my involvement) during the main course. Nico had read my mind. It *was* the Sweetbreads, accompanied by *Spanakopetackia* (spinach, green onions, and feta cheese, wrapped in phyllo pastry).

For dessert, we had *Loukoumades* (deep-fried yeast dough that puffs up and is served with honey and a dash of cinnamon). It was then that I broached the subject that had brought me to the restaurant—Matt and Delane Denning, their marriage and their finances.

"Ahh, the Dennings," Nico said, shaking his head. "There is old Greek saying, Katie. 'A fool travels in the company of fools.' That crowd."—he gave a small snort through his beak and a dismissive gesture with his hand—"They spend three times what they make so that others will think they are twice as rich as they really are. Everything mortgaged up to their eyeballs. The only guy who profits in long run is bankruptcy lawyer."

"Did you know them well, Uncle Nico?"

"Naw. Barely. That crowd, they think Nico a peasant because I no speak the good English, I no drive the foreign cars, I no live in the mansions, and I no give or go to fancy parties. I work my ass off and when I get done with work, I go home to bed. And,"—he shook his finger at me—"I no pack my nose with the drugs. But when they need money for their charities, who do they come to?"

"You, Uncle Nico?"

"You betcha, me. I the only one who *got* any money. All that crowd got is debt. So they always ask your Uncle Nico to be on board for this and on board for that. I got closet full of plaques saying what a philanthropist I am. But I no get invited for dinner or golf."

He shrugged it off. "What do I care. I no play golf and I no like their food or company, anyhow. And the money they get from me, it goes to help needy. I got Delia; I got Khristophoros; I got Artemis and three beautiful grandbabies; I got restaurant; I got old friends; I got church"—he reached over and squeezed my hand—"and I got you, Katie. What I need with fools, heh?"

"So you don't know anything about the Dennings' personal life?"

"Personal life? Like what?"

"The Delane Denning I got to know seemed madly in love with her husband, Uncle Nico. But from what her neighbors told me, she's had affairs."

Uncle Nico sighed. It came from deep down inside of him and made the corners of his mustache flutter as it exited his mouth. Then he shrugged his broad shoulders and said very quietly, "Sometimes, Katie, that can happen. Even with people in love."

"Did it happen with Delane Denning?"

Again the shrug. "Who can say? Not your Uncle Nico. I know nothing about the Dennings' man-and-wife business. Just their business business. Mr. Denning is not the hotshot money-man he pretends to be. Other fools in his band of fools trust his judgment and lose shirts big-time. Irving Baumeister, over at First Tennessean, is old and dear friend. Smartest money-man I know. He calls Matthew Denning a putz."

* * * *

As I drove home, I reflected on the evening. It hadn't been a total waste of time. I had gotten to see Uncle Nico and had gotten fed. Also, while I waited for Carlos to bring Liddy around, Chris had come out with a doggie-bag of baklava and we firmed up dinner plans for the following Tuesday at The Opryland Hotel's Cascades Restaurant. I'd count the days.

Your loss, Daffy.

While traveling down I-65, I caught sight of a billboard that had most likely been rented by one of the Game Wardens. It read, "The Foresters Present: *Encore to Murder*—Thu, Fri & Sat at 8:00—Sun at 2:00" and gave a phone number to call for ticket information.

Still bothered about not finding Delane's shoes and clothing that I had driven all the way to Cove Creek to see, I tried to recall what Barbie (Taylor Hollingshead) had said on Thursday when she introduced herself at the Denning home.

The local community theatre group here in Forest Hills? Over on Otter Creek Road just before you get to Granny White Pike?

From Liddy's digital clock, I figured I'd just about make it there as the play ended, excellent timing for going to a community theatre production. But I wasn't interested in the play, just a few words with Ken or Barbie or the managing director. What was his name? Bobby? Yeah, Bobby.

* * * *

No one manned the lobby ticket desk at The Hunting Lodge, the name given their theater by The Foresters. I quietly slipped into the auditorium, eased the door closed, and stood with my back up against it. With the packed house, I watched silently as the play built to a climax.

A conversational grouping of furniture (a large sofa with twin love seats on either side) sat in the center of the stage. Up right was a bar. A fireplace had been erected stage left. In an alcove, down right, was a desk, drawing board, and a wall of bookshelves, obviously a small home-office of some sort.

"You just couldn't keep your big mouth shut, could you, Roger?" a man whom I recognized as Jason Scarborough (Ken from last Thursday) said contemptuously to a much older, portly man.

Jason waved a revolver back and forth, aiming it first at a man sitting on the desktop, then to another man half lying on the sofa. "Don't anyone move!" he ordered.

The man on the sofa pulled himself up to a sitting position on the sofa's arm. "What now, Mr. Dunbar? You've got nowhere to go."

"I don't *have* to go anywhere, Chief," Jason replied, continuing to wave the revolver around in jerky little movements. "You already answered one prowler-call tonight. Gunshots fired, remember? Well your prowler is about to strike again and Roger and I will be two very frightened and sad witnesses to the tragedy."

"No!" the portly man playing Roger commanded. "Absolutely not!" He calmed his voice as he slowly approached Jason. "No more, my boy. No more killing." He sounded like a father talking to a wayward child and extended his hand. "Give me the gun."

It looked as if Jason would comply, shifting his aim from the other two men and holding out the revolver toward the one called Roger. Then he sneered and said, "You whimpering old fool," and pulled the trigger twice in rapid succession.

While everyone else in the building gasped, I quickly shoved the knuckle of my right index finger into my mouth and bit down on it hard. It was either that or burst into uncontrolled laughter.

With the sound of the gunshots, the actor playing Roger (two-hundred-and-fifty pounds if an ounce) rose up on his tippy-toes, performed a perfect three-hundred-and-sixty-degree pirouette, staggered for three or four more steps, then melodramatically fell onto the back of the sofa and rolled off onto the floor with a gigantic thud.

I felt a snort-laugh about to burst through and knew if I let it, I'd blow packing all over the place and start the nose bleeding again. Hurriedly, I slipped back out into the lobby as quietly as I had entered. The door had no sooner closed behind me when I let the laugh loose through my mouth, spitting all over the front of my shirt as I did so.

"Is there something funny?" a middle-aged woman asked. She was rather short and heavy-set, with close-cropped brown/gray hair. Her icy tone left no doubt about the correct reply.

"Oh no, ma'am," I said, quickly wiping myself down and pointing to my bandaged-up schnozz. "It's just my nose. Sometimes it…uh…acts up and…tickles the back of my throat. I tried to get out as quickly as I could so that I wouldn't ruin the moment for your patrons."

Am I good, or what? The lady with the icy tone thought so and thawed immediately.

"Are you going to be all right?" she asked, coming over to me and reaching up to put a comforting hand on my shoulder. "Can I get you anything? A glass of water, perhaps."

"No, I'll be just fine in a second or two. What you could do, though, is point out the managing director to me as everyone leaves. I think his name is Bobby something-or-other."

"I'm Bobbie Deerfield," she said. "It's me you want to see."

"Oh," I replied, feeling ashamed that I had betrayed my gender by automatically thinking the managing director to be a man. Then I stuck out a hand in Bobbie Deerfield's direction and said, "My name's Caitlin O'Rourke. I was the one with Mrs. Denning when she was shot."

After five minutes or so of replaying the scene for her (much to her delight and my dismay), I trotted out the lie I had conjured up on the way over.

"I left one of my blazers and a pair of shoes in the closet up at the Dennings' Cove Creek home. When Jason and Taylor picked up Mrs. Denning's things yesterday, it was mistakenly put in with them."

"But the kids didn't pick up anything at Cove Creek," Bobbie said. "They only went to the Denning home here in Forest Hills."

"Are you sure?"

"They were gone less than half an hour. They couldn't have driven anywhere else."

"I guess the maid must have cleaned out Mrs. Denning's things from the lake house beforehand. Could I look through the bags that were picked up?"

"You're welcome to see the one containing Mrs. Denning's shoes, Caitlin. But Jason took the clothing bags directly to the dry cleaners. They won't be delivered until sometime late Tuesday morning."

The play had ended during our conversation and the patrons were streaming out, gushing about how wonderful the acting was. A beaming Bobbie Deerfield quickly turned me over to one of the volunteers and went to mingle with the crowd, graciously accepting her directorial accolades.

Debbie, the chubby, effervescent young girl that I had been entrusted to, took me to a closet where the trash bag of shoes had been temporarily stored. I looked at every single pair, selectively verifying that they were seven-and-a-halfs. However, none of them were the shoes worn by Delane during our Cove Creek stay.

Thanking Debbie, I took my leave, promising to return on Tuesday to look for my jacket. Hey, if you're going to lie, you have to stick with it, don't you?

On the drive home, the coldness of it all struck me. I could understand someone wanting to get rid of a late spouse's clothing so that they wouldn't be constantly reminded of the death. It's a perfectly natural reaction. We did the same thing when Da died and again when Ma passed away. But we didn't do it the very next day. And for all that clothing from Cove Creek to be gone, someone, indeed, had to clean out the lake-house closets either late Thursday night or very early Friday morning.

I guess we all deal with grief in different ways.

* * * *

I opened the back door to Kehough's at about ten-thirty and Bryan Mulcahy's lilting tenor, singing about *The Green Fields of America*, trickled through from the pub. The Saturday-night *ceili* was well underway. Deciding to take care of a few personal items before looking in on the festivities, I mounted the stairs to my quarters.

As I neared the top, two things caught my attention—a light, shining through the crack under the door, and the sound of voices from within. The light by itself didn't really bother me. Because of my erratic schedule, I have four lamps set on timers so that poor W.B. won't have to sit there all by herself in the dark. The voices, though, were somewhat disconcerting.

CHAPTER 11

A bit gun-shy after my coming-through-the-door experience of Thursday afternoon at the Denning home, I opened the door to my quarters very slowly.

"Well, it's about time," Pat said, hoisting himself out of the La-Z-Boy. "Where have you been?"

As surprised as I was to see Melinda Huntington, sitting at the end of the sofa where Delane Denning had sat the night she was mugged, I temporarily ignored her and answered my brother.

"Sorry, *Da*," I said, effecting a little-girl voice and using as much sarcasm as I could muster. "I didn't realize it was a school night."

It's no big feat to exasperate Pat; he exasperates easily. And when he does, he gets the typical Irishman's flushed face.

"Well, hell, Katie. Ms. Huntington's been here for well over an hour. I thought Ozzie told you to go home. About four hours ago."

"Yeah, but I didn't realize that meant I had to go *straight* home. Lighten up, will you?"

I crossed to the conversational grouping of furniture and extended a hand to Melinda Huntington. "Sorry to have kept you waiting, Ms. Huntington. To what do I owe the pleasure?"

"It's perfectly all right, Caitlin," she said, not rising because of W.B., curled up on her lap. "And, please, call me Mel."

After first stuffing the lace handkerchief with which she had been daubing her eyes into the side pocket of her dress (the same black sheath that she had worn to Delane's memorial service earlier in the day), she reached up to shake my hand. Her grip was very firm.

"Only if you'll call me Kate," I answered, sitting across from her in the La-Z-Boy that Pat had vacated. (It's *my* home and *my* favorite chair and he's my brother, not company.) "What can I do for you?"

"Convince me that my sister's killer will be brought to justice."

Even though she had been born, raised, and continued to live in Chattanooga, Melinda Huntington's approach was very unSouthern-like. There were no preliminaries, no small talk, just an opening salvo of words as if fired from a blunderbuss. She made the statement matter-of-factly, looking me squarely in the eyes and showing very little emotion.

I didn't reply but, to my credit, I didn't let my mouth drop open either. I swallowed hard and glanced up at Pat, who still stood beside my chair. In that unspoken language between family members, my expression said, "Care to field this one, big brother?"

"Let me assure you that the police are conducting a very thorough investigation, Ms. Huntington," he said, getting my message.

"I was given to understand, Detective O'Rourke, that you have precious little in the way of any hard evidence," Melinda countered.

Obviously, they hadn't been discussing the case in the hour they had spent together waiting for my return.

"We have a prime suspect who looks very good for your sister's murder," Pat replied.

"Then why were Kate and that black policewoman at the memorial service this afternoon all but accusing *me* of the crime?"

"As I understand it, *Detective* Osborn wasn't actually making an accusation, Ms. Huntington. She was merely getting a clarification on one of the items that had been reported stolen."

"You weren't there, were you?"

"Well…no," Pat sputtered.

"In fact, Detective, you aren't directly involved in this investigation yourself, are you?"

"Not exactly." His face had turned rhubarb red.

"Then, with all due respect, I'd really like to talk to Kate about it, since she *seems* to be."

"My sister is *not*…"

I reached over and squeezed Pat's hand, interrupting him as his voice rose. "I'm only involved as a potential witness, Mel, but I'll be happy to tell you what little I know." Again I looked up at my brother, but this time didn't rely on telepathy. "Pat, why don't you go see how the *ceili's* going and let Mel and me talk for a bit. Okay?"

He started to protest, but after I gave his hand another squeeze, this time a knuckle-buster, he pulled it away and walked to the door, leaving without saying another word.

Once he had gone, I matched Melinda's bluntness with some of my own. "You're right, Mel, it *was* a veiled accusation this afternoon. I had been told that you inherited everything and when I saw you wearing that necklace, I thought that somehow you might be involved with Delane's death. I hope you won't hold it against Detective Osborn. It was totally my fault. I jumped to conclusions and steered her wrong. I'm sorry."

"In a way, I'm glad you feel so strongly about wanting to bring my sister's killer to justice. Tell me, Kate, do they know anything? Really?"

"They know for sure that Junior Lee Thigpen stole Delane's purse. That's fact; I saw it happen. Anything beyond that is only supposition. I didn't see who killed Delane and I didn't see who hit me with the shotgun."

She nodded and, after a pause, asked, "Then you can't say for certain who *didn't* do it, can you?" Her eyes narrowed and her lips tightened into mere slits as she waited for my reply.

I took in a deep breath, but didn't give her an immediate answer. Nor could I make eye contact. I just sat there focusing on W.B., still curled up in Melinda Huntington's lap and loving every second of the ear-scratching she was getting. Even though the implication of the woman's question was obvious, I chose to stall for thinking-time, asking, instead, for clarification.

"You mean Matt?"

"Or…anyone else."

She gave a slight shrug, but I could tell that's precisely whom she meant. Apparently there had been some significance to the air-kisses I had witnessed between her and her brother-in-law at the memorial service.

Raising my eyes from the cat to the lavaliere, I said, "I know for certain that Matt did not kill your sister, Mel. Just before I heard the gunshots, I saw him pull into the driveway. He waved to me." That much was true and only after I said it could I look up and meet her gaze.

All the while she spent digesting my words, Melinda Huntington kept her light blue eyes locked onto mine. The effect was almost hypnotic. Finally she said, "But you aren't sure he wasn't in on it, are you, Kate?"

I guess I should forget any notion I may have entertained of becoming a professional poker player. Okay, so she knew I had some doubts. But deciding just how much supposition I should share with this woman was another matter entirely.

My Yankee friends talk about some foolishness up North called ice fishing and about how you have to test the thickness of the ice before you wander out and put your whole weight onto it. Every year, so I'm told, there are always a handful of morons who lose cars and snowmobiles because they fail to take this simple precaution.

Doing my own version of ice-testing, I said, "I had a run-in with Junior Lee Thigpen downstairs in the pub four days before he stole Delane's purse. He's a doofus and a doper. He may very well have killed Delane during a burglary as the police suspect, but, then again…" I left the sentence unfinished.

"How is it possible that Matt would have known this…this Junior person, Kate?"

Expelling a deep breath through my mouth, I ventured further out onto the ice. "Matt was here the night of that run-in. When my brothers tossed Junior out of the pub, Pat told me his name. In Matt's presence."

Again there was silence as Melinda considered this last little bit of information. She bit her lower lip and nodded her head slightly.

After about ten seconds, I said, "My turn, now, Mel. Did Matt know that Delane had started divorce proceedings and that she had changed her will?"

"Not to my knowledge."

"Did *you* know?"

"Yes, Kate, I did."

"Did Matt know that Delane had found out about his extramarital affair?"

"No, I don't think he did."

"Did she tell *you*?"

"Yes, when she told me she had visited her lawyer."

"Did she know who the other woman was?"

"No. She had become suspicious. You know, perfume odors on his clothing from scents she didn't wear. Evening meetings that were scheduled at the last minute that he didn't get home from until late. Even though she knew he was under a great deal of pressure at work to produce, something just didn't ring true. One evening when Matt went into the den and closed the door to make a call, she picked up the extension. He was arranging a tryst. After ten minutes or so, he came out and said he had to meet with a client. The next day she called her lawyer."

"What is your *own* financial status?" I asked, expecting to hear a cracking sound and a big sploosh as I fell into the frigid water.

After only the slightest of hesitations, where I'm sure the phrase, "None of your effing business," went round and round in her mind, she said, "Alimony from a fairly well-to-do ex-husband. I'm not wealthy, by any means, but very comfortable. Tell me, Kate, what will happen now?"

"The police will find Junior Lee Thigpen and question him. Believe me, Mel, this guy's not going down by himself. *If* anyone else is involved, Junior'll sell him out for a reduced sentence. Count on it."

"So we just wait?"

"As my brother Pat is fond of saying, 'Eighty percent of police work is tedious investigation, another fifteen percent involves paperwork, and only the remaining five doing what you see cops do on TV.'"

She gave a little laugh. It was the first time I had seen a face other than the somber one. As quickly as it had appeared, though, the smile vanished and once more Melinda Huntington resembled the newspaper photo of her sister.

"I'll be staying here in town at the Maxwell House for a few days," she said. "Taking care of some legal matters. Would you let me know if there are any developments? The police won't tell me a thing."

"After my screw-up this afternoon at the mortuary, Mel, I'm afraid I've been benched. I'm, as they say, out of the loop."

"But surely your brother isn't."

"I'll have to badger him, but, if I find out anything, I'll give you a call."

She started to rise but I could see that she wasn't sure what to do with W.B. I got up, scooped the cat from her lap and put it over my shoulder. W.B. meowed a single protest, then fell back asleep, leaning her head against my neck.

With the kitten again purring contentedly, Melinda and I walked to the downstairs door in silence. After exchanging goodnight handshakes, she entered the pub and crossed to the front door while the Tara-Diddles played *Humours of Kilfenora*. Any other Saturday night I would have put on my hard shoes, *Humours* being one of my favorite hornpipes. This night, however, nose throbbing, I remounted the stairs to my quarters.

Although still unable to take a decent shower, I badly needed to wash my hair. I hadn't done so since Thursday afternoon's swim up in Cove Creek and my locks felt like Medusa's, ready to begin writhing at any moment. After shampooing my mane in the sink and settling, yet again, for a neck-down shower, I put on a royal blue sleepshirt with the Regina Caeli crest over my heart and bobcat paw prints traveling up the front from left hip to right shoulder, then down the back again to the left hip. Reclining in the La-Z-Boy with W.B., I considered how different Delane Denning had been from her sister. I just couldn't imagine Melinda Huntington kissing me goodnight.

Thoughts of Delane made me cry. It was counterproductive, however. Not only didn't it make me feel any better, the tears loosened up my bandages and I had to redo them on my nose guard before going to bed.

That night, the dream that replayed itself over and over again was a slow-motion clip of me running up the steps to the portico of the Denning home, looking in through the front door, and seeing Delane lying there. Each time, as my eyes focused in on the garnet-and-pearl lavaliere, I felt the pain of getting smashed in the nose. Then the clip would start up again from the beginning.

No matter how hard I tried, I never could take my eyes off that necklace to see who it was that hit me.

Chapter 12

On Sunday morning I made it to 9:30 Mass at Our Lady, Queen of the Universe, with three minutes to spare and no traffic ticket for Pat to fix. As I slid into the pew next to Seamus, Mary Grace leaned forward, purposefully looked at her watch and whispered past Tim and Seamus, "Where's Pat?"

"Not my day to watch him," I whispered back.

Both my brother and nephew stifled snickers; however, Tim didn't manage nearly as well as his father. Mary Grace rewarded him with a smack on the back of his head. Church or not, discipline would be maintained in the Mary Grace O'Rourke household.

After Mass I declined an invitation to brunch, planning instead to grab something to eat back home, then go over to the Y later on and watch the Sunday afternoon B-ball game. No sooner had I inserted the key into Liddy's ignition when a black Chrysler Cirrus pulled into the parking spot next to me. I thumbed the button to lower the passenger-side window.

"You're either an hour-and-a-quarter late or forty-five minutes early," I told brother Pat as he exited his car. "What's up?"

"They've found Junior Lee Thigpen," he growled, opening the right-side door and climbing in beside me. "*That's* what's up."

"Great!" I said. Then, remembering what Carlos the valet parking attendant had suggested the night before, I added, "Any chance of me getting to talk to him?"

"Not you or anybody else. He's dead. Let's go."

"Where to?"

"Ozzie wants to see you."

Super, I'd been put back into the game!

* * * *

During the ride, Pat filled me in on Junior's untimely demise. Well, maybe not so untimely, for a snowbird.

A routine security patrol had spotted a white Plymouth Colt Vista at the rear of a warehouse parking lot back by Brick Church Park. A young woman lay slumped over in the passenger seat, a bullet hole in her right temple.

About ten yards into the overgrown park they had found the body of Junior Lee Thigpen. He, also, had been shot once in the head, during what looked to be a botched drug buy. He still clutched a half bindle in his right hand and white powder covered the front of his clothing. No one doubted what the analysis of the powder would show.

Although there was no purse with the woman in the car and Junior's body had no wallet or ID, the first officers on the scene had recognized him from the APB and had notified Homicide. Detectives Osborn and Sykes had responded. While Sykes stayed with the crime scene, Ozzie checked up on the owner of the Plymouth. The woman to whom it was registered, Swallow (I kid you not!) Sedlacek, lived not too far away and turned out to be the female victim.

A hastily arranged search warrant for her apartment turned up Delane Denning's purse and jewelry box. Ozzie wanted me over at Swallow's place to ID the lavaliere before she contacted Matt Denning for corroboration.

* * * *

Remember the apartment building in the movie *Rosemary's Baby?* Dark, old, once grand, but seen its better days and now slowly becoming seedier and seedier with each passing year? Such was the Normandy Arms, over on Trinity Lane, west of I-65.

A uniformed police officer stood sentry outside the door to apartment 2-B. He and brother Pat exchanged smiles and greetings as we entered.

"Don't touch anything," the cop whispered to me as I went past.

"Okay," I whispered back.

His patronizing wink and nod said, "Good girl." Not wanting to embarrass my brother, I tolerated it without comment.

Swallow Sedlacek's landlord, an extremely fat, elderly black man by the name of Ernie Hammerman, sat stiffly on a worn, purple velveteen couch in the middle of a threadbare faux-Persian carpet. An overstuffed chair (some of it oversticking out), a cheap end table, and matching coffee table were the only other pieces of furniture in the room, with the exception of a relatively new glass stereo cabinet, complete with state-of-the-art components.

On top of an old, nicked, and scratched Sony TV sat a new double-bay Sony VCR unit. On top of that, a high-school graduation picture showed a young Swallow Sedlacek.

She could have been the poster girl for the Anorexia Foundation, with an emaciated face, hollow cheeks, and bony shoulders sticking out of a pink strapless gown. All the potions of Merle Norman couldn't hide the dark circles under her eyes. In spite of her pitiable looks, Swallow's lips were curled up into a hopeful little smile. Her face said, "This is as pretty as I can get. Won't somebody love me?"

Unfortunately that somebody turned out to be Junior Lee Thigpen, and his drug habit had gotten her killed. I felt sorry for the girl. How big a loser do you have to be to rate only Junior Lee Thigpen for a boyfriend.

Detective Osborn must have just come from church, also, or been beeped out of the service. Instead of one of her workday pantsuits, she wore a cranberry-and-camel plaid wrap skirt, a cranberry blazer, a white mock turtleneck sweater, and high heels (two-and-a-half inches). As she had done the day before at the mortuary, she also had used makeup on this Sunday morning. The overall package looked striking.

Ozzie ceased her attempted interrogation of Mr. Hammerman when Pat and I arrived, rose, and gave the big man's shoulder a squeeze, then motioned us toward the kitchen with her head. Pat tugged slightly at my sleeve and I bent over toward him.

"Put your hands in your pockets," he directed in a whisper.

"What?" I whispered back.

"Put your hands in your pockets. It'll prevent any reflex urge to touch anything. You screw with any evidence and Ozzie will shoot you dead on the spot."

I complied, sticking my hands deep into the pockets of my boot-length denim skirt. At least Pat didn't follow up with a wink and a nod or a "good girl." He knew better.

The alternating charcoal-gray and pink linoleum floor tiles in the kitchen (some cracked and some missing) gave away the apartment's age. An old Kelvinator growled a protest from the corner by the pantry. It, like the white porcelain-coated range and sink, showed a chronology of chips.

Around the age-yellowed, white formica-and-chrome kitchen table were four chrome chairs with vinyl-padded seats and backs. Duct tape held the stuffing in place on the three dirty-white ones (part of the original set, I guessed). A fourth, much newer chair, covered in black vinyl, completed the grouping.

I considered myself fortunate that I hadn't yet eaten breakfast. With the smell of rotting food that permeated the room, I had all I could do to keep from gagging. Remnants of the Indian takeout that Swallow and Junior had eaten for dinner the night before sat atop a relatively new microwave oven. Old containers of Chinese food lay scattered about the sink and counter top, as did a quarter-filled bucket from the Colonel and three pizza boxes with moldy crusts.

Now I knew where Junior had holed up since the incident in the alley last Monday.

"Do you recognize this purse or any of the jewelry?" Ozzie asked, pointing at the table top. She was being very professional, not prompting me a bit.

A tan leather saddlebag purse and an expensive wooden jewelry box, made in the form of an English tea chest, sat on the far side of the table. An assortment of rings, pins, earrings and pendants had been laid out in front of them.

"I never saw Delane's purse," I replied. "It was too dark in the alley that night. The engagement and wedding rings look like hers and that's definitely her necklace."

The garnet-and-pearl lavaliere that I had fastened and unfastened at least a half-dozen times for Delane lay in the upper left-hand corner of the display. Tears welled up in my eyes and my right hand instinctively left my pocket and reached out for it. Brother Pat caught my wrist before the hand had traveled three inches.

"Do you need to examine it more closely?" Ozzie asked, noticing my reaction.

"No. I'm pretty much certain that's it." I shook loose from Pat's grip and returned the hand to its pocket.

"Pretty much doesn't cut it, Kate. Barry, can she touch the necklace?"

A studious-looking young man who appeared to be just out of high school entered from the panty, wearing a pair of surgical gloves. He pulled a second pair from the pocket of his white smock and handed them to me.

"Don't touch the jewels themselves," he said. "There's blood evidence I need. Just the chain. And wear these."

I gently picked up the lavaliere by the tiny clasp and ring, fumbled with them for a moment, then unfastened and refastened them. I had thought it difficult before. It was even more so with gloves on.

"Yeah, Ozzie, this is it," I told her. "No doubt." I set the lavaliere back from where I had gotten it.

"Okay. Thanks for coming down, Kate. You can go."

"What now?" I asked, stripping off the rubber gloves.

"I just told you, Kate. You can go."

"I mean with the case."

"You saw Junior Lee Thigpen assault Mrs. Denning in the alley behind your bar and steal her purse, right?"

"Yeah."

"The identification and credit cards in this purse belong to Mrs. Denning, so this must be it."

"Okay," I acknowledged.

"Also, you just confirmed that these rings and this necklace were those worn by Mrs. Denning when she was killed, right?"

"Yeah."

"And the rest of the jewelry corresponds to the list provided by Mr. Denning of the items stolen from his home."

"Okay."

She reached out and plucked the gloves from my hand. "Case closed, Kate. Go home."

"But shouldn't we follow up on the murder-for-hire aspect?" I asked.

Please, Coach, don't take me out and make me sit on the bench again. Let me play. Please?! I even sounded pathetic to myself.

"Remember what I said this afternoon, Kate? There *is* no *we* anymore."

"But, I thought…"

"There *is* no *us*. Go home and let me do my job. I've conducted murder investigations before. I think I know who to talk to and what lines of inquiry to follow. Go home.…Please!"

Before I could protest and become even more pitiful, Pat took me by the arm and turned toward the door with me.

"Don't embarrass me," he whispered between clenched teeth. "Let's *go*!"

I went, taking one final look as we exited the kitchen. Ozzie had returned the surgical gloves to Barry and the two were engaged in conversation. Although not yet out of sight, I was already out of mind.

Guarded by a uniformed female police officer, Ernie Hammerman still sat stoically on the living room couch, but a single tear-line glistened down one immense jowl. Most probably he cried for Swallow Sedlacek. I felt like joining him. Not for Swallow, though; I hadn't known her. And certainly not for Junior; I couldn't have cared less about him. He got what he deserved, the son of a bitch. I wanted to cry for me. Coach Osborn had benched me again.

* * * *

We drove back to the church parking lot in silence. Since the 11:30 Mass was still going on, the spot next to Pat's car was occupied. I pulled up behind it and slammed the gearshift lever into PARK.

Pat opened the car door to get out and I said, "So? What will happen now?"

He left the door open but turned in his seat to face me. "I assume you're talking about the Delane Denning murder case?"

"No, I'm talking about global warming. Of *course*, the Delane Denning murder case, you moron!"

"It's not my case. How would *I* know?"

My mouth dropped and I sat there looking at him for a few seconds until I could recompose myself. "Because maybe your little sister is involved with it?"

"Excuse me, but I distinctly remember Ozzie telling you not more than twenty minutes ago that you were no longer involved with it."

"Hey, whose side are you on, anyway?"

Pat glanced at his watch. “Let’s take a walk,” he said with a huge sigh, getting out and slamming the car door. “Park over there.” He gestured to a spot on the far side of the lot.

Once I had done so and gotten out of the car, my brother ushered me toward the oak grove that served as the parish picnic grounds. I looped my arm around his and we walked side by side along the cedar-chipped path that meandered its way though the small woods. There was something in his tone of voice that told me to keep my mouth shut and listen, so I did.

“Remember the summer between your freshman and sophomore year in high school?” he asked.

“Yeah. Ma and Da had passed away that year and I was just getting used to living with Seamus and Mary Grace.”

“That, too. But I was referring to the CYA basketball camp.”

I gave a slight laugh, having completely forgotten about that incident in my life.

* * * *

The parish newsletter had announced the tryouts for the special Catholic Youth Association Summer Basketball Camp. The top fourteen finishers in each age group (twelve through seventeen) would get to spend two weeks at Vanderbilt, staying in the dorm and getting both team and individualized instruction from the Commodore coaching staff.

I could hardly contain myself, talking about nothing else for a week. Finally, after nagging and pleading and whining and making a general pest of myself, Mary Grace had relented and had written out the five-dollar check for me to send in with the entry blank from the newsletter. Within a week, I had gotten confirmation and had received a tryout time.

Permission letter in hand, I showed up bright and early on the appointed day, ready to impress the coaches with my prowess in the four designated categories (foul shots, lay-ups, dribbling, and a round-robin one-on-one competition). My smiling Black-Irish eyes welled up with tears, however, at what the official told Seamus.

"I'm sorry, Mr. O'Rourke. The camp is for boys only."

My brother waved the newsletter notice in front of the man's face. "Where the hell does it say that?!"

"But it's a CYA league function, Mr. O'Rourke. The CYA only has a boy's league. Sorry."

"Sorry, my ass. This notice doesn't say anything about boys only and, besides, you took her money."

"I guess nobody realized that *Caitlin* was a girl's name. I'm sorry, sir. She can't compete."

"Are you aware, *sir*, that Turlough McInerney, pastor of Our Lady, Queen of the Universe, is my brother-in-law?"

A brief discussion between the officials followed. I imagine the gist of it went something like this: "What the heck, let her compete. These boys will wipe up the floor with her anyway and we can avoid a nasty little incident."

They would have been better served to have told Seamus *no* right there on the spot. A nasty *little* incident would have been preferable to the nasty *big* one which ensued. After I had placed first in foul shots, fourth in lay-ups, sixth in dribbling, and second in the one-on-one, they then told me I couldn't go to camp.

Seamus called Turlough; Turlough called the Archdiocese; the Archdiocese not only upheld the boys-only rule but reamed out Turlough but good for having dropped the controversy onto their doorstep and given them bad press over it.

Maybe it was a coincidence that all of Turlough's seminary classmates had since made Monsignor at the very least, while he alone remained a simple parish priest but, then again, maybe not.

* * * *

"So you remember?" Pat asked again.

"Oh yeah, but I fail to see your point."

"The police department has, for the most part, been a boys-only club, Katie. And a white-boys-only one, at that. Do you have any idea how Ozzie has had to bust her black butt to be twice as good as a white woman and four times as good as a man to get where she is?"

I shrugged.

"Could you have played on a men's college basketball team?"

"Maybe."

"And maybe not."

I shrugged again. As much as his comment stung, he might have been right, not one of the starting five, anyway.

"Could you have played in the NBA?"

"No."

"Because, although you were a terrific *female* player, you flat out couldn't compete with the best of the men."

This time I didn't even bother with the shrug, just bit down on my lower lip and fought back the tears.

"Well, as a detective," Pat continued, "Ozzie *is* good enough to play for our version of the NBA and she's doing a damn fine job of it. Twice now, you cost her credibility points. Stay the hell away from her, Sis. She doesn't need that kind of grief."

Not only had I been benched by Coach Osborn but, now, by my big brother as well. I said nothing in return.

"Well?" he asked.

"Point taken," I replied, unable to look at him.

* * * *

With an hour or so to kill before B-ball, I decided not to stop home for anything to eat after all, opting, instead, to go for a drive. I had hoped to shake the lousy mood Ozzie and Pat had put me in, and just started off with no particular destination in mind. Somehow, though, I found myself on Marylebone Drive in Forest Hills.

As I coasted past the Denning residence, I had an urge to stop, but couldn't tell from the street whether or not anyone was at home. Even if Matt were there, I didn't think it my place to tell him about Junior's death. Besides the police would be doing that as a matter of procedure. He would have to provide the official identification of Delane's things.

So, rather than give in to the urge, I took a swing down Tottenham Court Road through Forest Creek Park to see where Junior had effected his escape. The trees, mostly Japanese Black Pines planted in seven staggered rows, completely screened the back yards of the Marylebone Drive homes from the Tottenham Court Road traffic.

A small service road…(In Forest Hills, they don't call them alleys. In fact, I also misspoke when I used the term *back yard* a second ago. The estates in Forest Hills have *rear grounds*.) Anyway, a small service road ran behind the lots, connecting with Tottenham at about every fifth house. I cut through the trees at where I estimated the Denning home should be, was off by four, and drove down to the wrought iron fence.

Seeing the layout confirmed my opinion of the day before. Junior would have had to enter and exit through the back gate. There's no way that scrawny little SOB could have climbed the fence, especially not while carrying a jewelry box.

But the detectives had probably been correct on another point. Junior would have had to park his car elsewhere. Had he left it on the service road or driven it through the gate onto the Dennings' rear grounds, he risked being spotted by the neighbors.

Leaving Liddy there (after all, I had nothing to hide), I walked up through the tree line to Tottenham. The shoulder was wide enough to accommodate a parked car and anyone who might have noticed it wouldn't have thought anything amiss. In fact, from my position I could see four vehicles along the roadside.

In the park itself, an elderly gentleman walked an equally elderly (in dog years) yellow Labrador Retriever; two shirtless, well-built young men in their late teens (yum, yum) tossed a football around; and a pair of young lovers had spread a blanket for a picnic lunch (I hoped they both got food poisoning).

Yes, I know that sounds petty. After watching them for a minute or so, I let a sigh of envy escape and promised to write *I will not be bitter* three-hundred times, then turned away and started back through the trees.

Halfway to the service road, a frail-looking woman in her mid-seventies, carrying a shoebox, accosted me. "Have you found any more of them over here?" she asked in a shrill voice, eyes flaring with anger.

At first I took her for a bag-lady. She wore faded bib overalls, a blue-and-black checked flannel shirt, and leather sandals. Her long steel-gray hair had been wound around on top of her head and an attempt had been made to fix it into a bun. The attempt had failed miserably. Wispy strands stuck out every which way.

"Any...any more what?" I answered, still walking apprehensively in the direction of my car.

"Why, our little feathered friends," she said, holding out the shoebox toward me and lifting the lid ever so slightly.

The glassy eye of a crow, very stiff and very dead, stared back at me.

"N...no, but I haven't really been looking," I replied, still moving. "I was just...just admiring the park."

"It is beautiful, isn't it," she said, her gaze and voice both softening somewhat. "That's why my late husband and I moved here. The park. With the birds and the squirrels and the cute little bunnies. When my Gilbert and I built our home, we were the first ones in this subdivision.

Did you know that? The very first ones. Back then there were fox and raccoon, too. But no more. Not for a long time, now."

So much for her being a bag-lady. Besides, it was at about that moment I noticed the designer label on the outside of her overalls.

"Most of the people here are just lovely," she continued. "But some of them, the more ethnic ones, if you get my meaning, have absolutely no appreciation for the beauty of nature. Oh, they have money, all right, and can well afford to live here, but they have no breeding...no refinement. They might just as well be living up in...well, you know the section of town I'm talking about. Some of them even grow crops on their property. *Corn*. Can you believe it? In Forest Hills? And then they do this." She gestured again with the shoebox and shook her head in disgust.

"Someone killed the birds?" I asked.

"About a dozen of them. Over there." She gestured down the tree line in the direction from which she had come. "With a shotgun, no less. Just because birdies do what the good Lord put little birdies here on this Earth to do. So the little darlings eat a few morsels from their precious gardens. So what? They're God's creatures and they were here in this park long before the..."

She looked at my face as if really seeing me for the very first time, then put a hand to her mouth and said, "Dear me, you aren't Italian, are you?"

I snickered and shook my head. "Believe it or not, I'm Irish. Dark skin and all."

She glanced around conspiratorially, then whispered, "Long before the dagos moved in. That's what my Gilbert used to call them. Dagos. They're not like us at all, you know, dear."

Taylor Hollingshead and Jason Scarborough (Ken and Barbie) would have loved this woman. I wondered if she were a Foresters' Game Warden like the Dennings.

"You said *a dozen*?" I asked, pointing to the shoebox.

"That's what I've found so far. And it had to have happened within the past few days. They weren't here when I took my walk on Wednesday and I've been laid up with a summer cold since then. This is the third little birdie casket I've filled. Poor darlings. I'm going to bury them so that the nasty cats won't get at them."

Mary Grace would have been proud of me. In deference to the woman's age, I kept my mouth shut and let the cat-remark pass. Instead, I said, "That's very kind of you." After all, that *is* what she wanted to hear from me, isn't it?

The old woman smiled and kept right on talking. "I just can't imagine anyone being mean enough to shoot a poor defenseless creature with a shotgun. Can you?"

I nodded my head, blinking back the tears as the image of Delane Denning, lying in her foyer with her pretty oval face blown away, came to mind. "There are some really mean people in this world ma'am," I answered. "Really mean."

Chapter 13

I didn't bother going over to the Y on Sunday afternoon as I had originally planned. Seeing the Denning home again and having it trigger the vivid memories of Delane's death had turned my merely-lousy mood into a major downer. Instead, I came home and did the week's laundry. Whoopee, what fun!

W.B. sat in front of the washer and dryer during the entire time her blanket was being laundered, worrying her furry little head off that she'd seen it for the last time. When I did put it back in her basket and she got it adjusted to her liking, she never came out of that bed for the rest of the afternoon. I guess she was afraid that if she did, I'd steal her blanket again.

Perhaps for a cat, happiness is having your own bed, but I looked forward to Tuesday night's dinner with Chris Panacopoulos. Maybe, just maybe, something might develop with that relationship. I had that feeling, you know?

After a meal of pasta salad and tomatoes vinaigrette, I watched a little TV (not actually a *little* TV, but a big-screen TV for a little while) until the phone rang. Earlier that afternoon I had tried calling Melinda Huntington to let her know about Junior's death. Getting no answer, I had left a message with the desk clerk at the Maxwell House. The phone call was from Melinda. She had just gotten back to the hotel after spending the afternoon and evening with her attorney.

"Not nearly painful enough, after what that little bastard did to Delane," Melinda said, responding to my description of how Junior had been killed. "What will happen now?"

"The way I understand it, Mel, not much of anything. Junior had Delane's purse and he had her jewelry. The case is pretty much closed."

Although I had hated hearing that from Ozzie, it sounded so very logical when it came from my own mouth.

"They no longer think Matt had anything to do with it?"

"What they *think* doesn't matter. There's no evidence that he did and now, without Junior, there most likely won't be. Oh, I suppose the police will check to see if they can make a connection between Matt and Junior aside from that one night here in the pub, but I wouldn't hold out a lot of hope."

"Then we'll never really know, will we, Kate?"

"Probably not, Mel."

She thanked me for the call and I promised to let her know if I learned anything new, but cautioned her not to expect to hear from me on Monday. I had a nine-o'clock appointment the next morning to get my schnozz fixed. After hanging up, I went through the ritual of the hair, then turned in early.

The dreams that night were more bizarre than usual. Junior and Swallow played monkey-in-the-middle (I was the monkey, complete with big ears and a tail), tossing the garnet-and-pearl lavaliere back and forth and keeping it just out of my reach. A bleeding, faceless Delane Denning lay at my feet and I kept tripping over her as I tried to get the necklace.

* * * *

Some moron began slapping my cheek and calling my name. "Caitlin? Caitlin? You have to wake up now, Caitlin."

I couldn't open my eyes. I didn't *want* to open my eyes. All I wanted to do was sleep.

"Caitlin? Caitlin? You can't sleep now. You have to wake up. Then you can go back to sleep."

That didn't make any sense at all. *Leave me the hell alone,* I thought. *I want to sleep!*

Although I still couldn't force my eyelids open, I had a fairly good idea where the voice was located. If only I could move my arms, I'd be able to land one good punch and then maybe the moron would leave me be.

"Caitlin? Caitlin? That's a good girl."

Lights swirled around me and a ghost hovered over me as my eyelids cracked ever so slightly.

"She's coming around, now, Dr. Neely."

I started to fade back into sleep just as another ghost appeared within the vortex.

"The oxidation was a concrete sorceress, Katie," it said and a hand patted my shoulder. Or was it, "The operation was a complete success." I can't remember which.

Finally, after more badgering from the first ghost, my eyes began to focus. Unfortunately, so did my brain—on the pain in my nose. If any of you know what it's like to have an ice pick plunged squarely between your eyes and into your skull, I envy you. My pain had to have been far worse. I tried to talk, but there was a tube down my throat and I gagged on it.

"If you promise to stay awake, Caitlin, I'll remove the tube."

Yeah, yeah, anything. Just take the damn tube out, okay?

"There, there. How's that?" Nurse Ghost asked after extracting the tube. "Are we doing better, now?"

To quote a friend, "There is no we." I don't know about you, moron, but I'm doing frigging terrible. "W...water," I rasped.

"Here, how about a little cracked ice."

I wanted water, but the ice was better than nothing. "Pain," I rasped again.

"I'm not the least bit surprised, Caitlin. But you'll have to wait for just a bit until we can give you something."

That *just a bit* turned out to be nearly a half hour, until I was fully conscious, more or less. Even then, the shot only deadened the pain by half. After another forty-five minutes of sitting in a chair while Mary Grace and Seamus fussed over me and kept my cup of Diet Pepsi full, the nurse pronounced me ready to travel. I looked at the big wall clock. It read one-fifteen.

"Who's minding the store?" I asked as an orderly helped me into a wheelchair. "And please don't tell me it's Jimmy Tuohey." Visions of Jimmy, drunker than a lord and slumped over the bar next to an empty cash register, filled my mind.

"Seamus put up a sign on the door," Mary Grace replied. "We won't be opening until half past three. Quit your worrying, now."

* * * *

I fell asleep in the second seat of Seamus' Windstar on the way home, then awoke briefly to make the trek upstairs to my quarters, leaning on Seamus and Jimmy Tuohey for support. Both Jimmy and old Mickey Ryan had been waiting there on the doorstep, worried that the pub might never open again.

Once upstairs, Mary Grace shooed the two of them out and helped me undress. All I remember is sitting down on the side of the bed and holding out my arms so that she could get my shirt off. The next thing I knew it was five hours later and I was wide awake, in pain, and voraciously hungry.

Although a little light-headed, I was slept out. I took my now-routine neck-down shower and got the first good look at my face when I did a wipe around the edges with the wash cloth.

God, I hope some of the swelling goes down before my big date tomorrow night. I look like hell.

After taking a couple of pain pills, I dressed, pony tailed the hair, and was about to head downstairs when the door to my quarters opened.

"And just where do you think you're going, young lady," Mary Grace asked, entering with a tray. On it, in addition to food, was a beautiful terrarium chuck full of cacti.

I'm going to have to check my place for hidden microphones or video cameras. She has this uncanny knack for always knowing what I'm doing?

"I was hungry," I answered.

"Not surprisingly. Here, I brought you this." She set down a bowl of Lamb and Vegetable Soup, with two slices of buttered Brown Soda Bread and a cup of green tea.

"Jeez, thanks, Mary Grace, but I could have come downstairs for it. Honest, I feel well enough. In fact, I thought I'd take a run over to the Y tonight. Just to watch. I haven't seen the guys in a week."

"You'll do no such thing, young lady. Now, sit and eat your dinner, and if there's anything else you'll be needing, you call. One of us will bring it up to you. And here, this just arrived. It's from a Mel Huntington." She placed the terrarium on the counter between the kitchen and living room. "A boyfriend you haven't told us about?"

"Mel is a girl, Mary Grace. Short for Melinda."

My sister-in-law's expressions can often speak much louder than words. She slowly turned her head toward me and arched an eyebrow as she peered over the gold rims of her glasses.

"She's Delane Denning's sister," I said, rolling my eyes toward the ceiling. "They're a thank-you gift for keeping her informed on what little progress the police are making on the case."

"Oh," was Mary Grace's only response.

As my nurse/warden left, I wondered how I'd manage to sneak out later on. I certainly wasn't going to sit around here all evening. I needed to *do* something.

At 8:00 with dinner finished, I downed two pain killers and rinsed the dishes in the sink. Now for plan B. Dialing the number for the pub, I prayed that Seamus would answer. He did.

"Pretend it's someone else," I told him, interrupting his "Kehough's Irish Pub, the finest in food and spirits."

"Like who?" he answered.

"I don't care who. *An Taoiseach.* Anyone but me."

"The answer is *no.*"

"You haven't heard the question, yet."

"I don't *need* to hear it. Whatever it is, Mary Grace is bound to be against it, otherwise you wouldn't be calling me on the sly....No, it's just someone asking about facilities for private parties, dear. No, I'm telling him that. I don't want to be rude, you know. I'm sorry, dear, I didn't mean to snap....I'm hanging up, now, Katie. Good-bye."

"Wait! Is Pat there?"

"No."

"All I need is a little diversion so that I can sneak out. Come on, Seamus?"

"No way....Yes, dear, I'm telling him. He's asking about our off-day. Sunday afternoon. What do you think?...We're just starting to talk money, now, love. I'll let you know....I'm hanging up, Katie. Right this minute."

"But, wa...*Damn!*"

So I'd have to do it without a diversion. But, then again, maybe not.

When I was on the road in my playing days (both college and pro), my roommates and I would routinely turn on the TV in our hotel room before going out to dinner. We thought by doing so we'd confuse any would-be burglars, making them think the room was occupied. Either it worked extremely well or there were no burglars in the hotels at which we stayed because our room was never broken into.

Here's a tip for any of you who may be tempted to use this little ploy. Pay attention to which station you tune the TV.

Once when the Bobcats were down in Texas playing Hardin-Simmons, we missed our American Eagle connection in Dallas and had to bus it the remaining hundred-and-eighty-some miles to Abilene, which put us on a tight schedule. We checked into the hotel, Laurissa and I threw our bags on the bed, flipped on the TV, and rushed back out for practice and a very late dinner. Getting back to the room about ten o'clock, we switched off the TV and went directly to bed.

Even though our rooms were paid for by the College, each of us was responsible for any charges of a personal nature—room service, long distance, that sort of thing. Since neither Laurissa nor I had made any calls, I was surprised when the checkout clerk said we owed an additional thirty-six dollars.

"There must be some mistake," I protested. "We didn't charge anything."

"It's for the movies, miss," he whispered. Then he winked at me. "See, right here?"

The bill listed *Lesbian Warriors of Mars*, *Leave it to Cleavage,* and *Top Tongue*. The station to which our TV had been set was the pay-per-view sex channel. Rather than stand there with a lineup of people behind me and argue that I really wasn't watching dirty movies all evening, I quietly paid the thirty-six bucks and slithered, red faced, out to the bus.

After making sure W.B. had enough food and fresh water, I tuned the TV to the *ABC Monday Night Movie*, eased my door closed, and quietly tiptoed down the stairs. At the bottom, I waited for about fifteen seconds, holding my breath, fully expecting Mary Grace to come bursting through the door to the pub, wailing like a banshee. Nothing happened. I opened the back door to the alley and there stood Jimmy Tuohey.

"Hi, Katie, where to?"

"H…hi, Jimmy. Where to what?"

"The directions to the Y, I guess. That's where Mary Grace said you'd be wanting to go. I'm supposed to drive you there, stay with you, then bring you back home. But I suppose I could drive you somewheres else. She didn't say I couldn't."

So much for plan B.

"And if I don't let you?" I asked, even though I knew it wasn't an option.

Poor little Jimmy didn't realize that and scrunched up his face, imagining what it would be like to have to go back inside and tell Command Sergeant-Major Mary Grace that he had failed in his mission.

"She said she'd flail me alive. I'm not sure what that means, Katie, but I don't guess I'd like it a whole lot."

"No, I don't guess you would, Jimmy. Here," I said, digging the keys out of my purse and handing them to him. "The little one's to the garage door."

His face relaxed and he gave an enormous sigh of relief, then bounded off like a little puppy across the alley. When he reached the garage, he stopped and turned. "Oh, yeah, I forgot. Mary Grace said to tell you that you shouldn't count on booking any private parties in here on Sunday." With that, he shrugged, turned away from me and opened the door to Liddy's stall.

* * * *

About half the guys I play ball with at the Y are white. I don't think Jimmy Tuohey noticed that half. He took one look at the big black guys and almost wet himself. No sooner had I finished with the introductions then he climbed up to the highest row of the bleachers and stayed there, trying his best to attain a state of invisibility.

Whether black or white, most of the guys came up to me, took a good look at the plastic nose guard taped to my face, and muttered some sort of condolence. Reggie, the jock from Middle Tennessee State, tried to be a smartass.

"Guess some people will do most anything to keep from getting beat, huh?" he said, flashing a big old Gomer grin.

Obviously his memory didn't go as far back as the previous weekend when I had put on my little B-ball and V-ball clinic at his expense.

"Shit, babe," Bobby Curtis said, shaking his head, "you've come to witness a fucking massacre. Without you, this Reggie dude is whipping our asses but good. Again. We're already down two games to zip."

"Let's not be a defeatist, Bobby," I told him. "Get your team over here for a minute."

He did and I ran them through some quick rudimentary drills to see who could jump, who could move, who could hit, and who just took up space and needed to stay out of everyone else's way.

"Okay, guys," I said, wishing that I could play myself in at least three positions, "Jerry, you're in the back-right; Mitch, back-left; and Jamal, you play between them and back up Jerry and Mitch in case they miss it." (Wasn't that nicer than saying "Stay the hell out of their way?")

"Bobby, you're middle blocker and setter. Dewayne, you're down-left and Ahmad, you're down-right. Reggie is not going to finesse, believe me. He's going to try and ram everything down your throats. So you three guys in front, double block every shot. And everybody, feed the ball to Bobby. He'll set it up for Jerry or Mitch. Okay?"

They all bobbed their heads up and down, then took their positions.

After winning the next game fifteen to two, my strategy seemed downright brilliant. Fond du Lac, here I come. I couldn't help but needle Reggie, telling him if I had been playing, he wouldn't even have scored the two points.

The fourth game was well underway with my team leading eight to one, when play stopped and the guys all made animal noises. I turned toward where they directed their attention and saw Detectives E. Osborn and Patrick O'Rourke. I assumed the catcalls were for Ozzie.

She must have assumed the same and knew just how to stifle them. Pulling out her badge and ID she yelled, "Anyone here care to have his locker searched?"

An abrupt silence answered her question.

"Go ahead, guys, keep playing," I told them. "It's for me."

The game continued, still in relative silence, as I walked over to Ozzie and Pat.

I figured, like Pat, Ozzie would meticulously wear a different outfit every day. Thursday had been sage, with navy and russet on Friday and Saturday, respectively. Somehow Monday just seemed like it would be a red day. For me, perhaps; not so for her. She wore a black pantsuit with a white blouse that had black stripes.

Resisting the urge to say, "Hey, Ref, where's your whistle?" I said, instead, "Hey, what brings you out and about?"

"Operation went well, I see," Pat remarked. "Sorry I couldn't be there."

"Don't worry about it. Mary Grace and Seamus fussed enough for three."

"Glad you're all right," Ozzie said. "We need to talk. How's about if we go outside?"

"*We*?" I asked innocently, pointing at my chest. "But I'm not part of a *we* anymore, am I Detective Osborn?"

Pat threw up his hands and stomped out the door to the parking lot. If they had come in his car, he probably went right for one of the Snickers bars in the glove box. When Pat's ticked off, he eats.

Ozzie expelled her breath audibly through her nose, but didn't reply. She just stood there, examining the cracks in the gym floor.

"I was told there was no *us* and that I was to go home and stay out of it," I continued. "I didn't realize you meant that I could never leave home again for any reason. Is that why you're here? To arrest me because I broke curfew? I'm so very sorry, Detective. Can you ever forgive me?"

Ozzie looked up at me. "Are you through?"

"For the time being."

"Do you still have those sandals you told me about?"

"Yeah. They're out in my car."

"Good. Let's go."

"*Let's?* You mean as in, *you and I*?"

"Yes, Kate. Let's *you* and *I* go."

"Where?"

"The morgue."

"What for?"

"Trish Zelasko, the Assistant Medical Examiner, wants to have a look at those sandals."

Chapter 14

Since brother Pat had ridden over to the Y with Ozzie in her Sunfire, she went on alone to Trish Zelasko's office. He and I took Liddy, stopping by the pub just long enough to drop off Jimmy Tuohey with a promise that the little fellow's drinks would be on the house for the remainder of the evening. Jimmy left us, all smiles, his usual cheerful self again. Not only hadn't he got beaten up by colored guys, he'd drink freebies until the pub closed. Life just didn't get any better than that for him.

Pat was uncharacteristically quiet during both legs of the trip. I chalked up this reticence to either: number one, he was still ticked off because of the way I had talked to Ozzie back at the Y; or, number two, not having his own car, he hadn't been able to scarf down any Snickers bars.

When we arrived at the Simkins Forensic Sciences Center, over by Metropolitan General Hospital on Hermitage, Ozzie introduced me to her partner, Detective B. J. Sykes, and to Dr. Patricia Zelasko. Dr. Zelasko called me Ms. O'Rourke and didn't ask me to call her Trish.

While I remembered that Ozzie had arrived at the Denning home with a male partner, I must have been too groggy for anything to have registered about him other than that he was white. Had I been more alert at the time, I certainly wouldn't have forgotten this guy.

B. J. Sykes resembled a stock car driver I had seen on TV—tall, lanky, gaunt-faced, with jet-black hair slicked back with bear grease or something. Do they still make Brillcream? If so, B. J. Sykes used more than just a little dab. Had Mamo (my maternal grandmother) still been alive, she would have referred to the pencil-thin line of hair above his upper lip as a Lee Bowman mustache.

I figured his age somewhere in the mid-fifties. He sat on the corner of Dr. Zelasko's gray Steelcase desk, wooden toothpick hanging from the side of his mouth. I'd have bet money that under the collar of that Panhandle Slim shirt I'd find a neck colored on the top end of the spectrum. I'd also bet his initials stood for Billy Joe, Bobby Jim, or the like. I wouldn't find out from him, however.

"Just Sykes will do, Kate," he said with a big, friendly good ol' boy grin, as he grasped my hand in reply to my, "Nice to meet you, Detective Sykes."

"You probably don't remember me," he continued, "but you're looking a damn sight better then when we first met. Yessiree, Bob, you are. Hey, Paddy, long time."

"Five years, at least, Beej."

Trish Zelasko, all business, broke up the little reunion between my brother and Sykes with a throat-clearing "Uhumph!" and pointed at the sandals in my left hand.

"I'll take those, Ms. O'Rourke. Just have a seat for a few minutes...please." The *please* definitely had been tossed in as an afterthought.

I handed over the sandals and she left without another word. Ozzie ushered me into the swivel chair behind the desk and Sykes picked up a manila folder and swung around on his corner perch to face me. Brother Pat made himself comfortable in one of the two guest chairs and let his homicide colleagues get on with their work.

"Sykes has six photographs in that folder, Kate," Ozzie said. "He's going to lay them out in front of you and I want you to tell me if you recognize anyone."

Although B. J. Sykes was by far the chronological senior of the two detectives, Ozzie clearly was in charge of the case. But that didn't seem to bother him, not that anyone could see. They made an odd couple, the laid back, middle-aged good ol' boy and the young, aggressive black woman.

"Don't say anything until all six are down in front of you," Ozzie continued, "then take a *good* look."

I tried to comply with her instructions, but when Sykes placed the fourth photo I couldn't help but gasp. Both detectives glanced at each other for just the briefest of moments, then Sykes continued with photos five and six. I took a second or two to scan the half dozen pictures, all of very attractive Caucasian women in their early forties holding numbers in front of them, then looked up at each of the detectives in turn.

"I can't prompt you, Kate," Ozzie said. "You have to tell *us*. Do you recognize any of these women and, if so, from where?"

Tapping number four with my index finger, I said, "That's Delane Denning. Different color and style of hair, but that's definitely Delane. When was she arrested, and for what?"

"The picture you're pointing at, Kate, is of a high-class hooker by the name of Courtney Howell," Sykes said.

I turned to brother Pat. "Come over here and look at this. Tell them it's Delane."

He simply shook his head. "No can do, Boo. Sorry."

"What do you mean, *no can do*? Haul it over here and look at picture number four!"

"He's already looked, Kate," Ozzie said, putting a hand on my shoulder. "He didn't recognize any of them. Now that you've picked one, he can look again, but we can't use it as corroboration."

Pat got up and crossed to our side of the desk, picked up photo number four and studied it. He shook his head and handed the picture to Sykes. "Not even now, Katie. Remember, the Delane Denning I saw had mud on one cheek and held an ice bag to the other the whole time

I was there. Any of these six pictures could be her. Hell, so could Trish Zelasko, for that matter. She's the right age, race, and body type."

"I'm telling you, this is Delane Denning! Even though the hair is dark here, I know that face. I spent three days with the woman. What are you guys saying?"

"What we're saying, Kate," Sykes took over, "is that if this *is* the woman you spent three days with, then you spent those three days with Courtney Howell, not Delane Denning."

"Then this woman was shot last Thursday to make it *seem* like Delane Denning was killed?"

"No, Kate, Delane Denning *was* shot last Thursday. Delane Denning *was* killed. There's no doubt about that. Nosiree, Bob. The dental records proved it conclusively."

"Then what?"

Trish Zelasko strode back into the office, grim faced, sans sandals, but carrying a brown paper bag. "I can't say that it's a hundred percent, but there's a very strong possibility...a *could be*...a *might be*. The strap is in the same location. We'll see if the lab can come up with anything on it, but I wouldn't place any bets. The sandals are polyurethane with straps made from a marine nylon webbing, and they're completely clean, like somebody washed them off."

Rather than admit to being the somebody who washed and wiped the sandals before putting them in my suitcase, and not seeing the relevance anyway, I shouted, "Hey! Is someone going to tell me what's going on here?"

Trish gestured to Ozzie and the detective sat on the desktop, facing me. "Earlier tonight a body was pulled from the Cumberland River over by the Baptist Seminary. It had been tied and weighted down, but not very well. A white female between the ages of thirty-five and forty-five. She had a broken neck. Although her face had been beaten beyond recognition...after she was killed, by the way...her fingerprints IDed her as a hooker we have on file. Courtney Howell. Photo number four."

"No!" I stood, picking up the photograph as I did so.

"She still had on one of her shoes," Ozzie continued. "A size six. And there was a Band-Aid on her pinkie toe. Trish called me to say it looked like it covered a rub mark that could have been made by a sandal strap."

"I want to see her."

"No you don't, Kate."

"I *want* to see her!"

Trish Zelasko crossed over to us. "Ms. O'Rourke, have you ever seen a body that's spent a couple or three days in the water?"

"Of course not."

"Then you don't want to start now, believe me. I do this for a living and *I* have trouble with these cases. Besides, there's nothing you'd be able to tell from the body. Not in the condition it's in. I *would* like you to take a look at these, though."

Sykes tugged the photograph from my fingers and put it and the other five back into the folder, then both he and Ozzie vacated their positions on the desktop. Trish Zelasko opened the bag she had brought with her and spread the contents out in front of me.

I sat back down and fingered the damp, torn bluejeans and white cotton sweater, ignoring the undergarments and the single brown penny-loafer. They were completely unfamiliar to me. For a second my mind flashed back to Cove Creek as I finished getting ready for the trip back home.

Delane stood there in a black-and-white linen coatdress and white pumps with a black patent leather cap-toe and heel. *I haven't seen my man in three whole days*, she had said, by way of an explanation on why she had gotten so dressed up. *I want him to realize what he's missed.* She had given a throaty laugh as she walked away and then struck a sultry pose in the doorway. *So, what do you think?*

"The Delane Denning I knew, was dressed like the Delane Denning you found shot to death in her home," I said. "I've never seen these clothes before."

Sykes again took the photo of Courtney Howell out of the folder. "The woman in this picture was wearing these clothes when someone killed her and dumped her body in the river."

"That son of a bitch!" I said, tears forming in my eyes.

"Matthew Denning," Ozzie agreed, nodding her head.

I still found the situation hard to believe. "He set up the whole mugging incident? Had his wife killed, using *me* as an alibi? Then killed his decoy?"

"Most probably had Junior Lee Thigpen do it, then killed him and the girlfriend, too," Sykes added. "Unfortunately, we'll never know."

"That son of a *bitch*!" I repeated, then the words that the detective had just spoken registered with me. "What do you mean, *we'll never know*? You go over there, roust his ass out of bed, and arrest him!"

There was silence as the AME, Pat, and Sykes looked at Ozzie.

"Now we focus our investigation on Mr. Denning and search for corroborating evidence," she said quietly.

"You *what*?!" I asked, coming out of my seat and looking down at her, a foot or so below me.

Pat had been standing to one side and slightly behind me. He motioned with his head at the other three as he reached up, put a hand on my shoulder, and slammed me back down into the chair. The jarring force to my nose brought more tears to my eyes, this time, though, tears of pain. The doctor and the two homicide detectives huddled in conference by themselves on the far side of the room.

"What the..." I started to yell.

"Shut your mouth, Katie!" he yelled back at me. "And listen!"

I glared at him, but did, in fact, shut my mouth. I might have been bigger than him and twice as strong, but he *was* my older brother.

"We have your word and your word alone...which we believe," he hastily added as I started to rise again, "that Courtney Howell is the woman Matt Denning introduced to you and me as his wife. But do you think he's going to admit it? Hell no. He's going to say that, at the very least, you're mistaken. Probably that you're crazy. And his attorney is going to put me on the stand and ask *what*, Beej?"

Sykes crossed over to us and said, "Were you there the night of the mugging, Detective O'Rourke."

"Yes, sir, I was."

"In fact, you filed the initial police report, didn't you?"

"Yes, sir, I did."

"Whose name did you list as the victim?"

"Delane Denning."

"You're a trained investigator, aren't you, Detective O'Rourke?"

"Yes, sir, I am."

"When shown a photograph of a prostitute named Courtney Howell, were you able to identify her as the woman you knew as Delane Denning?"

"No, sir, I was not."

"Well, screw me," I said, slowly shaking my head.

"Yessiree, B..." Sykes started but Pat shook a finger at him.

"Don't even think it, Beej," he growled.

The good 'ol boy chuckled all the way back to the other side of the room.

"All right," I said, placing my palms on the desktop. "So it's my word against his. Is that what you're telling me? Okay, what now?"

"A uniformed team is on its way to Courtney Howell's town house with a search warrant," Ozzie said. "Sykes is going to meet them there. You're invited."

I nodded and a smile crept across my lips. Coach Osborn had put me back into the game. "What about you?" I asked.

"I'm going to, as you so colorfully put it, roust Matt Denning's ass out of bed. But I'm not going to arrest him. We have no evidence. I'll just drag him in for questioning. Put a little fear into him and make him sweat. Then we'll keep an eye on him and see if he panics."

"I want to go with *you*," I said.

"No, Kate. It's Sykes or home. Your choice."

Okay, so it was to be the second string. But, still, back in the game, and infinitely better than riding the bench. Pointing to Sykes, I looked over at my brother and said, "Follow that man, driver. And don't let him out of your sight. First off, get me a glass of water. I gotta take some pills. This nose is killing me."

* * * *

I was now a veteran and knew the drill. Before the uniformed cop at the front door could say anything, I jammed my hands into the pockets of my jeans and smiled at him. He smiled back, nodded, and winked.

The contrast between Swallow Sedlacek's apartment and Courtney Howell's was like midnight to high noon. While, no doubt, both girls performed the same services for the men in their lives, Courtney's choice of clientele was the better by far. Her Elm Hill Pike town house, just off Briley Parkway near McGavock Pike, could have been featured in *Better Homes and Gardens*, without the garden, of course.

But I found it extremely difficult to imagine her kind of work being conducted amid soft, warm wood tones, violet-and-white Laura Ashley fabrics, and stuffed bears throughout. Every room had a look of little-girl innocence to it.

The manager had nothing but praise for his tenant—no complaints from the neighbors; no loud parties; in fact, very few visitors that he had noticed. With her schedule, home during the day and leaving at dusk, he had always assumed that she was a nurse, working the night shift in one of the hospitals. She was always polite, pleasant, and tipped extremely well anytime she needed something repaired or rearranged in her unit.

Apparently Courtney didn't conduct business out of her home after all, using it, instead, as a refuge from her professional life. For some reason that made me feel good inside.

Why do we differentiate between a whore and a high-class call girl? Because, I guess, even if it is only price, there *is* a difference. No way could I think of Courtney as a whore.

The light on the answering machine blinked rapidly and the message count showed thirteen. I thought the low number odd for someone in her line of work until a beep sounded from a console table behind the overstuffed sofa.

Sykes pointed at a pager sitting there. "She was a smart one, yessiree, Bob," he remarked, nodding in admiration as he wrote down the number.

"How so?" I asked.

"Didn't let them know where she lived," Pat said. "They'd beep. She'd call *them*. Or not, as she saw fit."

Sykes pressed the button on the answering machine. With the exception of one call which I assumed was from her...agent ("Call me about next weekend, Courtney. There's a private party aboard a yacht. An extremely *expensive* yacht."), the other twelve were from the same person, a woman named Greta, and clearly a friend. According to the automatic date and time stamp, they had started late Thursday night and continued on into Monday evening. With each call, the woman sounded more worried. By the last one, recorded about three hours earlier, I could tell she was on the verge of panic.

"It's Greta again. Please, Court, if you're there, pick up. Please? I don't know what to do or who to call. I knew this was a bad idea. I just knew it. Please call me as soon as you get home...no matter what the time. And if I'm not here, beep me. I just need to know that you're all right. Please, honey?"

Sykes took the tape, replacing it with a fresh one. His preparedness surprised me, but I guess he'd done this once or twice before. He also took an address book and the mail that had accumulated in the downstairs box. With each item he confiscated, he announced it aloud and Pat scribbled a description in a notebook.

There were quite a few photographs displayed—parents; headshots of Courtney during various stages of a would-be modeling or acting career (one of which Detective Sykes took for evidence); and one with another woman, roughly the same age. It was taken on the Old Mill Scream ride at the old Opryland Park, shot by the camera at the drop-off. The photo captured both women in mid-squeal as the boat plunged downward. They clearly were having a delightful time.

Despite the chestnut brown hair, worn in a flip, I had no doubt that Courtney Howell was the woman with whom I had spent three days in Cove Creek, not the solemn-faced Delane Denning of the newspaper photograph.

Using my memory of Courtney as a reference point, I figured the other woman to be almost my size. With her fair skin and crystal blue eyes, I imagined the blond hair to be genuine.

Could this be Greta? I wondered. She certainly looked like a Greta to me.

Although I didn't really expect to find the clothes Courtney had worn up in Cove Creek, I checked out the closet anyway while Sykes poked around in it. They weren't there. With phone messages unplayed and mail in the box that predated Thursday, it was obvious that Courtney Howell had never made it home from Forest Hills. I *did* notice, though, that all the shoes in the closet were size six.

"What will they do with the body?" I asked.

Sykes looked over at Pat. "They keep it a week or so, I think." My brother shrugged his shoulders and Sykes continued. "If nobody claims it, it's cremated. I'm not sure what's done with the ashes."

"If no one comes forward, I'll take care of the funeral arrangements," I said. "Who do I tell?"

Pat raised an eyebrow. "Are you sure, Katie?"

"Positive."

He gave another shrug and gestured toward Sykes.

"I'll let Trish Zelasko know," Sykes said.

I told him "Thanks" and walked out into the hallway, fighting back more tears. I really had gotten to like this woman, first as Delane and now even more so, after seeing her town house and possessions, as Courtney.

* * * *

Pat and I rode home in silence. There was nothing that needed to be said. Sykes had promised that either he or Ozzie would call the next morning and fill me in on how it went with Matt Denning. I secretly wished that Matt would pull something incredibly stupid with Ozzie and that she'd have to shoot him in the gut, and that he'd die a slow and excruciatingly painful death.

In trying to analyze my feelings, I couldn't decide whether they were strictly born out of a sense of justice and retribution because of the killings for which he was responsible, or because he had duped me. I really hoped I wasn't so petty as to wish someone else dead out of spite. But, at that point, I could only be sure of one feeling toward Matt Denning. *Die, you son of a bitch! And rot in hell!*

With Liddy secured in her stall, I turned down Pat's invitation for a nightcap and lumbered upstairs to my quarters, head throbbing as if a jackhammer were attached to my nose. I needed another dose of painkillers. Yes, I know it had only been an hour or so since I took two at the ME's office, but my nose couldn't tell time.

"In a minute, Dub," I told the kitty as she wound herself around my legs in greeting. "Mom needs medicine first. Desperately."

After downing another two Orudis, I collapsed in the La-Z-Boy and put my feet up. W.B. hopped into my lap and I tried to slump there as immobile as possible, except for stroking my little buddy's fur. In fifteen minutes or so the throbbing had diminished from jackhammer status down to blacksmith-hammering-on-an-anvil. I got up and gave W.B. a fresh drink, opened a can of Turkey & Giblets Dinner for her and poured a snifter of Baileys for myself.

Yes, bad Katie-Kat, mixing alcohol with painkillers, but I had to try something to exorcise the blacksmith.

On my way back to the recliner, I noticed the blinking light on my own answering machine and poked the PLAY button.

"It's Mel Huntington, Kate. What's going on? Phillip Kaplowitz, my attorney, just called and said that the police had picked up Matthew. Matthew called him, but since Phillip doesn't practice criminal law, he's recommended someone else. Do you know what this is about? Have the police found new evidence? I've phoned down there, but, of course, no one will tell *me* anything. Please call me when you get in. I'm at the Maxwell House."

Maybe the Matthew Dennings and Melinda Huntingtons of the world knew the Maxwell House's phone number by heart, but I had had to look it up on Sunday afternoon when I called. The scratch pad on the desk still had the number written on it. I dialed, then pulled the phone over to the living room and nestled back into my La-Z-Boy. The hotel operator put me through and the room phone rang only once before an anxious Melinda grabbed up the receiver.

"Melinda Huntington."

"It's Kate, Mel. I just got in. Hope I didn't wake you."

"There's no way I could sleep. What's happening?"

After thanking her for the terrarium, I did a quick recap of my trip to the ME's office, including the information about the sandal.

Melinda was flabbergasted. "So, in order to murder my sister," she said, finally, "Matthew killed this prostitute, too?"

"And Junior Lee Thigpen and his girlfriend."

"Will they be able to make it stick?" she asked.

I hesitated, then decided I might as well be honest with her before she got her hopes up. "They didn't really arrest him, Mel. There is absolutely no evidence that anything I just told you is true. Until and unless they can come up with a direct tie-in between Matt and Courtney Howell or Matt and Junior, it's strictly my word against his. They picked him up for questioning tonight in the hopes that they can scare him into doing something stupid. Make a mistake of some kind. My guess is, with a lawyer, he'll be out in an hour or so."

"Then what?"

"Then he'll know that *I* know what really happened. But if he's been careful and covered his tracks, he'll also know that he has nothing to worry about."

"That son of a bitch!"

"My sentiments exactly, Mel."

"You'll let me know if you hear anything more?"

"Count on it."

After we hung up, I got to thinking about not being able to identify Courtney's clothing down at the ME's office. I located Ozzie's card in my wallet and tried her work number first. I got Sykes.

"Hey, I just got to thinking. Both Courtney Howell and Delane Denning were dressed identically on the day Delane was killed. If Matt Denning didn't ever think we'd find out that there were two different women, which we wouldn't have except for the sandal, maybe he bought both outfits at the same time. One for his wife and one for Courtney. Would you pass that along to Ozzie?"

As soon as he began his reply, I regretted placing the call.

"Golly, Miss Kate," he started, doing a perfect Goofy Dog impression. "We dumb cops sure do thank you for pointing out those facts to us. Yessiree, Bob, we do, yup, yup, yup. Cause that probably would never have crossed our tiny civil-servant brains for at least...well, let's see now. For at least..."—he dropped the impression—"at least a minute and a half after we realized a switch had been made. And no, I won't pass it along to Ozzie because, while I find this call amusing, *she'd* be pissed...*mighty* pissed. Good night, Kate. We'll call you tomorrow...as promised."

I finished the Baileys, poured another, and finished that, too. Then, feeling quite the horse's ass, brushed out my ponytail and went to bed.

The repeating slow-motion dream of Saturday night, where I'd run up the steps to the portico of the Denning home, look in through the front door and see Delane Denning lying there, replayed itself. But tonight, new characters had been added. As I looked up from Delane's lavaliere, Courtney Howell, standing at the open French doors with crows sitting on her shoulders, blew me a kiss. As she ran out, I felt the pain of getting smashed in the nose, then the sequence started up again from the beginning.

As it had been before, though, no matter how hard I tried, I could never see who hit me and, again, I awoke in a cold sweat.

But the presence of Courtney Howell and the crows opened my eyes to an entirely new aspect of the case. The real Delane Denning must have already been dead before Courtney and I arrived at the house. The gunshots I heard had been fired out through the open French doors into Forest Creek Park, killing the old woman's little feathered friends. Then Junior hit me and he and Courtney made their way out through those same French doors, across the rear grounds, and out the back gate.

Did Courtney know that Delane Denning was going to be murdered? Somehow I couldn't bring myself to believe that she did, and imagined the shock she must have experienced upon seeing the bloody body of a woman dressed identically to herself. I wondered when it had dawned on her that she, too, would be killed. Had she realized it during her run through the trees, before getting into Swallow Sedlacek's Plymouth, she might have been able to save her own life.

After another two Orudis, downed with a double shot of Baileys, I cried myself back to sleep. Within seconds of closing my eyes, the dream started up again.

Chapter 15

At about the umpteenth time my dream assailant swung the shotgun butt at my nose, the sound of metal on concrete rang out. I sat up in bed wide awake, listening for a second noise.

Zilch.

Rolling over, I checked the bedside clock. The illuminated digits read four-forty. I couldn't have imagined the sound. Nothing in my dream made a noise except for the gunshots, and me, of course, first hitting the wall, then the floor. But the sounds of me were dull thuds, not steel on concrete.

Duke! I thought, hopping out of bed and rushing first to the closet for my Big Bertha seven-iron, then to the kitchen window that overlooked the alley. *That frigging dog has knocked over a trash can again.*

I could just barely make out the row of cans, dimly lit from the bulb in back of Claridge Cleaners, but they were all in place with their lids on, weighted down by cinder blocks.

Where are you, Dukie? Show your spotted little butt, you SOB.

As I scanned the alleyway, it looked to me as if the door to my garage was ajar by about four inches. I distinctly remembered locking it after Pat and I returned from Courtney Howell's town house. Although only dressed in my Bobcat sleepshirt (which covered my sports bra but not totally my black silk panties), I jammed my bare feet into the Luccheses and took the stairs three at a time down to the back door.

Somebody's gonna learn the hard way not to screw with Katie O'Rourke, I thought, still clutching the golf club.

I slowly opened the back door about a foot, stuck my head out and listened for a few seconds. Still no noises came to me other than typical summer night sounds. From this vantage point, however, I could clearly see that the garage door was open. I tiptoed across the alley and stood motionless next to it. Again nothing. Nothing that I could hear, but something I could definitely smell—gasoline.

Who the heck breaks into a garage to siphon gasoline? This doesn't make any sense.

Now here's a tip for any of you who might decide to go skulking around after a would-be burglar in the middle of the night. Call 911 *first*! Wishing that *I* had, and also that I had brought a lob wedge instead of the seven-iron, I choked down on the club, yanked the garage door open and stood in the doorway.

"Okay, morons," I yelled. "You've got just one chance to get out of here with all your…" I was going to say *teeth* but everything went black before I could get the final word out.

* * * *

God, my head hurts. That's the first thought that came to mind as I drifted out of the blackness into a brief state of semi-consciousness. The back of my skull hurt so badly, I no longer felt any pain at all in my nose. Then the blackness swallowed me up again.

The second time I faded back in, through clouded and spinning vision, I saw the flames. But I couldn't move and again slipped back into oblivion.

A growling and snarling from about eight feet away brought me back for a brief third bout with reality. *Oh, God,* I thought, *am I going to die from a fractured skull, be burned to death here in my own garage, or be eaten by a wild beast?*

The report of a single gunshot pierced the silence of the night, accompanied by a yelp. I tried to look around, thinking, *None of the above. Maybe I'll be shot to death, instead.*

Just before lapsing into unconsciousness once again, I felt an affinity with the early Christians as I realized my fate would be the wild beast, after all. Sharp teeth and slobbering jowls ripped at my sleepshirt, tearing the fabric to shreds before grasping the back of my sports bra. I tried fighting the animal off, but couldn't get my arms to respond to the message from my scrambled brain.

* * * *

"Miss? Miss? Just lie still. You're going to be all right."

It was like being teleported into that Bill Murray movie, *Groundhog Day*, where he had to relive the same events over and over again. How many times was I going to wake up with a pain in my head and someone calling out to me?

I knew full well from my previous two experiences that if I opened my eyes, I'd become nauseated. But I did so anyway. Dummy me.

Two paramedics had just hoisted me onto a stretcher. One fixed a head-immobilizer collar around my neck while the other held a flashlight. By moving my eyes, I was able to see the fire fighters continuing to hose down what little remained of the line of garages. A skeleton of a Land Cruiser stood amongst the rubble.

Aw, jeez. Poor Liddy. What have they done to you?

"You're a lucky lady," one of the paramedics said as he cinched a final buckle around me. "It's a good thing you've got such a loyal pooch. If he hadn't pulled you out of there, you'd be one crispy critter by now."

"What?"

I glanced to my left. Duke the Dalmatian lay on another stretcher a couple of feet away, tongue lolling out of the side of his mouth and a doggy grin on his face. Seeing me look at him, he tried to sit up, but gave a whine and stayed put, panting in pain.

"Well, thank you, Duke," I said, reaching up an arm to pull on one of his velvety ears. "I didn't know you cared. Please, feel free to help yourself to the trash can of your choice. Anytime."

"He wouldn't leave your side," the paramedic continued. "We had all we could do to convince him that we were friends."

"Take it easy, boy," the second paramedic said, patting the massive spotted head. "We'll get you to a vet just as soon as we can."

"He's hurt pretty bad," the first medico explained. "Probably jabbed himself on a piece of metal. He's lost a lot of blood. Where do you want us to take him?"

"He's not mine. Belongs to the Larsen's. About midway down on Plainview, other side of the street. Yellow house with a chain link fence. But take him to the Ross Animal Clinic over on Nolensville Pike. They have someone on call around the clock. Tell them to send me the bill."

"I've patched him up the best I can. We'll have one of the police officers run him over there. Regulations, you know. No animals in the ambulance. We'll be right back."

Both paramedics raised Duke's stretcher so that the wheels folded out and they started to push it in the direction of a police car. The dog began to bark.

"Go ahead, Dukie," I yelled after him. "It's all right, buddy. And thanks again."

"Glad to see you've come around, young lady," a uniformed police officer with sergeant's stripes said, walking over to me. His name tag read, SWIRSKI, and he looked like a Swirski—square head with graying, once-blond hair in a crew cut.

Young lady? Is this guy going to give me a Mary Grace type of lecture? Sure thing.

"The smell of gasoline is pretty heavy," he continued in a tone of voice I immediately began to resent. "Mind if I ask just what you were doing in there at this time of the morning?"

"Trying to catch whoever it was that burned down my garage."

"There was someone else here?" The skepticism hung in the air like a cloud.

Duh, I thought, then let my smart-aleck streak take over. "No Sarge. I torched my own garage, then hit myself over the head with a golf club. Damn that fool dog for pulling me out."

"There's no need for sarcasm. We'll check out that possibility and *if* we find…"

"It's *when*, Sergeant, not *if.* And it's not a possibility, it's fact. Get Detectives Osborn, Sykes, and O'Rourke to meet me at the hospital. I'll talk to *them*. You and I are done."

Out of respect for the uniform, which brother Pat had so proudly worn for his first ten years on the force, I refrained from calling Sergeant Swirski a moron.

"We're done, young lady, when *I* say we're done." He hitched up his pants in an attempt to disguise the bit of a belly he had developed. It didn't work.

"Detective Sergeant Pat O'Rourke is my brother," I shot back at him. "*Now* are we done?"

The paramedics had returned for me. Since the sergeant had not yet replied to my question, I said, "Let's go, guys. And don't spare the siren. My head feels like it's going to split wide open any minute now."

In response to their look, the police officer simply growled at them. "Get her out of here. We've got work to do."

* * * *

"Ahh, we meet again, Miss Caitlin O'Rourke," the ever-cheerful Dr. Kamul Bhitiyakul sang out as he entered the examining room. "My oh my, but you certainly do get yourself beat up quite often, do you not? Yes, indeedie, you do."

He placed three x-ray films on the light board and studied them, muttering to himself as he did so. "Good, good, and very good. All good, as were your CT scans. Yes, indeedie."

The ambulance had arrived at the hospital at six-thirty-seven. I had been unconscious in the alley for over an hour. Now that I think about it, that time in never-never land was much more pleasant than that which I spent waiting in triage, then waiting in a hallway, then waiting in another hallway outside of Radiology, then waiting again after being returned to the first hallway.

At least the x-ray technician had given me one of those flimsy gowns to wear. It wasn't much, but it beat the remnants of my dog-jowl-shredded sleepshirt.

There was something, though, that irritated me more than the waiting. Neither of the homicide detectives nor my brother had shown up.

You'll be sorry, Sergeant Swirski.

Dr. Bhitiyakul crossed over to me and took my face in his tiny brown hands. "Your nose, it looks to be in excellent shape. Yes, indeedie. I commend Dr. Neely on his exceptional surgical skills."

"I'm sure he appreciates it, Doc. But what about the *back* of my head?"

"Ahh, another slight concussion, nothing more. You have a very thick head. The blow, it did not even break the skin. You will have a very, very bad headache for the next few days, but that is all. If you get plenty of…"

"Why the hell didn't you have someone call me?" brother Pat bellowed out from the doorway to the examining room. "The Fire Marshall got Seamus out of bed about an hour ago to ask him some questions and he finds out you were taken away in an ambulance. Christ, Katie, Mary Grace is worrying herself sick."

"Glad to see you, too, Pat. I'm fine, thank you. Nice of you to ask. Dr. Bhitiyakul, here, was just…"

"Well, shit, I can see you're fine. That's not the point. Why didn't you call someone?"

"At about six-fifteen this morning, I asked a Sergeant Swirski to call you, Ozzie, and Sykes. My guess is it didn't happen."

"Why the hell would you have him call Ozzie and Sykes?"

Since arriving at the hospital, I had had plenty of time to think about the morning's happenings. I had decided, among other things, that whoever broke into my garage, didn't do so in order to siphon ten-bucks worth of gasoline.

"Someone lured me down to that garage, Pat, hit me over the head, then set the garage on fire. I'm no detective, but I'm thinking that maybe it has something to do with a couple of murders where it's only my word against somebody else's. What do *you* think?"

My brother looked at his watch. "Six-fifteen?"

I nodded. Even that slight movement sent my head spinning.

"You're sure you made it clear to Swirski that he was to call us?"

"Oh yeah. No doubt about it." I successfully fought off the urge to nod again.

"That son of a bitch." Pat turned on his heel and stormed out of the room.

Dr. Bhitiyakul had been standing silently beside me. He simply glanced over at me and said, "Your brother Patterick, he is very excitable, is he not?"

"He is that, Doc. Yes, indeedie, he is."

"Ahh, you make the joke at my expense, Caitlin O'Rourke. That is okay. I do not mind. Now, as I was saying, if you get plenty of rest, you will feel much better much sooner. If you do not, and something tells me you will not, your head, it will hurt much longer. Are you still taking Orudis for pain in nose?"

"Yeah."

"It will help pain in head, also. Continue taking it and when you see Dr. Neely for follow-up nose visit, stop by here and have me look also at your head, yes?"

"Will do, Doc."

"Will do? Not, yes, indeedie? Until the next time you get yourself beat up, Miss Caitlin O'Rourke, I will say good-bye."

* * * *

Pat drove me home. There we were met by Seamus, an almost hysterical Mary Grace, two men from the arson squad, and Gary Muldoon, our insurance man. The arson guys had finished their preliminary investigation and had pronounced the fire the work of an arsonist.

Duh! No kidding!

Gary tried to be funny and told Seamus that as long as it didn't turn out to be me who set the fire, we'd get paid. Mary Grace rewarded him with a sound smack to the back of his head and ran him off.

I had no doubt that the claim would be settled expeditiously since Gary's agency had the office at the Plainview end of our little strip of five connected buildings. The entire line of equally-connected garage/storage buildings had all been lost to the flames, Gary's included.

Veterinarian Janette Ross had called and left a message. Duke the Dalmatian had not punctured himself on a piece of metal as the paramedics had thought; he had been shot. The bullet had gone through, not damaging any bones or muscles and my doggy-hero would recover nicely. Pat had the arson investigators go over the alley again looking for the bullet, but none could be found.

My head hurt; my nose hurt; and I was filthy and scratched from having Duke drag me across the alleyway. Nose be damned, I needed a real honest-to-goodness shower. I untaped the nose guard and stood under the water, letting the hot needles spray over my entire body for about twenty minutes. It felt wonderful to wash my hair the way God had intended for it to be done, instead of in the sink.

I emerged, toweled off, donned a fresh sports bra, panties, and Bobcat sleepshirt, took two more Orudis, reinstalled the nose guard, and crawled into bed. The sleep for which I longed would have to wait, though. She with ears like a bat must have heard me pull back the covers because, within three minutes, there she stood with a tray of brunch, and Seamus, Pat, and Detective B. J. Sykes lined up behind her like three little ducklings.

My relatives looked relieved at the sight of a cleaned-up me. Sykes carried a manila folder with him and looked mighty ticked off, but, fortunately, not at me.

* * * *

As I lay there, propped up on three down pillows, alternately slurping spoonfuls of leftover Lamb and Vegetable Soup and munching buttered slices of Barm Brack, Sykes brought me up to speed on the case.

After a completely fruitless two hours with Matt Denning and Michael Kahn, a criminal lawyer that Phillip Kaplowitz had recommended, Ozzie had cut Matt loose but had stationed a patrol car outside his Forest Hills home. According to the officer on duty, Matt hadn't left the house during the night nor had he any visitors.

"Did you put someone on Tottenham Court Road or on the service drive?" I asked.

"What for?" Sykes asked.

"Well, duh," I said. "The garage opens both front and rear. How do you know he didn't leave and return through the back gate?"

The detective left the room to use the telephone. When he returned a few minutes later, his mood had worsened. "From our man's position on the street, he couldn't see the back of the house. Sorry,"—he shook his head in disgust—"but we hadn't considered he'd try anything like this."

"Can't you get a search warrant and examine the car?" I asked. "Check it for something that might tie it to the alley here."

"Not a chance."

"Why not?"

Sykes looked at the faces around the room, then said, "May I speak to you in private, Kate?"

"You can say whatever you have to say in front of my family."

"My pension's involved. It's either in private or not at all."

"Seamus, why don't you and Mary Grace go downstairs and get ready for business," Pat said. "I'll be down in a little while."

My sister-in-law started to protest, but Seamus took her firmly by the arm and started out of the room. "Pat will handle everything, love," he said. "Let's you and I go open up for little Jimmy and poor old Mickey Ryan."

Stopping at the bedroom door, Mary Grace turned and shook a finger in Pat's direction. "Don't you dare let her get herself hurt again, Patrick."

Pat held up his hands in submission as Seamus half-dragged Mary Grace out of the room. At the sound of the apartment door closing, Pat sat on the edge of my bed and folded his arms across his chest. "There's private and then there's private," he said to Sykes. "And this is as private as it gets, Beej. Consider me a fly on the wall."

Sykes took a moment or two to mull over Pat's comments, then nodded and parked himself on the clothes hamper. "Okay. Here's the situation. Very early this morning, at about five, so I'm told, Matt Denning's lawyer Michael Kahn paid a call at the Mayor's home. Got him out of bed. Why did the mayor let him in, you ask? Kahn is a personal friend of His Honor. The meeting lasted about forty-five minutes. At that point in time Kahn left and the mayor called his aide, Ray Bob Gardner, and got *him* out of bed. Ray Bob then called Ozzie and me and got *us* out of our beds with orders to be in the mayor's office at 0700 sharp. I'll spare you the gory details, but the bottom line is that we're off the case."

"What?!" both Pat and I screamed in unison.

The few spoonfuls of broth left in the bowl sloshed over onto the tray as my brother came to his feet.

"Step back, Paddy," Sykes said, "and look at this objectively. Just what minuscule shred of evidence have we got to support what we think happened?"

"We have…" Pat started out with a bellow, then stood there with a perplexed expression on his face.

"Yes?" Sykes asked, cocking an eyebrow. "We have what?"

"How about my word," I chimed in. "Isn't that worth something? Huh, guys?"

"To us, it's golden," Pat said, sitting back down on my bed and patting my leg. "But Beej is right. We have no evidence at all against Matt Denning. As far as his wife's murder is concerned, we can tie it to Junior Lee Thigpen. Period. And the evidence says Junior died in a drug deal. Case closed in the Delane Denning killing."

"But what about Courtney Howell?" I asked. "She posed as Delane Denning."

"So you say, Kate," Sykes answered. "But we have no corroborating evidence. And as for *her* murder, there's absolutely no link to Denning. And I can show you the files of seven murdered prostitutes that I have on my desk that are covered with cobwebs. They don't get solved. They don't even get worked on."

I couldn't believe what I was hearing. "What about last night? After Ozzie picked him up for questioning, Matt had to realize that I'm the only one who can testify against him. So what did he do? He tried to eliminate me. Doesn't that say something?"

"Did you see him?" Pat asked.

"No, of course not."

"Did you hear his voice?"

"No."

Neither Pat nor Sykes bothered telling me that meant there was no evidence. They both just shrugged their shoulders.

"Okay," I said. "But even though you're officially off the case, you're going to continue investigating, aren't you? Unofficially?"

Sykes shook his head. "Nosiree, Bob."

"Why not?!" I set the brunch tray on the night stand so that I could swing my legs around over the side of the bed and face him directly. You'll be happy to know, though, that I had the presence of mind to keep the spread wrapped around me so as not to arouse any lustful thoughts in old B. J.

"Your brother will understand this, Kate, even if you don't. Ozzie and I each have something damned important at stake, here. For me, it's a pension. For Ozzie, it's a future. If we deliberately disobey this order to stop *harassing* Matt Denning, and that's the word both Denning's lawyer and the mayor used, we jeopardize my pension and Ozzie's future. So you see, Kate, a *police* investigation is out of the question."

"What other kind is there?" I asked, in response to his emphasis on the word *police*.

Sykes picked up the folder he had brought with him and looked over at my brother.

Pat grimaced, shook his head, and groaned, "Mary Grace will kill me, Beej."

"For what?" I asked. "What are you two talking about?"

"Well?" Sykes said, still looking at Pat. "Your call, Paddy."

My brother simply gestured to me and left the room, still shaking his head. Within a minute, I heard the refrigerator door open.

"What?!" I asked, for what seemed to be the dozenth time.

Detective B. J. Sykes nodded. "Okay, Kate, here it is. Ozzie and I, and that goes for Paddy, can't do anything more without some sort of evidence against Matt Denning. Yes, it's politics, but that's life. If we had anything at all, no matter how small, we could justify reopening the case. That's where you come in, if you want to."

My head still hurt and I wasn't thinking too clearly. "I don't understand." I told him.

"No one was ever supposed to know that Courtney Howell impersonated Delane Denning," Sykes continued. "And, had it not been for that sandal, no one would have. The case really *would* be closed."

He handed me the manila folder he had brought with him. "We, that is, Ozzie and I, think you may just know something else that you're not aware you know. And that might explain last night's attempt on your life because Matt Denning realizes that you know it. This is a copy of the complete Denning file. Every interview, every report. Although we can't continue to investigate, maybe what's already in here might just help you remember that all-important something else. Look it over. And let's hope so, Kate, because unless you figure out what it is that you know, there's no guarantee that Denning won't try again to silence you."

Chapter 16

Detective Sykes left my place at about 10:30 that morning. I shooed Pat out, too, even though I only managed to half convince him that I'd be all right during the day with Seamus and Mary Grace downstairs in the pub. He reluctantly agreed, but with one stipulation, and a big one, at that. I had to allow him to move in with me and spend the nights here for the foreseeable future. There was no dissuading him; his big-brother instincts were too strong.

I hoped the case would be wrapped up soon. Although there would be no problem tonight, this being only my first date with Chris Panacopoulos, I had expectations of many more to come. Since Chris had not yet found an apartment of his own and was back in his boyhood room at his parents' place, Pat's continued nightly presence would be an immense cramp in my style.

The sleep that I had so longed for before Sykes' visit had been totally forgotten. I slipped on a bathrobe, took a couple of painkillers, and curled up in the La-Z-Boy with cat, case-folder, pad of yellow lined paper, and black felt-tip pen.

Ozzie and Sykes had done a thorough job of investigating, as far as I could tell. Some of their queries I would never have thought to make. For instance, a check with the Peabody Hotel in Memphis, courtesy of Memphis PD, turned up both a desk clerk and a room-service waiter who remembered seeing Matt Denning on Tuesday, Wednesday, and Thursday, alone on all three days. Memphis PD had also interviewed the clients with whom Matt had met. His last appointment had ended at about eleven on Thursday morning.

Although they had questioned Matt's neighbors and maid, as well as his co-workers and secretary at Reis-Wiedenkeller, neither Ozzie nor Sykes had come up with any leads on his suspected paramour. Matt had apparently successfully kept not only her identity, but her existence, a secret from everyone—everyone except his wife.

Sykes had scrawled a note in the margin of his report. It read: *Smart money's on the secretary Sharon Ross. I think she's in love with Denning.*

Sharon Ross—Miss Mousy at Delane's funeral. So that's who she was, Matt's secretary for the last fifteen years. That would certainly explain her actions at the mortuary. For one thing, I now had a better understanding for her tears. They hadn't been for the dearly departed Delane; they had been for Matt, because she thought him to be hurting and that, in turn, hurt her.

I found myself agreeing with Sykes, but only up to a point. No doubt the prim and proper Miss Ross had been devoted to her boss, and secretly in love with him as well, not so unusual a situation. However, the detective and I differed in our conclusions based on that bit of supposition.

Oh, sure, Sharon Ross would probably have welcomed an affair, but she didn't impress me as the type to have been an accomplice in a murder. And that's what I figured Matt Denning's lover had to be. If Ozzie and Sykes had not been pulled off the case, I'm certain they would have come to that same conclusion. I say this because, while the investigation into Delane Denning's death prior to the discovery of Courtney Howell's body had been thorough, the investigation since had barely begun. The key, at least to my way of thinking, was that Matt Denning hadn't considered the possibility that anyone would ever find out about the wife switch.

My theory went something like this. Courtney had probably been the one whom Matt Denning had been seeing on the side. Why a great looking guy like Matt felt he had to pay for it boggled my mind. Thinking back to that newspaper picture of the real Delane, though, she didn't look like the type who would be very...oh, let's call it adventuresome. Maybe he liked something kinky that only a hired lover would provide.

Delane discovered his affair accidentally, as Melinda had told me, and ran straight to her attorney. Somehow Matt found out about his wife filing for divorce. Maybe she flung it in his face out of spite. You know, something like: "You'll be left with nothing but the shirt on your philandering back, you son of a bitch!"

I figured the incident in the bar that night where Matt saw me deck Junior had just been serendipity. Matt then enlisted Junior and Courtney so that: number one, the police would automatically suspect the mugger who had stolen Delane's purse; number two, Courtney (as Delane) could fill me with blarney about how much she loved her husband, further throwing suspicion off of him; and number three, he would have a rock-solid alibi by letting me see him pull into the driveway just at that moment when the fatal shots were fired. He had plenty of time to drive back from Memphis after his last appointment that morning and set things up.

I now suspected Courtney's true motive for stopping at the Marriott on our way back from Cove Creek, and it hadn't anything to do with her bladder. I made a note to have Pat run a check on the pay phones in the hotel lobby for that date and time. Finding that a call had been placed to the Denning home from one of them would not come as a complete surprise.

To my regret, with this theory I had to revise my earlier opinion of Courtney's innocence, and that greatly saddened me. If she *were* the mistress and in on the plot, she *had* to know that Delane would be killed. Matt probably led Courtney to believe that he was madly in love with her and that once his wicked old wife had been disposed of, he would marry her and make a respectable woman out of her.

Remembering Courtney's town house, I could well imagine how something like respectability might appeal to her. Even though, somehow I still couldn't think badly of her, just worse of Matt Denning, that son of a bitch.

So. Courtney calls Matt from the Marriott. Either he or Junior shoots Delane. Matt gets into his car and leaves, parking somewhere until he sees Courtney and me arrive, then pulls into the driveway and honks the horn. That's the signal for Junior. Junior fires two shots out through the French doors and waits for me to enter. He lets me get just the quickest of looks at the dead Delane, then bammo with the shotgun butt to my nose.

How's that sound? Pretty good, huh?

But back to the key. If Matt Denning thought no one would ever find out about Courtney Howell, then that's what I figured I should concentrate on—Courtney, the proof thereof. And then it hit me. Fingerprints! Courtney's fingerprints! They would have been left all over the place—on the purse, in the Denning's Cove Creek home, in Liddy, and in my apartment.

I checked the file. A forensics report stated that no prints of any kind had been found on the outside of the purse nor on the wallet. The only other prints found on items inside the purse matched those of the murder victim, identified from dental records as Delane Denning.

So, Junior had wiped his own and Courtney's prints off the outside of the purse and his own off the wallet after he had lifted the money from it. With the thorough cleaning the Cove Creek home had received, it would be utterly useless to check for prints there. But as for Liddy…

Was that why the garage had been burned? To eliminate both me, who knew too much, *and* Liddy, whose interior was probably covered with Courtney Howell's prints?

But what about my apartment? Unfortunately, Mrs. Nash had been here on Wednesday, so any prints Courtney might have left on that Monday night would be long gone. However, Matt didn't know about Mrs. Nash. Did that mean the pub was next on the list for a fortuitous fire?

I decided that, first, I'd better check the batteries in the smoke detectors and, secondly, I'd better not take too long recalling what it was that Ozzie and Sykes thought I was supposed to know. As a tertiary item, and with no disrespect to Mrs. Nash intended, I made another mental note for Pat. Perhaps he could get a forensics specialist to check out the wood arms of the sofa and English Oak end table near where Courtney Howell had sat last Monday, just in case a stray fingerprint managed to somehow escape Mrs. Nash's dust cloth.

Going through the file again, I realized that someone extremely important to this case had been missing from the entire investigation, from Monday night when the mugging occurred, to Thursday afternoon when Delane Denning was murdered. Courtney Howell and I were in Cove Creek. Matt Denning was in Memphis—alone. Anita Mendoza, having been told not to come in Tuesday, Wednesday, or Thursday, was at home. Presumably Swallow Sedlacek and Junior were at her place.

Chester Murdock, the locksmith, had said in a statement given to Sykes, that the Dennings' Forest Creek home had been unoccupied the day he came to change the locks. He did his job, then FedExed keys to Mr. Denning at the Memphis Peabody and another set to Mrs. Denning (Courtney) in Cove Creek.

But what about the *real* Delane Denning? Where was *she* while all this was going on? The homicide detectives had been taken off the case so soon after we realized that a switch had been made, no one had ever asked that question.

W.B. picked that particular moment to hop down and get herself a drink. As she did so, she bumped my pad, balancing on the arm of the chair, and knocked the pen to the floor. It bounced twice and, true to

Murphy's Law, both times away from me. I had papers all over my lap. Not wanting to disturb them by getting up, I tried stretching for the pen. Even with my orangutan-like arms, I couldn't reach it.

After being saved by Duke the Dalmatian, I had begun to think more kindly of dogs. "If you were a Labrador Retriever," I shouted, as the cat disappeared into the kitchen, "you'd bring that pen to Mom." As usual, my little furry buddy paid no attention to me whatsoever.

Had I gathered my papers together as soon as the pen had fallen and gotten up, I would have had it by now and been once again ensconced in my chair. Having wasted time stretching for it and failing to reach it, I tried taking the pad and using it as an extension. Even that extra eleven inches wasn't good enough.

Still too lazy to get up, I looked around for something else to use. If I had been wearing a belt, I might have tried tossing the buckle-end of it in the hope of snagging the wayward pen. But there was nothing on either end of my bathrobe sash that would serve as a hook.

Three thoughts flooded my brain in a kind of montage. B. J. Sykes sat on my clothes hamper saying, *Ozzie and I think you may just know something else that you're not aware you know.* Matt Denning sat across from me downstairs in Caitlin's Corner, answering a stupid question I had asked the first night we met about him being a fisherman. *With a passion. Got a small place down on Nickajack Lake.* And Melinda Huntington stood there at her sister's memorial service showing Ozzie and me a head-and-shoulders shot of two girls, both blond and attractive, one in her early teens, the other a few years younger. They both carried fishing poles.

I dumped the papers from my lap onto the butler's tray coffee table as I bounded out of the chair toward the telephone. Bad move. My head started spinning and I had to grab hold of the kitchen pass-through counter in order to stop the room from spinning. The pad beside the phone still had my chicken-scratch of the number for the Maxwell House. The clerk rang Melinda Huntington's room and I said a quiet prayer that she'd be in.

Yes, I know it's incredibly stupid to do that. She's either in or she's not. And if she's not, the good Lord is not about to teleport her from wherever she is just for my convenience—or would he? Hey, I'm an Irish Catholic; what more can I say?

Either she *was* in or God *had* just teleported her to the hotel room because Melinda answered on the third ring. I'll leave it to you to decide which.

Dispensing with any preliminary courtesies, I jumped right in. "Mel, it's Kate. Do you know where Matt Denning's fishing place is down on Nickajack Lake?"

"Well, yes, of course. But how does that figure into the case?"

I told her my whole scenario. Although I'm not sure she believed all of it, her desire for Delane's killer (Matt) to be brought to justice overcame her skepticism.

"It's sort of hard to find, Kate. Have you a map?"

I set the phone down, dragged out a road atlas and turned to the Tennessee page. "Shoot," I said, picking up the phone again.

Between the lines on the map, the notes I took, and a little luck, I figured I could find the place. I thanked Mel and started to hang up when she yelled, "Wait, wait, wait! Are you still there, Kate?"

"Just barely. What?"

"A month ago when I was at the cottage, they were doing construction on State Road #28 between U.S. 41 and the interstate. It was horrendous. If it's still going on, you'd be better off taking the next exit, Highway #27, and then doubling back. Call me if you find anything. In fact, call me even if you don't. And just in case I'm not here when you get back, let me give you my cell phone number."

I wrote it next to the number for the Maxwell House and thanked her, promising to call when I returned.

Sykes had given me the case folder in the hopes that it would jog my brain into remembering something that would justify their reopening the case against Matt Denning. While it hadn't done that, the review *had* fueled my speculation on where the real Delane might have spent those three days.

I know I should have called the police and let them handle it, but my hunches had gotten Ozzie into trouble twice before. Initially, the information about the sandal (although it had later turned out to be extremely important) had caused problems between her and Trish Zelasko. And my hunch about Melinda's necklace at the mortuary had given Ozzie all sorts of grief. Not wanting to screw things up any worse for either her or Sykes with a might-have-been, I decided to do a little preliminary investigating on my own.

After dressing, I got hold of Pat and asked him about checking the phone records for the Marriott and dusting my sofa arms and end table for Courtney's fingerprints. He agreed and promised to have the forensics guys come out that afternoon. I didn't tell him about my plans for driving down to Nickajack Lake. Had I done so, he would have called Mary Grace and that would have been the end of that. And besides, I figured on being back long before he knew I was gone.

Tiptoeing downstairs into the pub, I peeked around the corner of the hallway. The lunch crowd had just started to arrive and Mary Grace was busy in the kitchen. So far so good. I had hoped to catch Seamus' eye without her spotting me, except that Seamus wasn't looking in my direction. He was down at the other end of the bar with Mickey Ryan and Jimmy Tuohey. A soccer match on ESPN droned on in the background from the TV set above the bar.

"Psst," I whispered.

No response.

I tried a little louder. "Psst!"

Still nothing.

"Psst, psst! Seamus?!"

Jimmy and Mickey looked up. Seamus still had his back to me.

"Seamus, it's Caitlin," Mickey said, touching my brother's shoulder and pointing in my direction. "I think she's wanting to talk to you, lad."

"You must be mistaken, Mr. Ryan," Seamus answered without so much as a glance over his shoulder. "My sister's under doctor's orders to rest. You wouldn't think she'd be ignoring those orders, would you, now?"

"Mr. Ryan's right, Seamus," Jimmy chimed in, innocently. "It *is* Caitlin." He waved to me. "How you feeling, Katie?"

Seamus just shook his head, still not turning around. "I tell you, you're both daft. My sister's a bright young lady. College degree and all. If the doctor says for her to rest, you can be sure that's exactly what"—then he raised his voice—"she'd better damn well be doing!"

"What are you bellowing about?" Mary Grace shouted from the kitchen.

"Nothing, love. The boys, here, were just wondering how Katie's doing and I was telling them."

"Sounds like you were telling the whole neighborhood. Keep your voice down. If you wake her, there'll be hell to pay."

"Yes, love."

I stepped from around the corner of the hallway. "What's all that shouting about?" I whispered, rubbing my eyes with my fists. "I was sound asleep and someone woke me."

Seamus turned; fear showed in his eyes. "You wouldn't dare," he hissed, shaking his head.

"Keys to the Windstar," I replied, holding out a hand and wiggling my fingers.

"Not a chance."

"Who's making all the noise?" I whispered louder. "I couldn't…"

"All right, all right, here!" He rummaged around in his pocket and tossed the keys to me. "But you damn well better be back before she brings your dinner tray up, or we're both in deep trouble."

"Tell her not to bother with dinner, bro. That'll buy us another hour or so. I've got a date tonight. I'll be back around six to get ready for it."

"With who?" He came down the length of the bar, scrunching his brow into a frown and shifting into his overprotective-parent mode.

"Chris Panacopoulos."

"Nico's kid?"

"The one and the same."

"I thought he was in Detroit. And Married."

"Back. And divorced. Ta-ta; see you later." I turned and walked down the hallway toward the rear door.

Seamus followed me. "Katie, you know how strongly Da felt about you dating that Greek kid."

"Yep. And with no disrespect to our dear departed father, TS, baby. I'm gonna do it anyway. Besides, Chris isn't a kid anymore and neither am I." With that, I scurried out the back door, climbed into the Windstar, moved the seat as far back as it would go, and backed out of the parking space.

As I navigated my way around a dump truck, bulldozer, and the dozen or so workmen tearing down the remains of the burned out garages, I checked the rearview mirror. My brother still stood in the pub doorway, shaking his head and ringing his hands—an incarnation of our dear Da, if ever there was one.

Chapter 17

Although the cleaning service supervisor at Cove Creek had said he'd have the information for me on Monday as to who had placed the cleaning order for the Denning home, I hadn't bothered calling. To be truthful, with my nose operation that morning, sleep in the afternoon, and finding out about Courtney Howell that evening, it had completely slipped my mind. I made a mental note to call later on in the day if I happened to get home by five.

That didn't seem likely. It was already one o'clock as Waldo and I approached the State Road #28 exit on Eastbound I-24 and I could see the construction Melinda Huntington had warned me about still fiercely in progress. The usable roadway had been narrowed to one lane, backing up the northbound traffic for a good five-hundred yards. I took Mel's advice and kept on going, backtracking on U.S. 41 from the next exit.

Waldo, you ask?

Seamus' Windstar. I had to call him something, didn't I? How else would he know what I wanted him to do? And because painkillers had numbed half my brain and the other half was preoccupied with my quest, I really didn't have time to consider all the appropriate possibilities. *Waldo* came to mind first, so *Waldo* it was.

With two bedrooms, two baths, a kitchen, dining room, and living room downstairs, and a master suite upstairs, Matt Denning's fishing cottage turned out to be anything *but* a cottage. The gigantic redwood A-frame with wraparound deck overlooked the Minnedosa River a mile or so upstream from Nickajack Lake.

My reason for driving down was not to look for fingerprints; after all, the Dennings owned the place and it must be laden with Delane's prints. But, she had spent at least three days somewhere, most probably here, and, unless someone had kept her tied to a chair the entire time, I had hoped one of the neighbors might have seen her. Those hopes faded by a couple orders of magnitude, however, as I pulled Waldo into the Dennings' driveway.

All the dozen or so cottages on that stretch of the river were of similar design and cost. And all were set back into their heavily wooded lots, screening out the rest of the world. If anyone *had* seen Delane Denning, it would have been only by the merest of happenstance.

I made the circuit of the grounds. Not only couldn't I see any of the other homes from the Denning property, but I'm sure no one could see me unless they were on the river directly in front of the cottage. The lots on the other side of the river (all part of the same exclusive development) were staggered so that no two homes looked across the river at each other. From the Dennings' boathouse and dock I could see the boathouses and docks of the two properties kitty-corner across the river, but not the homes themselves.

Melinda Huntington had told me where to find the spare key (hidden under a pile of fake dog doo-doo on the south side of the driveway) and had given me the alarm code. After seeing how isolated these homes were, I didn't wonder why they were wired directly to a security service. On an if-come, I jotted down the address and phone number for Marion Alarm from a sign on the front door. Maybe the security company would have been notified if the alarm had been shut off during Delane's stay.

The inside of the cottage yielded nothing, not that I thought it would, but I'd have chastised myself all the way home had I failed to look. Besides, the pain medication had begun to wear off and I needed a glass of water to wash down two more pills.

My strategy in dealing with the neighbors was to pose as a guest of the Dennings and thoughtfully let them know about Delane's passing in case they hadn't already heard. To that end, I had attempted to look the part by piling my mane on top of my head and applying some makeup, as much as the nose guard and bandages would permit. Instead of my usual jeans, shirt, and boots, I had worn a white safari-style pantsuit with a pair of high-heeled sandals.

After getting the lay of the land, I decided to try the cottages on either side and the two kitty-corner across the river. If any of the neighbors had seen Delane, the odds were that it would have been one of them.

Durham Poole, the curmudgeon on the north side, hadn't heard about Delane's death and didn't seem to care very much.

"Never really met them formal like, you know?" he said, looking up into my eyes only after a quick glance at my boobs, then at my nose. "Oh, we'd wave if we happened to pass each other on the river, but that's about it. Too bad about her, though. She was sort of a looker, you know what I mean?"

"Well, I just thought I should tell the neighbors, Mr. Poole. No telling how long it's been since most of you have seen the Dennings."

"A month for me. Maybe two," he said, taking my bait. "Like I say, we weren't close like, you know what I mean?"

I thanked him and tried the neighbors to the south. Although the Petersons showed more emotion than Durham, they hadn't seen the Dennings recently, either.

Driving north for a couple miles, I found a bridge over the Minnedosa, then tried to locate the two homes diagonally across the river from the Dennings. I drove slowly, hoping to catch a through-the-trees glimpse of the redwood A-frame on the other side. No such luck.

There *was* no through-the-trees. That was the beauty of this development, the seclusion. All I could see from the road were mailboxes and driveway entrances.

I was just about to backtrack and check my odometer reading from the bridge to the Denning cottage when I spotted a driveway and knew in my gut that it had to be one of the two for which I had been searching. A yellow plastic tape about three inches wide had been stretched across the drive, blocking all entry. On the tape, in black block letters, the words SHERIFF'S LINE DO NOT CROSS were repeated end upon end.

Brother Pat has often pontificated that in police work there is no such thing as a coincidence. I had no doubt that Bernard Tibbets of 1285 Riverbend Drive, so proclaimed on the rural mailbox, *had* seen Delane Denning sometime during the previous week and had paid the ultimate price for that chance encounter.

So far Matt Denning had covered his tracks very nicely indeed—no Courtney, no Junior, no Swallow, no Liddy. And no nosy neighbor who might read about Delane Denning's death in the newspaper and voice his concern about a report that had her returning with me from Cove Creek when he knew she was here at Nickajack.

* * * *

"Robbery and murder, pure and simple, ma'am," Deputy Darryl Johnston said in response to my query about the happenings out at Bernard Tibbets' place. "Shot that poor old man once in the head and stole all his stuff. Stereo components, VCR, microwave. We figure it was a one-man operation because the big-screen TV was left behind. Too big for one person to carry."

I had driven up to Jasper and now sat across the desk in the Marion County Sheriff's Office.

"Any leads? I asked."

"Hell, lady, pardon my French. Stuff like that was probably fenced before we ever knowed it was taken. It happened sometime last Thursday night. We didn't get the call until Friday morning when one of his fishing buddies found him. No witnesses. No one suspicious in the area, not that any of them rich dudes would see anything out there in them woods. Oh, we went through the motions, all right. Called in the TBI, got fingerprints off of everything, ballistics on the bullet, but I ain't holding out no hope of catching whoever done it. Not unless he gets himself picked up for something else with that gun on him. What's your interest in this? You a reporter?"

"No, deputy. I'm working with Metro PD up in Nashville on a case that may be related."

"No fooling? You a cop?" He asked it in the same tone of voice he would have used had he said, "You a midget?"

"Not exactly. I'm running a parallel investigation of my own…with their blessing, of course. You can check with Detective Sergeant Patrick O'Rourke, if you like."

"Oh, a PI, huh? Well, if the Nashville boys are cool with it, I guess it's okay by me. What do you want from us?"

My bluff had worked. Had he called Pat, who still thought I was home in bed where I should have been, my brother might have decided to teach me a lesson by telling Deputy Johnston that I was an escaped mental patient and that he should lock me up until further notice. Rather than let the deputy know that I wasn't a private eye either, just a doofus with a hunch, I asked about the ballistics report from the Tennessee Bureau of Investigation.

The bullet, dug out of Bernard Tibbets' brain, was a .44-Magnum, the same caliber as used on Junior Lee Thigpen and Swallow Sedlacek, so said the file Sykes had given me. Deputy Johnston gave me copies of the Sheriff's report on the Tibbets' case, along with photomicrographs of the bullet to take back home. In return, I promised to have one of my Metro Homicide *colleagues* let him know if the bullet matched those in the Nashville killings.

From Jasper, instead of driving over to Kimball, I fought the construction traffic on State Road #28 down to the offices of Marion Alarm near the interstate. It was a waste of time. With the type of systems they install, they only get alerted when an alarm goes off and dials them up. They have no way of knowing when it's active or inactive at a client's home.

I thanked Billy Beasley, the owner, and got up to leave, only to see the southbound traffic at a standstill.

"This must be a pain in the butt for the businesses along this stretch," I remarked.

"Tell me about it. Before they started up a couple of weeks back, they sent around some government pencil-pusher to smooth our feathers over. To let us know that they're thinking...that's what he said, *thinking* of reimbursing us for some of our lost revenue. I won't hold my hand on my ass. Besides, it's not just the lost revenue itself, it's the lost referrals. These systems are damn good, lady. And for every one I install, I get a half dozen or so referrals. Maybe one in twenty results in another sale. How many of *those* am I going to lose in the next three months?"

"Bummer," I said.

"Tell me about it. You headed to the interstate?"

"Yeah."

"Go around the side of the building and take the back alley down to the gas station. You can get right on from their lot. And here,"—he handed me a fistful of business cards—"you tell your friends, Marion Alarm does first-rate work."

* * * *

I exited Westbound I-24 at the Bell Road interchange. When I got to Wooten I glanced at my watch—four-thirty-seven, still plenty of time. Instead of making my right turn and heading for home, I continued on Old Hickory Boulevard to Forest Hills. The clothing Barbie and Ken had picked up from the Denning home on Friday should have come back from the dry cleaners earlier in the day.

The doors to The Hunting Lodge were open. I found Bobbie Deerfield and a couple of Foresters on the stage, resetting furniture and props for a midweek rehearsal of *Encore to Murder*.

"Sorry to bother you," I called out from the back row as I crossed down toward them. "But you said Mrs. Denning's clothes would be back from the cleaners today and I thought I'd look for my jacket."

"Oh, yes, yes, yes," Bobbie cooed. "No trouble at all. Everything's still hanging together in the costume room. We haven't logged any of the pieces in, yet, or placed them in their final storage spot. Come on up here; we'll go though the back."

I mounted the stage and waited as she gave some last-minute instructions on where to place additional glow tape to keep the actors from running into the furniture during the blackouts.

* * * *

A sign on the costume room door, hand-lettered on astrobright pink paper, proclaimed: OFF LIMITS TO ANYONE EXCEPT THE MANAGING DIRECTOR AND THE WARDROBE MISTRESS. THIS MEANS YOU! STAY OUT!

Bobbie unlocked the door and flipped on the fluorescents to illuminate row upon row of bagged and numbered garments. There must have been a couple thousand of them. More impressive still was the near wall. Its entire length had been subdivided into pigeon holes, each containing a wig wrapped in cellophane.

As she explained to me in much more detail than I wanted to know or in which I am relating to you, each one of the items in storage had an identifying number sewn into it and a specific location assigned. A computer tracking method assured that the wardrobe mistress knew at all times the location for each wig or article of clothing.

Delane Denning's things had not yet been subjected to that process and everything hung, plastic bagged, on a separate rack. I made a quick check of all the outfits. None were the ones worn by Courtney Howell during her Delane impersonation up at Cove Creek.

I thanked Bobbie, mumbling something about probably leaving my mythical jacket elsewhere, and left the theater. Once again I had to admire Matt Denning's thoroughness. Even though at the time he hadn't known that anyone would stumble onto his wife-switch ploy, he had left nothing to chance. Most probably he had had Junior Lee Thigpen dispose of Courtney's clothing after having Junior dispose of Courtney herself.

Those thoughts of Junior brought back memories of Swallow Sedlacek's apartment. I climbed into Waldo and grabbed up the Marion County Sheriff's report on the Bernard Tibbets' robbery/murder. Tibbets' fishing buddy had given the deputies a list of what he thought had been taken from the old man's cottage—stereo system, VCR, and microwave oven. By my recollection, those were precisely the only three items in Swallow's hovel that looked relatively new.

Matt Denning might have been thorough, but I doubted that he had considered the full extent of Junior's greed. In addition to electronic equipment, I wondered if friend Junior had recently brought home some new clothes for Swallow.

* * * *

Ernie Hammerman sat out front of the Normandy Arms in a once green but now rusted metal lawn chair, contemplating life and a list of numbers that he had been manipulating. The differing degrees of corrosion on metal brackets affixed to the chair testified to its being reinforced on at least two occasions in order to support the big black man's bulk.

As I approached him, he looked over the rims of his glasses at me and dropped one hand out of his lap, setting it on the enormous head of an old Rottweiler that lay curled up under the chair. The dog didn't growl or make any attempt to get up, just lifted its graying upper lip and sneered at me.

Brave dog, I thought. I sure as heck wouldn't have laid under Ernie Hammerman's rusted out chair for all the Milk Bones in the world.

"Mr. Hammerman," I said, stopping a respectful four feet in front of him and his beast. "My name is Caitlin O'Rourke. I don't know whether you remember me or not but I was here last…"

"I 'member you, all right," he interrupted, nodding his head. "You was here with the police the day they found that poor little Swallow."

"Yes, sir, I was." Having him make the connection himself, saved me from stretching the truth and implying that I was still *with* the police.

"I told that Detective Osborn that Swallow was a good girl and I meant every word of it," he continued. "She didn't do no drugs. She didn't steal no jewels, either. No ma'am, she didn't. She was a *good* girl. Never made me no trouble. Paid her rent on time. And always called me *Mister* Hammerman. If you be looking for a doper and a thief, you don't need to look no further than that good-for-nothing boyfriend of hers. It be him who got poor Swallow killed."

Seeing his eyes go moist, I moved a few steps nearer and squatted down to be face to face with him. The dog snuffled me but didn't attempt a snap.

"We know that, Mr. Hammerman. The way we figure it, Swallow had absolutely nothing to do with the robbery we were investigating. Junior just used her place to hide out in. He was one bad-news fella any way you slice it."

"You done got that right!" Ernie Hammerman turned his head and spat on the weed patch that served as a front lawn, his contempt for Junior Lee Thigpen almost palpable.

"He hit her," Ernie went on. "I know he did. But she wouldn't say so. No, ma'am. Always claimed to have fallen down when I seed some fresh bruises. Can you believe he *hit* that poor little girl?"

"Yes, Mr. Hammerman," I replied, tapping my nose with the index finger of my right hand. "I surely can."

The old black man's eyes grew wide and bulged from their sockets. "He hit you, too?!"

I nodded, then smiled. "But when I'm hit, I hit back."

"Did you get him a good one?"

"Kicked him right square in the balls, Mr. Hammerman. Laid him out like a mackerel."

Okay, so I reversed the sequence of events. But I could see from Ernie's face what he wanted to hear so I gave it to him. And you can't argue with success.

"Hot damn!" he yelped, grinning with glee and smacking his hand on his thigh. "I wish I'd done seed that."

It was the first time I'd seen him smile. He had a gold front tooth the size of my thumb nail. Then, just as quickly, he became morose again.

"Too bad that little Swallow hadn't of done the same thing," he said. "Maybe she'd be alive today iffen she had." He gave a gigantic sigh and shrugged his massive shoulders. "I suppose you be wanting to see her apartment again?"

"Yes, sir. I know this is an awful inconvenience for you, with people traipsing in and out, but I need to check on one more thing."

He dug a ring of keys from his pocket and flipped through three of them. "This be the master key. With you a detective an' all, there's no point in me walking up them stairs with you. I be right here when you get done. If not, I be in apartment 1-A."

Taking the key ring from him, I rose and started toward the door.

He called out after me. "You got a lucky number, Miss Detective?"

I turned back to him? "Seventeen."

"Seventeen? Why seventeen?"

"March seventeenth. St. Patrick's Day. I'm Irish."

His eyes bulged again. "Shit, girl. You ain't no more Irish than I is." He pronounced it, *Arsh.*

"Haven't you ever heard of the Black Irish, Mr. Hammerman?"

He snorted and shook his head, then turned his attention back to the list of numbers. As I entered the building, I could hear him chuckling to himself.

"Black Irish. If that don't beat all."

* * * *

Not only did Swallow Sedlacek's closet contain every outfit that Courtney Howell had worn during our stay in Cove Creek, except for the duplicate of the black-and-white linen coatdress in which Delane Denning had been killed, but Courtney's size-six shoes as well. There was also a Samsonite three-suiter, monogrammed with the initials CAH.

Leaving the apartment as I had found it, I relocked the door and returned the keys to Ernie Hammerman, giving him three more lucky numbers—my height (73), weight (178), and age (that's between Ernie and me, if you don't mind).

I was proud of myself, and rightly so. Coaches Ozzie and Sykes had brought me in off the bench with our team losing miserably and I had gone on an unbelievable scoring streak to win the game. In my mind I pictured the entire Metro Police Force seated in Bobcat Gymnasium doing the wave and shouting, "Yea, Katie-Kat!"

The clothing I had found gave credence to my heretofore unproven wife-switch theory. With those outfits, Ozzie and Sykes could now tie Courtney Howell directly to Junior Lee Thigpen. And, if the ballistics matched (which I was sure they would), Junior's and Swallow's deaths would have something in common with that of Bernard Tibbets, the across-the-river neighbor of the Dennings. Using brother Pat's dictum of *there's no such thing as a coincidence*, the professionals could now justify reopening the case and putting the squeeze on Matt Denning.

All the way home I debated with myself on whom to call first—Pat, Ozzie, or Melinda Huntington. As it turned out, I didn't have to call anyone. Pat and Ozzie stood out in the alley, watching the workmen bulldoze away the last remains of the burned-out garages.

Tuesday must have been yellow day for Ozzie. Her pantsuit of that color contrasted nicely with her skin. I made a mental note, though, to tell her to ditch the mocha-colored blouse. It so closely matched her skin tone that from a distance, she appeared not to be wearing one. I wondered how many of the workmen had strained their eyes to spot cleavage before noticing the blouse.

"Where the hell have you been?!" Pat greeted me as I climbed out of Waldo. "We've all been worried sick about you."

"Hey, save your scolding until I take some more pills. My head's killing me." I walked past him toward the rear entrance to Kehough's, stopping just momentarily to tease Ozzie. "Make him be nice to me, Ozzie, or I won't tell you how to solve your case." I winked and gave her one of my patented bemused smiles as I continued on.

"There *is* no more case, Kate," she said to my back. "It's been solved. That's what I stopped by to tell you."

"What?!" I turned toward her, all thoughts of the pain in my head forgotten. "But how?! I've got the proof." I waved the manila envelope that contained the Marion County Sheriff's report at her. "It's all here. You can arrest Matt Denning. It'll hold up this time."

"Matt Denning is dead, Kate. He committed suicide sometime early this morning."

Chapter 18

Up in my quarters with two more Orudis futilely attempting to dissolve away the pain in my skull, Ozzie explained what had happened.

On Tuesday mornings, Anita Mendoza did the grocery shopping on her way to the Denning home, usually arriving somewhere between ten and eleven o'clock. This morning, unaware of Matt's car in the garage, she had lunch in the kitchen, then started on her daily cleaning chores. It wasn't until about one-thirty or so when she entered the den and found Matt lying on the floor behind his desk. The pool of blood from a hole in his right temple had already begun to coagulate. A Smith & Wesson Model-629 .44-Magnum revolver lay near his outstretched hand.

Trish Zelasko estimated the time of death at between seven and eight o'clock that morning and neither the police nor the Medical Examiner's Office could find any evidence to support a theory other than the obvious—suicide. The position and angle of bullet entry and the amount of powder residue on the side of Matt's head were consistent with a wound of the self-inflicted nature. His hands had been swabbed with diluted nitric acid and the swabs subjected to a Neutron Activation Analysis. The test showed gunpowder residue and proved that he had, indeed, recently fired a weapon. Also, the only fingerprints on the gun belonged to him.

Additionally, ballistics checks established with a ninety-seven percent certainty that the same gun had been used to kill both Junior Lee Thigpen and Swallow Sedlacek.

"When we picked up Denning the other night, it was to see if we could shake him," Ozzie finished up. "Obviously we did. He knew then that we were on to Courtney Howell, even though we couldn't prove anything. He wasn't stupid. After he botched the fire here this morning, he figured it would only be a matter of time before we closed in on him."

"What do you mean *botched*?" I asked. "It looks to me like he did a pretty thorough job. My car and any trace of Courtney Howell's fingerprints are long gone."

"*You're* still here, Katie," Pat reminded me. "As far as Denning was concerned, the attempt to shut you up was botched."

"But I don't have any more information than he already knew I had. After you guys were taken off the case, what more harm could I have done to him?"

Ozzie waved the Marion County Sheriff's report at me. "How about this. And the clothing you found at Swallow Sedlacek's. You did one hell of a job on this investigation, Kate, although you *should* have called one of us instead of going off by yourself. I'll have ballistics compare these photomicrographs to those from Denning's revolver and get forensics to check out the clothing. If we can find a few hairs that match Courtney Howell's and mud from your alley on the outfit she wore here that Monday night, that'll tie up any loose ends for the bureaucrats downtown. Time was running out for Denning and he knew it. Rather than face the humiliation, he used his last bullet on himself."

"Last?" I asked.

Ozzie nodded. "Something tragically poetic about that, isn't there?"

"I realize I'm a philosophy major and not super strong in math," I said, completing the mental arithmetic. "But I count only five bullets—Junior and Swallow in the park, Tibbets down in Marion

County, Duke the Dalmatian in the alley, and Matt Denning himself. Did that model gun hold only five bullets or is there another body yet to be found?"

Pat and Ozzie looked at each other and winced.

"The 629 holds six," Pat said.

"Maybe one missed its mark," Ozzie added hopefully. "If the dog tried to attack him, he could have fired twice. How many shots did you hear?"

"I only remember one, but I couldn't swear to it, not in the condition I was in.…Has anyone seen Sharon Ross lately?"

"Denning's secretary?" Ozzie asked, raising an eyebrow.

"Sykes initially had her pegged as Matt's lover and accomplice, although there's not much doubt now that it was Courtney. Could she have known something that might have incriminated him?"

Ozzie didn't even bother asking if she could use the phone. She simply picked it up and dialed a number she had written in her notebook. When the connection was made, she identified herself and asked to speak with Miss Ross.

"I see," she said, after listening for a few seconds. "No, that won't be necessary; I just wondered if she had been told. I guess she has been. Thank you."

The detective recradled the receiver and turned to look at Pat and me. "Still alive and kicking. Or alive and crying, is more like it. That was her sister. Sharon Ross came home from work in tears early this afternoon after hearing about Matt's death. She's in her bedroom, still crying. Come on," Ozzie said to Pat. "You're buying."

As the two of them headed downstairs to celebrate, she called out to me over her shoulder. "Oh, by the way, the fingerprint guys came up empty when they were up here earlier. I'd sure like to borrow that Mrs. Nash of yours for a few days. There wasn't a fingerprint or smudge of any kind on that sofa arm where Courtney Howell sat or on the end table, either."

I passed up on joining them. Not only did I have to get ready for my date, I wasn't in the most festive of moods. Somehow I felt cheated. Yes, I *had* done a heck of a job investigating the case, but Matt had snatched victory away from me in the final seconds of the fourth quarter. It was like winning a game by forfeit. It shows up just fine on your won/loss record, but you know deep down inside that you didn't actually *win*.

Oh well, I had a date with Chris Panacopoulos and that definitely *was* worth celebrating, so I tried to put the whole Denning affair out of my mind.

Checking out the mirror in the bedroom I found that the makeup needed a good deal of freshening—a tad more eyeliner, eye shadow, and mascara, a bit more blush, and a deeper crimson lipstick. Rather than just add to what I had and, since nothing was going to detract from the nose, anyway, I ditched the nose guard, carefully washed my face and started over from scratch. Ignoring my good sense for vanity, I didn't reinstall the nose guard, vowing to be extra careful about where I stuck my big, still-tender schnozz.

I liked what I had done with the hair that morning, sort of the chic-unkempt image, so I left it piled on top of my head and just tidied it up a bit. Then I prowled through my good-clothes closet and selected a black jumpsuit.

Now I don't want you to get the impression that I was dressing up like Josephine the Plumber. It isn't that kind of jumpsuit at all. This one is made of silk and has flowing palazzo pants. It also has a halter top with spaghetti straps and a built-in bra that displays the tops of my boobs in a very sensuous manner.

To complete the look, I selected gold strap-sandals with two-inch heels, a hammered-gold three-inch cuff bracelet for my right wrist, and gold dangle earrings with a caged pearl at the end. Instead of wearing my stainless steel Omega Speedmaster, I decided to swap it out for a more ladylike gold Piaget Polo. After a quick spritz of Fidji, I chose my favorite necklace, a 14k gold pendant with my name inscribed on it in the ancient Celtic Ogham alphabet.

Caitlin the huntress was ready for her date, except that I couldn't fasten the tiny clasp on my necklace. Picking up a small black-beaded shoulder bag that contained just the bare essentials, I took off down the steps at about ten minutes to seven, pendant in hand.

"Here," I said to brother Pat, thrusting the necklace into his paw and turning my back to him. "Fasten this."

He struggled with it for a minute and a half; finally Mary Grace came by and took over. Thirty seconds later I sat perched on my customary stool, legs crossed, and effecting a sultry pose.

"Where's Ozzie?" I asked.

"Had one drink, then split for ballistics," Pat replied. "She was anxious to check that photomicrograph you brought back from Marion County. Excuse me for a second; I've got to see a man about a dog." He got up and hurried around the corner toward the men's room.

Why is it that guys can't just say, "Excuse me; I'm going to the restroom?" Do they really think that *we* think they actually *are* going to see someone about a dog? Of course, we don't just powder our noses, either, do we?

He was no sooner gone when Seamus approached me and put his cupped hand in my lap. "Here's something for your purse," he mumbled.

I couldn't believe it. He used to do the same thing when I was in high school, slip me a fiver, just in case my date got fresh and I had to call a cab.

"Really, Seamus," I said. "Don't you think I'm a bit old for this?"

"Not a bit. Now go ahead and take it, but don't let Mary Grace or Pat know I gave it to you."

We made the hand-to-hand transfer surreptitiously and Seamus quickly moved away from me, back down to the other end of the bar. Only after I had opened my purse to deposit the money did I realize that what I had in my hand wasn't a folded-up five-dollar bill, but a foil-wrapped condom. Before I could yell over at Seamus, brother Pat returned. I dropped the condom into my purse and closed the flap.

"Here," he said, sticking out a closed hand toward me. "Take this and put it in your purse."

"What the hell is going…" I started, but Pat interrupted.

"Just take the damn thing and keep your voice down, Katie. You never know when it might…" Too embarrassed to finish the sentence, he pushed the condom, bought from the machine in the men's room, into my hand and hurried over to check out the selections on the Wurlitzer.

Well, damn, I thought. *What do these two clowns think I am? Some sort of bimbo?*

The presence of tall-as-I, dark-as-I, and good looking-as-I (in a very masculine sort of way) Khristophoros Panacopoulos, entering through the front door in his black Armani suit, suddenly made me want to thank my brothers rather than strangle them.

"Wow," Chris said, stopping in his tracks, smiling broadly, and nodding his head in approval.

"Wow, yourself," I replied, shooting him one of my patented bemused smiles.

After introductions all around (my brothers and sister-in-law had not seen Chris since high school and all the regulars wanted a close-up look) he offered his arm and I looped mine through it.

Just as we started toward the door, Mary Grace called out. "Caitlin, may I speak with you for just a minute, please, dear?"

I turned around. She had retreated to the kitchen doorway and stood there with her finger crooked at me.

"Pull the car up," I told Chris, not wanting him to hear if Mary Grace said anything really embarrassing to me. "I'll make this short."

As he exited the pub, I stood there for a few seconds admiring his buns of steel, then answered my summons.

"What, Mary Grace? Are you going to give me a curfew?"

"No dear, come in here for a moment."

She ushered me into the kitchen, then removed something from her apron pocket and held out her hand to me. "Here, put this in your purse."

I'll be damned if it wasn't another condom.

"Mary Grace!" I started to protest, but she wouldn't let me finish.

"Now just because you have this, you don't have to feel compelled to have S E X, dear. (Yes, she spelled it out.) In fact, you know, the good Lord would prefer that you didn't until after you're married. But just in case you find yourself too weak to resist the devil's temptation, I'll feel much better knowing you have this."

While I stood there dumbfounded, she lifted the flap on my evening bag and slipped the condom inside. "There now,"—she patted my cheek—"you go and have a nice dinner with your young man. You can tell me all about it tomorrow." With that, she turned me around and propelled me through the kitchen door.

* * * *

If you ever get to Nashville, or within an hour's drive of Nashville, for that matter, you owe it to yourself to allot some meandering time and spend it wandering around the Opryland Hotel. Aside from the Convention Center, with its exhibit halls and meeting rooms, the Hotel consists of four uniquely designed areas, each having a different Southern theme.

The Magnolia and Veranda sections, the oldest of the structures, give you the feeling of being in the genteel Old South, with a grand staircase, lagoons, and decor reminiscent of the antebellum mansions.

The newest addition is the Delta section. With a river running through it, complete with small river boats on which you can ride, you get the flavor of the Mississippi and Old New Orleans.

Although the Cascades Conservatory is, in my opinion, the most beautiful section of the hotel, I have a hard time placing it in the South at all, unless maybe it's meant to represent South Africa or South

America. It reminds me of a rain forest. With its waterfalls, rock formations, and tens of thousands of tropical plants, it looks more like a set for a Tarzan movie than it does *Gone with the Wind.* Still, it's my favorite of the four areas and I always enjoy being there, whether for just a walk-through or a leisurely meal in the restaurant. I confess though, sometimes the circumstances can dictate how much you enjoy something, even in the most beautiful of surroundings.

There we sat in the white gazebo closest to the water display, silently watching the changing patterns of the Cascades Restaurant fountain. I made a mental note to have someone smack me on the back of my sore head. Less than a half hour into my dream date, I had asserted myself and trampled all over Chris' masculine ego.

Would it have been so bad, I wondered, as the water turned from bright yellow to crimson, *to have had the Stone-ground Mustard Rubbed Lamb Chops? I like lamb. Lamb is good. This lamb is probably excellent.*

But the choice of an entree was not the problem. The real problem was a cultural difference.

* * * *

The waiter had arrived, recited the litany of the specials, then looked at me. Before I could open my mouth, Chris said, "The lady will have the Crabmeat Soup, the Seafood Confetti, the Tropical Fruit Salad, and the Lamb Chops."

"Very good, sir," the waiter replied with a bright smile. "And for yourself?"

"That *was* for himself," I spoke up. "The *lady* will have the Malaysian Spiced Shrimp, the Asian-style Spinach Salad, and the Pasta with Portobello and Porcini Mushrooms, Westphalian Ham, and Shrimp."

Our waiter just stood there, eyes wide and mouth open.

"Did you get that?" I asked, somewhat snappishly.

"Y...yes, ma'am," he said, hurriedly writing down my order. Then he turned to Chris. "M...may I get you anything from the bar?"

"I'll have Gentleman Jack on the rocks," Chris replied. "You'll have to ask the *lady* what *she'd* like."

"M...m...may I..." he started.

"Baileys, also on the rocks," I said. And as he scurried away from the table, I called out after him, "Make it a double!"

* * * *

So there we sat, him sipping his Tennessee Whiskey and me with my Irish Cream, neither of us knowing what to say next.

Damn, damn, damn, I chastised myself. *It's a first date, you moron. Don't you know that on a first date your IQ is supposed to be smaller than your bra size?*

The plan had been to have dinner at the Opryland Hotel, then dessert, after-dinner drinks, and conversation at Zakinthos. Since Nico had come down with a cold and wanted to leave his restaurant early that night, Chris had to be there in his father's absence to schmooze with the guests and close up the place. The plans for afterward had been intentionally left indefinite. Now, I feared, they had been solidified—home as soon as he could get me there, and me in bed with W.B. Whoopee!

Stupid, stupid, stupid!

"Nice fountain," Chris said finally, still looking away from me and sipping his drink.

"Yeah. Really. Beautiful plants, too." I didn't look at him, either.

"Yeah," he said and, out of the corner of my eye, I saw him glance my way. "I'll bet the humidity from all this water is really good for them."

"Yeah. Must be," I agreed and turned to look at him. God, he was gorgeous. "After dinner we could take a walk through the conservatory...if...if you'd like. If we have time, that is." I hoped that didn't sound as desperate to him as it did to me.

He reached over and took my hand. "Let's make time. And...I'm sorry, Caitlin. Sometimes the Old World creeps up on me before I realize it."

I slid over on the semicircular bench toward him. "I'm sorry, too. Sometimes the New World comes blundering out of me before *I* realize it."

We attempted a kiss, but couldn't coordinate the positions of our aquiline noses. Because mine was so sore, I was extra careful, trying to correctly position his face with my hand. The result was both pitiful and brief.

"Maybe we can work on that in the conservatory," I suggested.

He smiled warmly. "I like the sound of that. Khristophoros Panacopoulos in the conservatory with Miss...excuse me...Ms. O'Rourke."

We both laughed and toasted each other, emptying the remaining gulp we each had in our glasses. Looking over toward the artificial rock cave that served as a bar, I had intended to flag down the cocktail waitress for a refill. Instead, I almost slid off the bench onto the floor, but not because of mixing alcohol with the painkillers. A well-dressed, portly, balding man in his middle fifties sat at a table for two, holding hands with an at-least-ten-years-younger, beautiful, buxom blonde—the same beautiful blonde as in the picture at Courtney Howell's town house.

"Hold that thought," I told Chris. "I'll be right back."

With the words of those frantic phone calls that were left on Courtney's answering machine running through my mind, I quickly exited our gazebo and crossed down to the bar area, coming up on the woman from behind.

"Excuse me," I said, touching her shoulder. "You're Greta, aren't you?"

She turned toward me and I could see the look of nonrecognition in her crystal blue eyes. Her dinner companion, however, looked positively frightened. His eyes widened and he glanced furtively about the dining area as if he were waiting for a lion to pounce from the shrubbery.

Damn, I thought as I looked down at her low-cut, sequined sheath and the realization suddenly hit me. *She's a hooker like Courtney. And she's working. This isn't a friendly dinner. It's a business transaction.*

"I'm sorry," I said. "We've never met, but I know you're a friend of Courtney Howell's and I just thought that..."

"Have you heard from her?" Greta asked, relief flooding her face. "I've been worried sick about her."

"I hate to interrupt your...your...your whatever, here, Greta, but can we go somewhere and talk for a few minutes?" I asked.

"Oh, God." The relief turned to panic as she picked up something in my tone of voice. "What's happened to her? Is she hurt? Where is she? Is she going to be all right?"

I took hold of the woman gently by the upper arm and guided her out of the chair. "Come on. Let's take a walk in the conservatory. We can talk there."

I'm afraid that my refusal to answer her questions right there on the spot telegraphed the truth.

"Oh, no," Greta whined, pulling back. "Please don't tell me she's dead. Please? Anything but that?" She had to grab onto the table to steady herself and then she began to cry.

By now the portly man had figured out that this *was* just a personal matter and not the blackmail setup he had initially suspected. Realizing that no photographer would jump out of the bushes, he had gathered a little courage.

"Hey!" he said, rising from his chair and grabbing Greta by the other arm. "What are you two little fillies trying to pull here? I paid for two hours."

Rather than play tug of war with him, using Greta, who was gradually getting limper and limper, as the rope, I tried another tack.

"Do you already have the room rented?" I whispered seductively, crossing over to him, putting my arm around him and pulling him in close to me. He was shorter than me and his double chin rested on the tops of my boobs.

"Yeah," he said, eyes getting bigger and rounder.

"I need to talk to my sister, here, I whispered, breathing the words directly into his ear. It's a family matter and it'll take only about fifteen minutes of your two hours. But we'll make it up to you; I promise. Why don't you go to the room and get ready for us."

"U…us? You mean, like the both of you?" He licked his lips and swallowed hard.

"We're both in the same business. Haven't you ever had a two-fer? With sisters?"

"N…no. N…never." He wet his lips again. "Honest to God? A…a two-fer?"

"Give me your room key," I told him. "Then go to the front desk and tell them you locked yourself out. When they let you in, take a nice hot shower and wait for us. We'll be there in a little while. Fifteen, twenty minutes. Half an hour, tops. Okay?"

"O…o…okay," he said, thrusting the room key into my hand, throwing a twenty on the table to cover the drinks, and then bolting away in the direction of the registration desk.

Seeing that Greta would never make it to the conservatory, I had her retake her chair. I pulled the second one around beside her and began the distasteful task of telling her about what had happened to the best friend she had in the entire world.

* * * *

Greta Bergstrom had been sobbing uncontrollably, head down on the table and buried in her arms. The sobs had only just recently tapered off to whimpers. I had given her the whole story, from the fake mugging in the alley to the recovery of Courtney's body from the Cumberland. During the course of the last forty minutes, she had downed a half dozen double Scotches while I nursed one Baileys. Maybe that's why her sobbing had tapered off. She was numb.

When the waiter arrived at my former table with the first course, I had waved over to Chris in a sort of sign language, telling him not to wait, but to go ahead and start without me. Now I wondered if I'd even get to take that walk through the conservatory with him. Greta was in no condition to drive and I certainly couldn't leave her there in her state of drunkenness. After all, it was I who had kept the drinks coming and had put her in that state.

"It looks like you're going to be tied up for a while longer," Chris said, coming down to us after he had finished eating and handing me a doggy-bag and a key ring. "Here's your dinner and the keys to my car. I've really got to get over and relieve Pop. I'll catch a cab."

I tried to mask the relief I felt. Giving me the car was his insurance policy that he'd see me again. And I had been wondering if, after tonight, he'd ever want to. I guess I underestimated my charm, or the low-cut halter. Whichever, I'd take it.

"Thanks, Chris. I'll bring it back to you tomorrow and explain everything then. I promise. And I'll make it up to you for tonight. That's another promise." Unlike the same promise I had made earlier to Greta's companion, this one I fully intended to keep.

We did a better job of nose-coordination with the goodnight kiss. Much better. I truly looked forward to seeing him the next day. Those condoms were starting to burn a hole in my purse.

Fifteen minutes and another Scotch later, even Greta's whimpering had subsided. She was almost comatose. A twenty-dollar tip for the waiter brought one of the bellmen with a wheel chair and we headed toward the Cascades Lobby entrance to ransom Chris' Town Car.

While we waited for the valet to bring the Lincoln around, a bus from the Second Church of Christ's Prophesy in Ashtabula, Ohio, pulled up. Out of it filed a group of orderly, polite, clean-cut youth missionaries, here for a four-day conference.

Two girls, aged fourteen or fifteen, spotting the wheel chair, approached Greta, and, in a solemn voice, one of them said, "If you truly believe that Jesus Christ is your Lord and Savior, he can make you well. We'll pray for you."

Greta raised her head slightly to give them an unfocused look, then nodded off again.

Rather than be a smart-aleck and ask if their Lord and Savior had any black coffee on Him, I smiled and said, "Your prayers are appreciated, but we have a friend here at the hotel who could use them even more."

Their eyes grew bright with the fires of evangelistic anticipation and I continued. "In fact, he could use some counseling, too. He's so depressed, I'm worried that he's on the verge of...of doing something with...uh...to himself."

"What can we do?" the spokesperson of the twosome asked. "We'll do anything we can to help. Is he a Christian?"

From my religious studies, I don't ever remember Christ asking what religion people were before he helped them. Rather than point that out to my two youthful zealots, though, I took the room key that Greta's companion had given me and said, "He desperately wants Heaven. Here. Get one of the adults and go to this room as quickly as you can. I've been away too long already and I'm really frightened for him."

The talky one grabbed the key and both girls ran over to a middle-aged woman with her salt-and-pepper hair in a bun. As the valet helped Greta into the car, I watched the three angels hurry off to save another poor soul.

Maybe I should have given them the condoms along with the key.

*   *   *   *

The combination of the half-hour drive to Greta Bergstrom's Brentwood condo, a cold shower, and a pot of strong coffee had sobered her up, reasonably so, anyway.

"It's all my fault," she kept whining over and over again. "Court's dead because of me."

"No she's not," I assured her, trying my best to be comforting but failing miserably.

"It's true!" she insisted. "I'm the one who told Court about the audition. If it hadn't been for me, she never would have gotten the part."

"Excuse me?…What part? What audition?"

"It was supposed to be the Julia Roberts' part. You know, like in the movie *Pretty Woman*? We were told that a businessman needed a make-believe wife for six days to fool a client into thinking he was married. It was only supposed to be a game. No one was supposed to get hurt."

"But wasn't Courtney Matt Denning's mistress?" I asked.

"No, of course not. We didn't even know the client's name. In fact, those of us who didn't get the part never even saw his face. Not even at the audition." Then came more tears. "And I'm the one who told Court about the audition. And now she's dead."

While Greta sat there sobbing, curled up in her four-poster canopied bed, I tried to figure out what had just happened to my entire scenario of Delane Denning's murder.

"Tell me about these auditions," I said. "Where were they and how did you find out about them?" I handed Greta a tissue. She dabbed her eyes and blew her nose, then after a tremendous sigh, she told me her story.

"A friend of ours, Wendy Tabor. She works the Printers' Alley area. Some guy came up to her and told her about it. Said it paid five-thousand dollars and that no sex was involved. That whoever got the part just had to pretend to be a businessman's wife in front of a client."

"Who was the guy? Do you know?"

"No. He was at the auditions but he never said his name. A little guy. Pimply face and a runny nose."

Junior, I thought. *It figures.* "Tell me, what sort of audition was it that you didn't see anyone but the little guy. His name was Junior, by the way."

"It was at the Opryland Hotel. In the Veranda section. Midway down the hall in two adjoining rooms. Everyone had a time-slot. Fifteen minutes apart. That was important to them, the timing. We were told that right up front. I don't think they wanted any of us to see our competition. If we were more than one minute early or late, we would be disqualified. We were to wear a bathing suit underneath a trenchcoat. We came to the first room and we'd wait there. Then this guy...this Junior would let us into the adjoining room where the audition was. There were bright lights shining in our eyes so that we couldn't see who was behind them. We figured it was the client, this businessman. Junior told us to walk to the center of the room, take off the trenchcoat, make a full turn, then stand there and tell him something about ourselves. Then he told us to put our coats back on and he let us out of the audition room into the hallway. We were supposed to go directly out to our cars and leave. Everyone got a hundred dollars just for showing up."

"The only voice you heard was Junior's and you never saw anyone else?"

"That's right. Apparently I wasn't what they wanted because I didn't even get to take my coat off. I walked to the center of the room while Junior went behind the lights. Almost immediately he said "Thank you," came back around to the front and let me out. Court, though, spent her whole fifteen minutes in there, walking back and forth in her bathing suit and talking. She told me that this Junior asked her if she would dye her hair, she said sure and he told her he'd be in touch. That was on Saturday afternoon. That night Court got paged and left Sunday morning."

"For where?"

"I don't know. And neither did she. She had me drive her downtown and drop her off by the Broadway Dinner Train. That's the last time I saw her, standing there with her suitcase and blowing a kiss to me as I drove out of the parking lot."

The sobbing returned, but Greta tried to continue in between convulsions. "I didn't like the idea of not knowing where she'd be. But she told me not to worry, that we take chances every day with every john. She promised she'd call me as soon as she got home."

I pulled the comforter up around her, sat on the edge of the bed, and stroked her hair. "If it's any consolation, both Junior, who killed Courtney, and the guy behind the lights, who ordered it, are both dead." Having said that, I kissed her on the cheek and crossed toward the door.

"Kate," she called out after me.

I turned. "Yes, Greta?"

"It's not really that much consolation at all, but what about the third person?"

"What third person?"

"In the audition room. There were two people behind the lights."

"I thought you couldn't see?"

"I couldn't. But there were two of them. I could…sense it…sort of."

"Get some rest," I told her, flipping off the bedroom light. "I'll let myself out. And Greta?"

"Yes?"

"It wasn't your fault."

"Then whose was it?"

I could hear her start to cry again as I closed the bedroom door. *It's as much my fault as anyone's,* I thought. *If I hadn't let Courtney go into that house by herself, she might still be alive.... Then again, we both might be dead.*

On the drive home I pondered the new information gleaned from Greta Bergstrom. If Courtney wasn't Matt's mistress and only an actress playing a part, then she had absolutely no idea Delane would be murdered. But if she wasn't Matt's mistress, who was? Sharon Ross? Hmmm?

Had I been wrong in my earlier assessment of Miss Mousy's capability for murder? Could her love, or lust, for Matt Denning have been that strong? And I had seen her organization skills at the mortuary, the way she had stage-managed the entire affair to keep everything moving along smoothly. From what Greta had told me, the *Pretty Woman* auditions had moved along like clockwork, also.

I decided to wait until morning to fill in Ozzie on the evening's developments. It was late; I was tired and hungry; my head hurt; my nose hurt; and I needed to think about things with a clearer brain rather than, once again, crying wolf.

*   *   *   *

Shoving my appetizer and entree into the microwave, I downed a pair of Orudis, got W.B. her dinner and a fresh drink, then started in on my now-wilted salad. The nuked pasta dish wasn't bad, but the Piri Piri sauce on the spiced shrimp turned out to be much too hot for me to handle. I sprung for the fridge, opened a bottle of Red Mountain Golden Lager, and downed the cool liquid in five gulps.

With dinner, such as it was, over, I took a narcissistic look in the full-length mirror on my closet door and thought about the lost opportunity with Chris. I assured myself that opportunity would, indeed, knock a second time, then I undressed, removed my watch, bracelet, and earrings, and sat there in front of the vanity in only my black, queen-size Underalls, trying to undo the clasp on my Ogham pendant.

After three or four futile minutes, I muttered, "Screw it! I'll have Mary Grace get it in the morning," and performed the ritual of the hair. Then I brushed my teeth, in an attempt to purge my mouth of the taste of Malaysian Spiced Shrimp, changed into my nighttime bra and Bobcat sleepshirt, collapsed on my bed, and fell asleep thinking of Courtney Howell.

Bad move. Those thoughts triggered my recurring nightmare and, as in previous dreams, it played out in slow motion.

This time, however, I wasn't in my usual starting position next to Liddy, waving at Matt Denning as he pulled his Mercedes into the driveway. I was already at the front door, looking in at the bloody, faceless body of Delane Denning.

At the sound of a car horn from behind me, I glanced up from Delane's garnet-and-pearl lavaliere to watch Junior Lee Thigpen fire two blasts from a shotgun through the open French doors and then frantically motion for a horrified Courtney Howell to exit.

Although she still had the crows from Monday night's dream sitting on her shoulders, she was now dressed in a trenchcoat that hung open in front, revealing her striking figure in a gold mesh bathing suit. Tears were streaming down her cheeks. She blew me a kiss and ran out into the yard as Junior started toward me, shotgun held by the barrel like a baseball bat.

Instead of watching him, though, my eyes were, for some strange reason, drawn back to Delane's necklace. Just before I got smacked in the nose with the gun butt, the garnet-and-pearl lavaliere morphed into my gold pendant with the Ogham inscription.

I awoke, drenched in sweat, heart racing, with both hands clasped around that pendant.

Oh my God!

I found the scrap of paper in my evening bag, dialed the number on it, and waited. When a sleepy voice answered on the other end of the line, I said, "It's Caitlin O'Rourke. I need your help."

Chapter 19

Checking my watch for perhaps the half-dozenth time in a space of less than two minutes, I wondered if, perhaps, the velocity of the folding chair on which I sat had somehow approached the speed of light. Time definitely seemed to be slowing down.

Come on! I thought. *Let's get this show on the road!*

I got up and turned to Ozzie. She had traded her tailored yellow pantsuit for an untailored green one belonging to the Opryland Hotel housekeeping staff. Now she looked like one of the many black maids that invisibly move among the guests.

Before I could open my mouth to speak, she whispered, "You look fine," then heaved a sigh of frustration. "You looked fine a half hour ago when you first asked, twenty minutes ago when you asked a second time, ten minutes ago when you asked again, and now. If you ask me one more time how you look, Kate, I'm going to take out my pistol and shoot you. Now sit down! Trust me. I've worked as a vice decoy and you could pass for that big, blond hooker any day of the week."

I sat, as best I could in the skin-tight jeans, brushed a lock of blond wig-hair from my eyes and looked at my watch again. Five more minutes to go.

* * * *

The early morning hours had been frantic. My first phone call, placed just after waking up from the dream, had been to Greta Bergstrom.

"I need your help," I had told her, then I had gone on to explain that I knew who the third person at the audition was but couldn't prove it without her.

"Did this person have anything to do with Court's death?" she asked.

"Probably planned it, Greta."

"Whatever you want, just tell me." Gone were the tears and the whimpers. Her words held a steely resolve.

After briefly outlining my plan, I had told Greta to stand by her phone, then I called Pat. He had been a much harder sell, but after I had gone through the entire scenario for him and he could come up with no alternate explanation to support the facts, he had called Ozzie. That call, in turn, had set up a chain reaction—Ozzie to me, Ozzie to Sykes, then to her lieutenant, then back to me again.

She had begun each of her phone calls to me with the identical sentence. "Are you certain about this, Kate?"

Each time I had given her the same answer. "Dead certain, Ozzie. Not a doubt in my mind."

* * * *

Pat had gotten Bobbie Deerfield out of bed and had driven her to The Foresters' Hunting Lodge. As I arrived in Chris' Town Car, Ozzie was just pulling into the lot with Greta Bergstrom. Apparently Greta's ride in the little Sunfire had been as uncomfortable as mine the day Ozzie and I had gone to the dentist. She unfolded herself, struggled out of the car, and rubbed her knees.

With the hundreds of wigs in The Foresters' costume room, Bobbie had no trouble matching one of them with Greta's natural hairdo. A bit of scissors and curling-iron work and in no time at all I looked like the big Viking's twin, from the back anyway. Our skin tones were miles apart. A trip to the makeup room minimized that problem.

Next, we (including Bobbie Deerfield, hairdressing equipment and makeup kit in hand) headed up to the Sheplers store on Gallatin Pike. Sykes met us there with the manager, still a bit blurry-eyed from being rousted out at that time of the morning.

With skin-tight black jeans, black boots, white sweetheart neckline blouses from the store and Wonder Bras (mine borrowed from Greta), she and I looked enough alike from a distance to be one and the same (or two and the same, depending on whether or not you had the same focal point as Detective Sykes).

The time had come for Greta to place *her* phone call. Thank God we had the managing director from a theatre group with us. This was probably the first time the big blonde had an occasion to act in a vertical position and needed plenty of coaching and rehearsal.

After about twenty minutes of working with Greta, Bobbie excused herself from her pupil and came over to where the rest of us nervously waited. Shrugging her shoulders she said, "This is as good as it's going to get, people. My advice is to go with it now before she loses her nerve."

The script had been relatively straightforward: *I know who you are and what you did. I saw you in the audition room with Matt Denning and Junior Lee Thigpen. The price for my silence is fifty-thousand dollars. Bring it in a briefcase to the Conservatory at the Opryland Hotel. Today. Enter the Conservatory from the Cascades Restaurant, stay on the lower level and take the path on the north side of the building. About halfway through, you'll go up a set of steps to a lions-head fountain. There are two benches opposite the fountain. At exactly twelve noon, place the briefcase behind the western bench, continue on the path, and head out into the*

Delta section. Keep moving and don't look back. Get on a Delta River flatboat and congratulate yourself on getting away with murder.

In case of any protest or interruption, Greta was to be firm and say, "Shut up, listen, and do exactly what I tell you or the next call I make is to the cops!"

Ozzie dialed the number for a cellular phone and handed the receiver to Greta. There had been no interruptions. The big blonde finished her spiel with only two minor hesitations and quickly hung up. Her entire body trembled. So struck with fear was she that her normal pale skin tone had approached that of an albino. While everyone else applauded Greta's performance, I gave her a big hug.

The site selection at the hotel had been carefully planned. From the specified drop-off point there was only one logical choice for an escape route—into the north corridor of the hotel, west about forty or so yards, and out into the parking lot. Although an extremely sweet girl, Greta was no rocket scientist. We wanted to make the plan as obviously simple as we could so that it would seem like she had orchestrated the operation herself. Also, a housekeeping storage room, located just few yards down from the fountain, provided a perfect spot for Greta and me to switch places.

Deliberately making the call four hours before the scheduled drop would not only give our target time to gather the money, but time to reconnoiter the drop-off site as well. During that time, Ozzie had Greta periodically walk the length of the Conservatory's upper level and look anxiously down at the lions-head fountain. Anyone waiting and watching would have no doubt about the identity of the person making the pickup, or that person's amateur status.

* * * *

"She's on the move," Sykes' voice crackled through Ozzie's hand-held walkie-talkie. "But, like we figured, it's not the target. Repeat. It's not the target."

From his perch high up in room 54242, the detective commanded a view of the entire Conservatory.

Our target would be too smart to deliver the money in person, that we all had agreed on, but would hire some schmo to do it, then wait outside to ambush Greta in the parking lot. Pat and about a half-dozen officers, dressed as bellmen or groundskeepers, went about simulated duties, but all the while kept watch on the path I would take from the exit door to Chris' Lincoln.

"The briefcase is in place," Sykes radioed. "Pigeon continuing on toward the east entrance....Okay, Greta's on her way....She's got it....Coming your way...and should be about...now!"

Ozzie flung open the door to the housekeeping storage room and the timing couldn't have been more perfect. As Greta and I passed each other, her coming in and me going out, she handed me the briefcase and Ozzie quickly closed the door behind me. The switch had been made in less than three seconds.

I continued into the north corridor of the hotel, made a left turn and headed for the exit. "In the corridor," I whispered, hoping that the microphone tucked away deep in my cleavage was working. "No one in sight except a maid cleaning one of the rooms."

I was now halfway down the corridor. Both rooms 50220 and 50222 had their doors open with the maid's trolley parked between them. A green-pantsuited woman with her back toward me bent over, stuffing sheets into a laundry bag. No sooner had I stepped around both maid and cart when I felt cold steel behind my right ear and a hand roughly grabbed my left shoulder.

"Into the room," a voice hissed and the hand shoved me into room 50220.

I recovered my balance, raised my free arm over my head, and just stood in the center of the room. In one corner, a young Hispanic woman huddled in her bra and panties, tied, gagged, blindfolded, and obviously scared half to death.

I heard the door close behind us and the voice snapped another order. "Toss the case onto the bed, then put both hands over your head."

"Sure, Mel," I replied. "Anything you say." As the briefcase bounced on the bed, I could hear Melinda Huntington gasp.

I turned around slowly to face her. "Boo," I said, using my childhood nickname. "Surprised to see me?" Since she just stood there, speechless, leveling a chrome-plated revolver at my mid-section, I continued. "Guess so. What now, Mel?"

She didn't take very long to recover from her shock. Still pointing the revolver at me, she backed me up with her other hand. "Sit down and keep quiet, Kate," she said, crossing to the window and looking through the curtains into the Conservatory. "You just couldn't leave well enough alone, could you?"

"But it wasn't well enough, Mel. Now, it almost is."

"What are you talking about?"

I cautiously reached down into my cleavage with thumb and forefinger and brought out a miniature transmitter. "Amazing the delights big boobs can hold, isn't it," I said, flashing my bemused smile at her.

Melinda grabbed the transmitter, smacked me across the face with the back of her gun-hand, and crushed the little plastic box under her foot. "That wasn't very bright on your part, Kate. Not very bright at all."

"Quite the contrary," I said, wiping a trickle of blood from the corner of my mouth while saying a private prayer of thanks that I had turned quickly enough and hadn't caught the blow on my unguarded nose. "Now I can explain the facts of life to you *off* the record."

"What facts. No one knows where you are."

"Oh, come on, Mel. How long do you think it's going to take the police to do a room-to-room in this one corridor? Fifteen minutes? Twenty?"

"By that time you'll be dead."

"Actually, I think not," I said, smiling again. "And here's why. Do you know who's out there with the police, Mel?" I took her silence for an unspoken, "No, please tell me?" so I did. "My brother Pat, Mel. And what I didn't want broadcast over that transmitter is his solemn vow that if I'm harmed in any way at all, he'll make sure that you're shot dead trying to escape. No arrest; no trial; no prison sentence. His own personal death sentence, Mel. The choice is yours."

Melinda gave it about three seconds worth of consideration, then shook her head and sat on one of the chairs. She still had the gun, so I didn't press the issue. I just waited for her to decide on whether her life was worth mine. The decision didn't take her very long.

"How did you figure it out?" she asked.

I could tell from her tone of voice that she had resigned herself to the inevitable, so I rose, crossed to her, and held out my hand. "Give me the gun, Mel."

The look in her eyes as she raised her face to mine showed one last flicker of trigger-pulling desire, then it faded and she handed me the revolver, butt first. "How?" she asked again.

"The detectives were sure all along that my subconscious knew something important about Delane's murder, but I only realized what it was last night." Backing up to my seat on the edge of the bed, I pointed at her garnet-and-pearl lavaliere. "It was the necklace, Mel. I finally figured it out."

"I don't understand."

"Two necklaces, one for Delane and one for you, made perfect sense at the funeral parlor when we didn't know about the wife-switch. But those two necklaces were actually worn by *three* women…Delane, you, *and* Courtney Howell."

She shook her head. Recognition still had not set in.

"Up at Cove Creek," I continued, "I must have fastened that necklace a half-dozen times around Courtney's neck."

"That was the plan," Melinda broke in. "So that when you saw it on Delane, you would be all the more convinced."

"But it wasn't *that* necklace on your sister, Mel. It couldn't have been. There wasn't enough time between when Courtney entered the house and I got to the front door for anyone to make the switch. Certainly not with a necklace having a clasp as difficult to fasten and unfasten as that one. That meant Delane had to have already been wearing hers when she was killed. And, if so, then where did Courtney get the one she wore at Cove Creek? It had to have been yours, Mel. Once I understood that, everything else fell into place."

Melinda reached up, massaged her eyes with both hands and sighed. As I watched, her face seemed to age fifteen years in mere seconds. All the vibrancy left her body with that one sigh.

"I couldn't prove that Courtney Howell had been the person with me in Cove Creek," I went on. "Matt, or you *and* Matt, burned down my garage, ruining my car so that her fingerprints couldn't be recovered from it. And you lured me down there to eliminate me as well."

I had expected—no, hoped—to get some sort of reaction from her with that last statement, but didn't. There was no protest, no, "Not me, it was Matt," or, "We never intended to harm you, Kate." She didn't so much as glance in my direction, but just sat there contemplating her fate. That absence of a direct response, though, confirmed that she *had* been involved and that my attack in the alley *had* been deliberate.

"When the fingerprint team dusted my sofa and end table," I continued, "they couldn't find Courtney's prints there, either. We didn't really expect them to, though. My cleaning lady had come in while we were up at Cove Creek and had given everything a complete going-over. In retrospect, Mel, there *should* have been fingerprints. Yours. From Saturday night when you sat in the same spot as Courtney did, all teary-eyed and clutching your handkerchief. Matt must have told you exactly where Courtney had sat and you used that handkerchief to try and wipe away any trace of her prints. Actually, the only prints you succeeded in eliminating were your own."

"Are you quite through?" Melinda asked, wearily.

"Almost, Mel. Then there was the fishing cottage down on the Minnedosa. You were so helpful. You didn't even hesitate to give me directions. After all, you had nothing to hide. Junior had gotten rid of the only person who had seen your sister there. But, Mel, the construction on State Road #28 only started a couple of weeks ago. For you to have known about it, you had to have been there *with* your sister while Courtney and I were in Cove Creek."

Melinda's eyes narrowed slightly and I could see that she was upset with herself over that slip-up. She had planned everything else so well.

"Just one last thing," I said. "You should have been a little more creative after you killed Matt. Remember, by then I had already figured out that Junior had fired two shots through the living room French doors to make it seem like he had just killed Delane. If Matt *had* committed suicide, there should have been one bullet left in the revolver. However, you both had handled it and *your* prints were on the gun, too, Mel. You couldn't just wipe it clean, it had to have Matt's prints on it. So, after you shot him, you wiped your prints from the gun, then placed it in his hand. But then you realized that the police would check Matt's hands for powder residue. Maybe they'd still have some from when he shot the dog earlier that morning in the alley, but, then again, maybe not. You couldn't take the chance. So you forced Matt's dead finger to fire the last bullet out through the French doors in the den."

That *did* get a reaction from her, but not one that I would have expected. Just a slight smile and an even slighter nod. I had seen it before, many times on the B-ball or V-ball court after I had made an exceptionally brilliant play. An opponent would just smile slightly and give a little nod of her head—an unspoken tribute that said, "Nice move, Katie-Kat. Nice move."

"Now I'm through, Mel," I told her. "Except for just one question.…Why?"

She gave a tired little laugh, got up from her chair and walked to the window. "You're a sentimentalist, Kate. You'd like me to tell you that Matthew and I were deeply in love and that Delane wouldn't let him go. But the truth is, I did it for the money. Pure and simple. The money."

"But your own sister?"

"Oil and water, Kate. Always were." Then she laughed again. "Except at the end. When Delane overheard Matthew on the phone arranging to see his lover, she didn't stay on the line long enough to find out that the lover was me. She hung up immediately and decided to divorce him. And I was the one she came to for consolation. Can you believe it? I was having an affair with her husband and plotting her death, and my sister came to *me* for consolation. Even rewrote her will, leaving me everything. Wasn't that touching? That's when I decided that I didn't have to share the money with Matthew. Once we had disposed of Delane, I could arrange his suicide and have it all for myself."

"You disgust me, Mel."

"You know, Kate, sometimes I even disgust myself." She laughed again, this time from down deep in her throat, then gestured toward the door. "Lead the way, dear. I wouldn't want that brother of yours to shoot the first person coming out of this room."

I stood, crossed to the door and opened it, saying, "It's okay, guys, I've got her gun and we're coming out."

No sooner had I finished when I realized that Melinda Huntington had not been silently contemplating her fate as I had supposed. She had been hatching her escape plan. A tearing sound made me turn to look at her. She had ripped her green pantsuit top away from one shoulder.

As Sykes and Ozzie rushed in past me, weapons drawn, and badge cases visible, Melinda started screaming her head off. "Oh, thank God you're here! Thank God! Get the gun, get the gun before she kills me! She's a blackmailer. She tried to extort money from me. Thank God you've come! Arrest her! Her accomplice is somewhere in the hotel. A woman dressed just like her. Oh, thank God!"

"What are you talking about?" Ozzie asked, looking back and forth from Melinda to Sykes, then to me. "It's you who's under arrest, Ms.

Huntington, for the murder of Matthew Denning and for conspiracy to murder Delane Denning, Junior Lee Thigpen, Swallow Sedlacek, and Bernard Tibbets."

"And the attempted murder of Caitlin O'Rourke," Sykes added.

"But *I* didn't kill anyone," Melinda protested. "My brother-in-law killed my sister and those other people, then took his own life. This woman, here, tried to blackmail me. The money's there in that briefcase. Her prints must be all over the handle. Arrest her!"

"We have you on tape," Ms. Huntington, Ozzie said, "Ordering Miss O'Rourke into this room and telling her to toss the briefcase onto the bed. It was clear from what we heard that you had the gun."

"I only tried to capture a blackmailer," Melinda argued. "I was getting ready to call the police when she overpowered me and took the gun. If you hadn't come in when you did, she would have killed me. Ask the maid," she said, pointing at the helpless little creature in the corner. "Ask her. She heard the whole thing."

Until then, neither detective had noticed the third person in the room. While Sykes kept Melinda covered, Ozzie holstered her weapon, then proceeded to unbind and ungag the woman—a big mistake.

"*Ayúdeme! Ayúdeme! Policía! Ayúdeme!*" the maid screamed, lashing out with hands and feet at Ozzie and catching the detective on the shoulder with one of her kicks. "*Policía*!"

"I *am* the police!" Ozzie yelled back, warding off the blows and pointing at the badge hanging from the pocket of her own maid's outfit. "Me, police. *Policía*. Okay?"

The maid quieted and nodded, wide-eyed, looking around the room in terror.

"Calm down," Ozzie told her, taking the bedspread and tossing it over the girl's near nakedness. "Tell me what you heard these two women talking about?"

"*No comprendo! No comprendo!*"

Ozzie stood up and turned away from the frightened maid. "Swell. She can't speak English. Any more bright ideas, Ms. Huntington? Shall I question the table or the chair? Why don't you just tell us the truth?"

"But I am," Melinda whined. "Someone called me and told me that if I didn't pay her fifty-thousand dollars, she'd link me to my sister's murder. I thought I'd play along and maybe learn something that would help the police. This is the woman who picked up the money. It's Kate. She's a blackmailer. And, quite possibly, a murderer, too."

Pat entered the room, glanced quickly at me to see that I was all right, then approached Melinda. "Nice try," he said, clapping his hands together mockingly. "Very nice."

Melinda backed up to the wall, yelling, "Keep him away from me! He's in on it with her! She told me that if I didn't give her the money, he'd have me killed."

"That's not what I said, Mel," I spoke up.

"You did! You said if I didn't pay, your brother would kill me."

"Actually, according to the tape," Pat broke in, "what Katie said was that if you killed *her*, I'd see to it that you were shot trying to escape. Now, of course, that was merely conjecture on my sister's part, mind you, because as an officer of the law, I'd never do any such thing."

Melinda took one look at the smashed transmitter on the floor, then at Pat. "What tape?"

In answer, Pat removed a cassette player from the pocket of his groundskeeper jacket and thumbed the PLAY button. Melinda's disembodied voice emanated from the small speaker.

Can you believe it? I was the one having an affair with her husband and plotting her death, and my sister came to me for consolation. Even rewrote her will, leaving me everything. Wasn't that touching?

"Quite touching, indeed," Pat said, shutting off the tape player.

Again Melinda looked at the shattered transmitter on the hotel room floor, then at me.

I reached a thumb and forefinger deep down into my cleavage for a second time, turning away from B. J. Sykes' hungry eyes, and withdrew a second transmitter.

"The bigger the boobs, the more delights they can hold," I said to Melinda and gave her another one of my patented smiles. Only this time, I didn't really care if it came across more like a smirk than bemused.

The phrase, *If looks could kill*, seems a rather inadequate description for the glare Melinda Huntington fixed on me. I'm sure that killing would have been far less painful than what she had in mind.

"Book her, Ozzie-O," I said, handing Melinda's revolver to the detective. "Murder-one."

Ozzie, Pat, and Sykes all laughed. Melinda Huntington glowered. The maid just sat there in the corner, clutching the spread around her, thoroughly confused.

* * * *

I didn't go with the detectives when they took Melinda in. Instead, I used the vacant room to wash the theatrical makeup off my skin and change out of the hooker apparel back into my own clothes.

The woman who had made the money-drop for Melinda Huntington indeed turned out to be an innocent, albeit greedy bystander. Melinda had given her fifty bucks and some story about not wanting her boss' wife to see her returning the guy's briefcase, which he had left in her room the night before.

After I had cleaned up, Greta Bergstrom and I had lunch at the Cascades Restaurant and talked about Courtney. Before he left, Sykes had told me that Trish Zelasko had released Courtney's remains and that I could have them picked up anytime. I mentioned that to Greta, along with my plans for seeing to Courtney's funeral.

"That's very sweet of you, Kate," Greta said, squeezing my hand. "But…I'll take care of the arrangements."

I nodded and told her I understood, then asked, "May I come, though."

"Oh certainly, Kate. You must! That isn't what I meant at all. It's just that Court and I were...very, very close."

Remembering the good-bye kiss that Courtney had given me, I really *did* understand. She may have given her body to men, but her love she reserved for those who didn't make demands on or take advantage of her.

"Since not many of our friends are as big as you and me," Greta continued, "would you consider being a pall bearer? I'm sure Court would like that."

I agreed. Greta told me she'd call with the details, (probably a Saturday-morning funeral). We cheek-kissed and went our separate ways, she to ransom her car, left there overnight, and I to the self-park lot and then on to the Panacopoulos residence.

I had to return Chris' car, of course, but mainly I intended to force old Opportunity into knocking twice.

Chapter 20

Nikolaos Panacopoulos could have lived anywhere he wanted. He could have bought and sold most of the people in Forest Hills. He could have built a mansion. But Uncle Nico had no use for mansions, nor the people who built them just to impress their associates.

"What I need with all that room?" he would ask, whenever someone brought up the subject. "Me and Delia, we would rattle around like...well, take my word on it. Delia and I, we would rattle."

Instead, the Panacopoulosses had a very nice, functional, medium-large home in West Meade that backed up onto the Hillwood Golf Course.

I still harbored bad feelings for Chris' mother Delia about her *shanty Irish* remark of many years ago and had hoped to avoid seeing her. All the way over, I prayed that Chris would answer the door himself and not invite me in. That we'd hop back into his car, he'd drive me to Kehough's, and we'd plan our next date together up in my quarters.

Some prayers are answered; some are not. Although, according to Turlough, all prayers are answered. There are times, he maintains, when God just flat-out says, "No." This must have been one of those times.

The chimes had not yet fallen silent when the front door opened and the angel of death stood there, outfitted appropriately in a black dress with long sleeves and a high collar. I took one look into that pinched and stern face, and the smile I had put on for Chris faded abruptly.

"Good afternoon, Caitlin," she said in a tone of voice that sounded like she wished me anything but. "Khristoph said you might stop by with car. Please, come in. He and Nico had some big emergency down at restaurant."

"W...will he be away long?" I asked, dry-mouthed, entering the foyer as if stepping into a dragon's lair. "If...if so, I could come back another time."

She lifted her palms and gave a shoulder shrug. "Who knows with these things? Some nonsense about fire hazards or so I think. I leave restaurant business to Nico. Come, we talk."

Swell, I thought, following her into the living room, then said, "I...I don't want to be any bother to you, Delia," as she motioned me to a chair. "I'll just call my brother and have him come and get me."

"Nonsense. You are no bother. We sit and we talk."

"O...okay. So how's Arti?" I asked, trying to deflect any conversation away from what I suspected was a sore point with Delia, my dating her son. At the same time, I attempted to get comfortable in the straight-backed chair where I had been directed to sit. "I haven't seen her for, oh, it has to be six or seven years. I guess, the wedding."

Delia crossed to the grand piano and picked up a silver-framed family portrait and brought it to me. "Three children. Two boys, one girl," she said, beaming with pride. "And a husband who dotes on her. She has good life."

Counting the number of chins on my former Regina Caeli B-ball teammate, I thought, *She also hasn't missed too many meals.* What I said was, "Good-looking kids."

"Yes, they have their father's nose, thanks be to God." She crossed herself and returned the photograph to the piano. "Now, let us talk about you, Caitlin," she said, turning to me and fixing me with black, hard eyes. "Was last night a for-old-times-sake dinner with my Khristoph or did you have something more in mind?"

Subtle, this woman was not, so I decided to follow suit. "Delia, I've never been sure exactly why, but I know you don't like me. If it's an ethnic thing, hey, I can accept that. My folks had Old World ideas, too. I'm sure they would have wanted me to settle down with a nice, redheaded, freckle-faced, Irish boy. But Chris and I are a generation removed from all that. Jeez, I don't know if we're right for each other. But I do know that we like each other, we have fun together, we've got some sort of chemistry going, and...and I don't mean any disrespect, Delia. Please believe me, I don't. But...but we're old enough to make our own decisions on this."

She didn't say one word in rebuttal, just stood there for about thirty seconds, lips tightened into a fine line, then gave a little frustrated shake of her head, muttered something in Greek, and said, "Yes, Caitlin, you are old enough. You are both old enough. I come right back."

Damn, I thought as she strode from the room. *I'm good. I'm really good.* I sat there, waiting. As each second went by, though, my anxiety rose. *What now?* I wondered.

"These are two pictures I want you to see," Delia announced walking briskly back into the room and crossing to the coffee table. "You come and sit here." She gestured me to the love seat opposite her.

After I had moved and gotten comfortable, she set two more silver-framed photographs in front of me. Both were of newborn babies, one relatively modern and in color, the other in black-and-white that appeared much older. However, the babies in both photos looked identical—and familiar.

"This is a picture of me!" I said with surprise, tapping the modern one. "I have one almost exactly like it at home but, in mine, I'm in a pink blanket, not a blue one. Where did you get this?"

Ignoring my question, Delia pointed to the older-looking of the two photos. "And do you recognize baby in this picture?"

As in the first photo, the nose was unmistakable. My folks must have had it taken deliberately in an old-fashioned format—long lace dress, little knit cap and all.

"That's me, too," I said. "But I've never seen this picture before. How did you get these?"

In perhaps the first human contact she and I ever had, Delia sat beside me, patted my knee and smiled at me—a weary smile, but a smile nevertheless. "This picture," she said, picking up the modern one, "is my Khristophoros, taken the day after he was born."

"It can't be!" I protested taking the photo from her and looking more closely at it. "It's me, Delia! I'm positive it is!"

"It is not, Caitlin. Believe me when I tell you, it is Khristophoros. A mother, she knows her own child."

"Then both of these are of Chris?" I asked.

"No, Caitlin. The other is Nikolaos, taken many years ago on Zakinthos. Picture of father, here. Picture of son, there. Now, what do pictures tell you?"

"You think that somehow we're related?" I asked, touching the side of my nose. "That there's a recessive gene from a common ancestor that just happened to pop out in me?"

Again she muttered in Greek and shook her head in frustration, then she took my face in her hands and looked directly into my eyes.

"You are bright girl, Caitlin. A college graduate. Yes, yes, yes, there is common ancestor for you and Khristoph. It is Nikolaos! He is father to you both!"

She let go of me, stood, and paced the floor. I just sat there, stunned and open-mouthed.

"Nico and I, we had difficulties back then," she continued. "All couples go though them. Your mother and father, they had difficulties, too. Your father, he was not happy with your mother's new life as bookkeeper. They fought. Nico and I fought. What we fight about is not important now. Your mother and Nico, they did not fight."

When I switched purses this morning, among the items I had transferred from my evening bag were the three condoms—one from Pat, one from Seamus, and one from Mary Grace. I remembered them now. Had my brothers and sister-in-law really been all that interested in keeping me from catching a venereal disease? I suddenly thought not.

"I do not hate you, Caitlin," Delia went on. "Not now or ever. Nor did your father hate my Khristoph when we make two of you break off date in high school. We simply did not want brother to go on date with sister."

"Why didn't anyone ever tell us?"

"There was no need. I say *no date*. Your father, he say *no date*. We thought problem solved. And when Khristoph marry and move to Detroit, I thought problem gone forever. Then he divorce Daffy...excuse me, Daphne...and problem, it come back. Now, I ask you same question as before. Was last night for-old-times-sake dinner with my Khristoph or do you have something more in mind?"

After a silence of perhaps fifteen seconds or so, I looked up into her face and answered. "It was strictly for old time's sake, Delia. Nothing more." And as I said it, I felt a piece of my heart shut down and stop functioning—a piece which would forever belong to Chris—a piece which would forever belong to my brother Chris.

Delia nodded, came to my side and patted my cheek. "That is good."

I telephoned Seamus. Until he picked me up, Delia and I talked about Arti, her life, her husband, and her kids. Gone were any hard feelings. We were like aunt and niece, having afternoon tea together. No more was said about Chris and me. There was no more to *be* said. There *was* no more Chris and me. There was Chris; and there was me.

* * * *

"Got a call from Pat," Seamus said as soon as I had closed the passenger door to his minivan. "He says you did good today, Katie. Melinda Huntington gave the police a full confession. Congratulations." He backed out of the driveway and headed in the direction of Kehough's.

I simply looked at him and asked, "Why didn't anyone ever tell me?"

"Tell you what?"

"Cut the crap. Delia told me the whole story."

"Ahh, did she, now? Probably time for it." He gave a pragmatic nod of his head.

"You and Pat both know?"

"And Mary Grace. But that's as far as it goes, Katie. I don't think Pat ever told Eileen."

"Why did Ma and Da tell *you*?"

"Hell, Katie, I was seventeen and Pat was fifteen when you were born. We weren't blind. Or morons."

"Why didn't you or Pat ever tell *me*?"

"We promised Ma and Da that we wouldn't."

"Didn't you think I'd like to know who my real father was?"

He glanced over at me and a puzzled expression came over his face. "Do you remember who it was that rushed you to the hospital when you had that bout with diphtheria?" he asked.

"Da did. Why?"

"And who was it that sat up with you when you had the chicken pox, kept you covered with Calamine lotion, and told you story after story about leprechauns and wee-folk to keep your mind off your itches?"

I hadn't thought of those tales in a very long time. "Da," I said, smiling.

"And who was it that worked his tail off to put food on your table and clothes on your back?"

"It was Da."

"And who was always there when you needed him, lass, from the day you were born until the day he died?"

"Da."

"Now, you tell me, who do you think was your *real* father?"

Even as my eyes teared up, I managed another smile. "Da was."

"Indeed, lass. Indeed he was."

We traveled the rest of the way in silence.

As he turned the Windstar into the alley behind Kehough's, an alley now completely cleared of debris, Seamus said, "Have you decided yet on the Wisconsin job?"

The day after Rissa first approached me, I had told my brothers and Mary Grace about the offer. Although they had made supportive noises ("Wasn't that nice of her;" "I'm sure you'd be a fine coach;" etc.), I could tell that they weren't overjoyed at the prospect of me moving.

"I've got until Friday to make up my mind," I replied. "That's when Rissa will be back from vacation."

"Pat asked me the other day if you had said anything more about it. I told him you hadn't.... Which way are you leaning?"

"I think I'm going to take it. I've got to do something with my life." Still reeling from my conversation with Delia, there was no doubt in my mind that now I would definitely take the job.

My brother snickered. "Most people would consider an Olympic bronze and gold something. And being named league MVP wasn't chopped liver, either, was it? What more do you need to prove?"

"I don't need to *prove*, Seamus. I need to *do*. Something. Something...meaningful."

"Mary Grace will expect you home for all the holidays, you know that, don't you?"

I could tell from the slight tremor in his voice that he, too, would expect it, and be mighty upset if I didn't return to Nashville on a regular basis. Reaching over and giving him a shoulder squeeze, I said, "Wouldn't consider spending them anywhere else."

Chapter 21

A very quiet Chris Panacopoulos called me Wednesday evening after having had a father-and-son sit-down with Nico, at the instigation of Delia, no doubt.

"About that making-it-up date we talked about," he said, then gave a little cluck with his tongue.

"Yeah," I replied. "I guess we're going to have to cancel it, huh?"

"I…I guess so."

From the sound of his voice, I could tell that he was as disappointed about the situation as I was, so I tried to introduce a little levity.

"Yeah, it's a…a family thing," I said, throwing his own brush-off line back at him from those many years ago.

He chuckled and picked up on my old response. "Believe me, I understand about…about family things."

"So, I guess I'll see you around, huh?"

"Yeah, I guess so."

After a few seconds of silence, I said, "Chris?"

"Yes, Kate."

"Try not to think of it so much as losing a girlfriend, but gaining a sister."

"Oh, super," he said tonelessly. "Just what I had hoped for."

"Yeah. Me, too."

*   *   *   *

After dinner at the pub, I borrowed Waldo the Windstar and headed over to the Y, even though I still couldn't play. Since D-day (Decision-day on the Fond du Lac job) was only two days off, I thought I'd better take another stab at coaching to see if that really *was* what I wanted to do with my foreseeable future.

The five games (15-9, 15-10, 15-6, 15-2, and 15-2) that my team won reinforced my convictions that I *could* coach. However, I still hadn't resolved the big question—did I really *want* to?

Maybe my dream that night hinted of some of the concerns that troubled me on the subconscious level. I was dressed in my snake-skin-print bathing suit and playing beach volleyball. First off, I must tell you that I consider beach volleyball an abomination to the sport and simply a recourse for the has-been athlete who can't compete in real V-ball anymore and doesn't know when to quit. Yes, I know it pays reasonably well, but, then, so does table dancing, but I wouldn't consider doing that, either.

On the other side of the net were Courtney Howell, in her gold mesh swimsuit, and Greta Bergstrom, wearing a fur bikini and a Viking helmet. The sidelines were crammed with dozens of Junior Lee Thigpens, all swilling beer and shouting, "Bounce 'em, baby! Let's see those boobs bounce!" As I played the two hookers one-on-two, snow started to fall in big fluffy flakes. Before long, we were knee-deep in the stuff, all three of us turning blue and covered with goose bumps, with our…well, you know what else happens when it's cold.

I awoke, goose bumps and what else intact, pulled the comforter up around my neck and lay there shivering, trying to interpret the dream. Could this really be a battle between the lesser of two evils?

Finally sleep came again, this time, thankfully, dreamless.

* * * *

I hadn't worked out since my last day at Cove Creek, a full week ago. The nose didn't hurt too badly on Thursday morning so I spent an hour on the Nautilus and felt every single minute of it. Showered, dressed, and breakfasted, I commandeered Waldo and set out on a search for a replacement for my dear departed Liddy.

A stop at the Toyota dealership turned out to be a short one. It just didn't seem right to get another Land Cruiser. Also, it would be grossly unfair to the new one, always being compared to her predecessor.

I struck out at the Nissan and Izuzu dealerships as well. And I certainly didn't want a Jeep. Nice vehicles, but everyone has them. Then, as I walked through the Mercedes lot, I heard a woman's voice call out to my mind with just the barest hint of a German accent.

"Buy me," it whispered ever so softly. "I'm the one, Kate. Buy me!"

Turning around, I came eyeball to headlamp with a shiny, emerald-green ML-320 Sport Utility Vehicle, loaded. It was love at first sight. I wrote out a check, told the sales-weasel to get it prepped, and rushed home so that Seamus could drive me back to pick it up.

* * * *

Since construction had started that morning on our new garages, alley parking had been temporarily posted as off limits. Seamus had hand-lettered three RESERVED signs and had mounted them next to the handicapped parking spots that straddled our front walkway, two on one side, one on the other. He took the single for Waldo and I parked Mitzi (the Mercedes) in space number one on the opposite side. Brother Pat was a quick study. When he showed up for lunch, he'd easily figure out which spot belonged to him.

As I entered through the front door, Mickey Ryan called out to me. "You made the papers again, Caitlin." He and Jimmy Tuohey sat huddled over a newspaper at their end of the bar.

"And this time they got a picture of you," Jimmy added. "A good one, too, Katie."

I crossed over to them and Mickey turned the paper around and held it up so that I could see. The headline on the second section of *The Tennessean* read, "Former Volleyball Star Setter Sets Up Murderer for Cops." The picture they had used was my college graduation photo.

"Jeez," I said with a wince. "Did I really look that young just a few short years ago?"

"'If I make the lashes dark,'" Mickey quoted, looking up at me with a twinkle in his rheumy old eyes.

"'And the eyes more bright
And the lips more scarlet'"

He stopped and I continued. "'Or ask if all be right,
From mirror after mirror,
No vanity's displayed:'"

We both finished together. "'I'm looking for the face I had
Before the world was made.'"

I put my arm around the old man and gave him a hug.

"Ahh," Mickey said, beaming. "The lass, she knows her Yeats."

"But not as well as yourself, Mr. Ryan," I replied. "You're still our resident expert."

"'Tis good of you to say so, lass," he murmured, giving my arm an affectionate stroke. "'Tis good of you."

The newspaper article took up the entire first page above the fold and detailed my involvement in the investigation of Delane Denning's murder and the capture of Melinda Huntington. I made a mental note to call Ozzie and thank her. She was quoted as saying, "Without Miss O'Rourke's assistance, five murders would still be unsolved and the perpetrator would now be a very rich woman."

"That calls for a drink, don't you think, Katie?" Jimmy asked, wetting his lips and nodding hopefully.

"What doesn't, Jimmy?" I asked flatly in return, then said to Seamus, "Set 'em up, bro. All around, on the house."

"You're generous to a fault," my brother responded with a chuckle, looking about the pub.

There weren't more than a handful of customers there at the time, but, to a man, grateful for the freebie, they raised their glasses and toasted me.

"To Caitlin," Mickey shouted.

Everyone echoed him. "To Caitlin."

While I drank my Golden Lager, I signed a poster that Beth Ann Downey had dropped off that morning for her daughter Heather Ann, then opened the mail. A short note from Cece Prendergast in Cove Creek said that, as of Tuesday, no one had called about the sandals. I took a pen and Kehough's letterhead and jotted down a note back to her.

Dear Cece,

You can take the photo of the sandals down from the lost-and-found board. I've located their owner.

Regards,

Kate O'Rourke

* * * *

Thursday night at the Y was B-ball night. Although I still couldn't play, I tried my hand at coaching that as well. My team lost by three points (67-64), but I considered it a successful evening anyway. The last two times, without me playing, they had gotten their butts kicked 82-43 and 79-55.

That night my dream again featured volleyball, but court volleyball this time. On one side of the net, Ozzie and Sykes were paired and played against Matt Denning, Melinda Huntington and Junior Lee Thigpen. The scoreboard read, GOOD GUYS—0-BAD GUYS—10.

I entered the game on Ozzie and Sykes' team, and cheerleaders Greta Bergstrom and Courtney Howell chanted, "Katie-Kat, Katie-Kat, Katie-Kat" over and over again. My playing bordered on brilliant. I blocked shots and set up my teammates perfectly. The final score read, GOOD GUYS—15-BAD GUYS—10

* * * *

On Friday morning, after the hour on the Nautilus, I decided that I really needed to get back into rigorous training. If I were going up to Wisconsin (which I had all but decided that I would be), I couldn't let those girls see me wheeze. Even though the nose still hurt some, I figured the pain was manageable and struck out for my six-mile run around the neighborhood, much to the delight of the construction workers in the alley.

I had stopped briefly in the kitchen on my way out. Just before reaching the Larsen's home, I opened the brown paper bag I had brought with me and removed a roast beef bone. A generous amount of rare meat still clung to it. Duke, my Dalmatian doggy-hero, sat waiting for me at the near side of his yard, barking and wagging his tail. The fur on his haunch had been shaved away and I could see the stitches clearly, still a bit red and swollen.

"Hey, Dukie," I said, waving the bone. "Look what Katie's got for her big, spotted buddy."

His eyes widened and he sat up on his hind legs, wagged his tail faster and, in anticipation, ran his big slobbery tongue from one side of his muzzle to the other. I tossed the bone over the fence and those powerful Dalmatian jaws caught it in midair. Whatever the record for stripping a bone of meat is (probably held by some jackal in Africa) Duke had to have come close to breaking it. In less than thirty seconds the bone glistened a shiny white. After a final lick all around, he carried it over to his water dish and laid it down next to his other prized possession—a blue, hard rubber ball.

Returning to the fence, he gave a lunge in the direction of the garage, then stopped and looked at me. After trotting back, he once more lunged toward the garage-end of his fence and, again, stopped and looked. I swear to you, that dog actually cocked his spotted head and raised an eyebrow. Then, I understood.

"You want to chase me, is that it, boy?"

Duke answered with a sharp bark and more tail wagging. I could read his thoughts in those big brown eyes. They said, "Come on Katie-Kat. I spend the whole day out here with nothing to do. Give me your best shot. What do you say? Huh? Huh?"

"So all this time when I'd run by and bang on your fence, thinking I was being mean to you, you thought I was playing? Well, I'll be." I took a three-point stance. "Okay, Dukie, you got it. Ready or not, here I come. Now!"

I sprinted the length of the Larsen's yard, smacking the chain-link fence with my hand. Duke kept right with me, barking and growling, and snapping, until, like always, he ran headlong into the garage. At the last second, like a swimmer making a lap-turn, he hit the side of the garage with all four feet and bounded away in the other direction, still barking for joy.

"See you tomorrow," I called out over my shoulder.

*   *   *   *

The lunch crowd had started to trickle in when I returned from my run, and with it, brother Pat. I stopped by his stool and stole a sip of his Golden Lager.

"Help yourself," he said. Then, looking me up and down, he nodded his approval. "Looks like you're getting yourself back to normal. Today's the big day isn't it?"

I sat next to him on my customary end-stool and continued to sip his beer. "Yep. I expect I'll hear from Rissa before the day is out."

"You don't sound overly-thrilled at the prospect."

I shrugged.

He continued. "You know, you'll have to explain to Mary Grace why you can't coach closer to home."

Like Seamus, Pat seemed to be laying a lot on Mary Grace lately. I had a hunch it was really *he* who needed the explanation.

"It's simple," I told him. "My degree's in philosophy, not phys. ed. And, on top of that, it's only a bachelor's degree. When they hand you your Ph.B., they also give you a little piece of paper with a phrase written on it that you can use when you enter the workforce. Do you know what that phrase is?"

"No. What?"

"'Would you like fries with that?' The only reason I'm getting this shot at Notre Dame is because of Rissa."

He seemed to accept that, taking his beer back from me and sipping from the mug. "You see the new addition?" he asked, pointing a finger toward Caitlin's corner.

I looked. Someone had framed the page of yesterday's *Tennessean* and had hung it in a prominent spot on the wall next to my other accomplishments. Recalling how adamant my sister-in-law had been about me not getting involved with the police, I said, "Mary Grace know about that?"

"Do you think it could have gotten up there if she didn't?"

"Point taken." I snatched his beer mug again and downed the remainder of the lager. "Thanks for the beer. I'm going to hit the showers then come back down for lunch."

"You had fun doing that, didn't you?" Pat asked, gesturing with his head at the framed newspaper article.

"Yeah, I'll have to admit it. It gave me a rush."

"Like playing in one of the big games?"

"Not quite, but similar."

"Will coaching give you that kind of rush?"

I looked down at my older brother and thought for a second. "I really don't know. Honest to God, Pat, I don't."

"Well, don't make any hasty decisions," he said. "Sometimes things have a way of working themselves out."

I kissed him on his bald spot, then headed up to my quarters. The light on the answering machine blinked a greeting and the message counter showed the number two.

Probably both from Rissa, I told myself as I punched the PLAY button and waited.

The first one was, anyway. "Well, girl, it's Friday and I'm back. Time to fish or cut bait. I need your answer by this evening. Is you is or is you ain't my new V-ball coach? Bye for now."

The second message turned out not to be from Rissa, but from a woman whom I didn't know. "M…miss O'Rourke? My name is Allison Parisio. Y…you don't know me, but I got your number from a policeman in the Robbery Division. There have been some rather expensive items that have disappeared from my home in the past week or so, but now suddenly they've reappeared. The police said they couldn't do anything, since no crime has been committed, but one of them suggested I get in touch with you." She left a number that I recognized as a Brentwood exchange.

Why the heck would someone in the police department tell her to call me? I wondered.

Because the call had piqued my curiosity, though, I decided to talk with this Allison Parisio before getting back to Rissa.

A young girl answered on the second ring, trying to sound oh-so-grown-up. "Parisio residence. This is Michelle."

"May I speak to Ms. Parisio?" I asked.

"There are two Ms. Parisios," the girl answered. "Actually, three, counting me. Do you wish to speak to Rebecca or Allison?"

"Allison," I said.

"That's my mom. I'll get her for you."

After about fifteen seconds of silence a woman came on the line. "This is Allison Parisio. May I help you?"

"Caitlin O'Rourke," I said. "Returning your call."

Her voice fell to a whisper. "I can't talk right now, but could you meet me somewhere later today? Please? I really would like to hire you. The detective who I talked to in Robbery said your fee was three-hundred dollars a day plus expenses. I'd gladly pay it, just for the peace of mind. But he also said you might be leaving for Wisconsin soon. Is that true?"

She sounded worried—worried *and* frightened.

I could feel the adrenaline start to flow and the hairs on the back of my neck stood out. It was like taking the court for the start of the big game. I was pumped.

God bless you, brother Pat!

"No," I answered without any hesitation whatsoever. "That trip has been canceled. I work out of a place called Kehough's Irish Pub. In Nashville, up on Wooten between Deford and Plainview. Why don't you come up here and we'll talk. How's three o'clock sound?"

"Oh, thank you so much," she said and I could hear an audible sigh of relief. "I'll be there promptly at three." She hung up without saying another word.

I recradled the receiver and picked up W.B. as the kitty wound her way through my legs. "Unpack your heavy fur, Dub. We're staying here."

END

The Ed McAvoy Mystery Series

Even with a left leg shattered by a drug dealer's bullet and a medical retirement from the Detroit Police Force, former homicide captain Ed McAvoy feels he's too young to be put out to pasture. Accepting the job as Police Chief of Peekamoose Heights, in New York's Catskills, he figures it will be sort of like running a country club. After all, how much crime can there be in a quiet, little village?

McAvoy soon discovers that his skills as a homicide detective will not atrophy from lack of use in Peekamoose Heights. Murder, as it turns out, is an equal-opportunity crime that not only resides in large bustling cities like Detroit, but in sleepy Catskill villages like Peekamoose Heights as well.

Wash & Wear
(Coming in November, 2003)

A bank teller and owner of a small Catskill print shop is killed by a known mob hit-man who, in turn, is killed by Heather Larrabee, a Peekamoose Heights Police Officer. Now Heather's house and car have been searched, as well as the teller's aunt's house. McAvoy must find what the mob is looking for before someone else gets killed in the process.

Encore to Murder
ISBN: 0-595-25624-4
From iUniverse

In the suspenseful prequel to *Stream of Death*, a former fashion model runs her car off a cliff at the Ashokan Pass on the outskirts of Peekamoose Heights in New York's Catskills—or has it been made to look that way? What McAvoy suspects and what he can prove are two different things. But the retired big-city homicide detective, and now newly-hired village Chief of Police, has a few tricks up his sleeve that may lead him to that proof.

"*Encore to Murder* is a story full of mystery, suspense, and with a cast of characters that keep the story moving fast.…I recommend that you go out and purchase Encore to Murder, get comfortable in a cozy chair, and just sit back and enjoy. It certainly is a wonderful way to spend a cold and blustery winter night."

—Sue Hartigan—All About Murder

"…this is an enjoyable read and a great introduction to the Ed McAvoy Series. Stackhouse draws on his playwriting background to create a fun, flowing mystery with a twist at the end that will surprise readers and appeal to lovers of both classic mysteries and police procedurals."

—Cynthia Chow—The No Name Book Review Corner

"*Encore to Murder* isn't quite a cozy, but it's close.…The characterizations of small mountain towns rings true, and if you like puzzlers, you really should enjoy this read, curled up safely in front of your own fireplace. I did!"

—Vicki Ball—Books 'n' Bytes

Hickory, Dickory
ISBN: 0-595-22596-9
From iUniverse

In this exciting sequel to *Stream of Death*, McAvoy's friend Sam Douglas has bought a Queen Anne tall-case clock at auction—at a bargain price. Trading it to Kate Winthrop for her lesser-quality Massachusetts clock and then selling the Massachusetts to a third party sight unseen seems to bode well for the antique dealer—until the third party winds up dead and, in her dying breath, identifies Sam as her attacker.

"With it's small town atmosphere and characters, which include McAvoy's police force and the locals, the story resembles a village version of an 87th Precinct police procedural with a little bit of Agatha Christie thrown in. I very much enjoyed *Hickory, Dickory* and await the release of Bill Stackhouse's next book!"

—Peter K. Ackerman—I Love a Mystery Newsletter

"…the outlandish, oddball, rural characters that populate Stackhouse's stories are likable and believable. The plot is well thought out and unique with lots of action. There are twists and turns and an ending that catches you by surprise. Okay, Bill, I'm ready for the next Ed McAvoy mystery!"

—Beverly J. Rowe—MyShelf.com

"…the book is a pleasure. Stackhouse has a sly sense of humor, a good feeling for characters, and a decent sense of plot. Future books by him are anticipated, while the current one is recommended."

—Mary A. Axford—Reviewing The Evidence

Stream of Death
ISBN: 1-890208-56-6
From Poisoned Pen Press

In the closing days of WWII in Sicily, the famed Isabela Pendant disappears amid a hail of machine-pistol bullets. When it temporarily resurfaces in Detroit after fifty-some years, six people are murdered. Now, four years later, a dog has dug it up in the woods near McAvoy's peaceful Catskill village of Peekamoose Heights.

"*Stream of Death* is an enjoyable regional mystery that links events over five decades apart. The well-written story line works because the minor subplots bring depth to the cast, making the key players seem genuine. In his debut novel, Bill Stackhouse writes like an old pro stacking his chances for success with this phenomenal police procedural that combines a hard-boiled investigation with that of a regional cozy."

—Harriet Klausner—BookBrowser Review

"Bill Stackhouse's *Stream of Death* is an excellent and original debut novel which blends the hard-boiled and softer elements of the crime fiction genre....The field of crime literature is already indebted to Bill Stackhouse for introducing Chief Ed McAvoy."

—Andrew McAleer—A Crimestalker Casebook Book Review

"...Well-written and engrossing to read....Keeps the reader intrigued to the end of the book."

—Sally Fellows—Mystery News

Sample chapters of these Ed McAvoy Mysteries may be downloaded at
http://www.billstackhouse.com